DEATH WAS IN THE BLOOD

LINDA L. RICHARDS

FIVE STAR
A part of Gale, Cengage Learning

GALE
CENGAGE Learning®

Detroit • New York • San Francisco • New Haven, Conn • Waterville, Maine • London

GALE
CENGAGE Learning

LIBRARY OF CONGRESS CATALOGING-IN-PUBLICATION DATA

Richards, Linda, 1960–
    Death was in the blood / Linda L. Richards. — First edition
      pages cm
    ISBN-13: 978-1-4328-2716-8 (hardcover)
    ISBN-10: 1-4328-2716-2 (hardcover)
    1. Women private investigators—Fiction. 2. Upper class
families—Fiction 3. Olympic athletes—Juvenile fiction. 4. Los
Angeles (Calif.)—History—20th century—Fiction. I. Title.
PR9199.4.R5226D423 2013
813'.6—dc23   2013005470

Find us on Facebook– https://www.facebook.com/FiveStarCengage
Visit our website– http://www.gale.cengage.com/fivestar/
Contact Five Star™ Publishing at FiveStar@cengage.com

Printed in Mexico
2 3 4 5 6 7 17 16 15 14 13

DEATH WAS IN THE BLOOD

Death Was in the Blood

CHAPTER ONE

He was a long, lean, cool drink of water, called himself Matty Sweet. He had a mug like a first-edition paperboy, but there was something in the way his skin stretched over the bones of his face that made you wonder what you were looking at. He was pretty, all right, I'll give him that. But there was something about him—just that, just something—that made you wonder if his name described him or if, like for a lot of people, it was just a name.

He'd been sitting in the waiting room chair for about a half hour when I noticed him fidgeting. I couldn't help but feel sorry for him. "Mr. Theroux shouldn't be much longer," I said with my most professional smile.

"He's been a while," he said, though he didn't sound overly concerned. I liked his voice. There was something assured and resonant about it. Something I figured I could listen to for a long time.

"Mr. Theroux's last appointment is still in there with him." I used the end of my fountain pen to indicate the door. "He's usually quite punctual," I said, which was actually something like a lie.

The kid smiled and maybe he let out a grunt, then went back to flipping the out-of-date magazines we kept in our little waiting room. From what I figured, a two-year-old edition of *Movie Play* was the freshest thing he'd find, and he'd be lucky with that much.

As he waited, I found myself stealing little glimpses of him and wondering what he might want with Dex. He was young enough, you figured it couldn't be very much. I made him to be two or three years older than I was, which would put him at twenty-five or six. He was well dressed, too. His suit fit him in a way that bespoke tailors, not at all like something you'd buy off the rack at Blackstone Department Store.

He'd put his hat down and aside when he came in, in proper style for a gentleman. That hat, too, spoke of money and time, something most people didn't have much of anymore. The easy way he'd put aside the hat, then relaxed into that waiting room chair, I figured he had enough of both.

After a while, I fidgeted slightly, knowing that Dex's previous "appointment" was his best friend, the fixer Mustard. Dex and Mustard had been in there some time. Left to their own devices, they'd be in there for a while longer still, swapping stories and pouring ever-deeper drinks and generally making like it was Saturday evening at Pico and Bundy and they had nothing to think about besides which speakeasy offered up the better class of rotgut and which long-legged roundheels might be most easily toppled into their respective beds.

"I think I'll just go and check on Mr. Theroux again," I told the young man pleasantly after a while, "make sure he remembers that you're here."

I tried not to show my alarm as I moved through the office and the sounds of Dex and Mustard's revelry became more plain. And I tried not to look surreptitious as I maneuvered myself quickly through the door in an attempt to avoid letting Mr. Matthew Sweet see beyond it. It was possible that what was currently behind that door might look less like a good shamus's office and more like a blind pig speakeasy, which wasn't a good bet for a Wednesday afternoon, any way you picked it up and turned it around.

Dex and Mustard greeted me with twin smiles when I closed the door tightly behind me and leaned against it: my mission accomplished.

"Nicely done," Dex said. "If the PI business ever needs a spy, I'll put your name out for the job."

"Me too," Mustard said loopily. "Why, she's as stealthy as a three-legged mouse in a room full of six-legged cats." Considering the state the two of them were in, I wasn't sure if it was a compliment or not.

"A three-legged . . . ?"

"Oh, all right," Mustard amended gallantly, "a huntress in high heels. Either way, you'd be perfectly cut out for espionage, Kitty. Especially with all the experience you've had sneaking around after Dex."

"I don't wear such high heels, Mustard," I said, indicating my sensibly heeled shoes. When I could, I rode the Red Car and Angels Flight and, now and again, Dex would give me a ride someplace. Most days, though, I ended up riding shank's mare. And when you're doing a lot of walking, the fact that a higher heel puts a prettier spin on your ankle doesn't help things at all.

"Not really the point, Kitty," Mustard said, grinning into his lowball glass, maybe assessing his next sip.

They'd been in there drinking for over an hour and both had likely started before that. The two of them were at the place where a little bit of drink can seem like a lot of fun. To them. From where I was standing, fun was a long ways off. I addressed Dex directly, ignoring Mustard, hoping he'd go away, I guess. At least disappear, though I wasn't optimistic of the chances of that happening. He's usually a pretty busy guy, but whatever business he had seemed to have been put on hold for the afternoon. For whatever reason, the two old army buddies looked as though they'd settled in for the duration.

"You have a client, Dex," I said, trying to keep tired out of my voice. "You know you have a client."

Dex looked at me. Raised his eyebrows. Held back a smirk. Despite the five o'clock shadow and the cragginess of a face that had slept not enough after too much fun, there was a boyishness about him when he looked at me then. Almost an elfin quality that was an odd juxtaposition against his strongly cut features. It sparkled through his eyes. "I'm not sure I care for that tone, young lady."

I guess Mustard couldn't help himself. The guffaw came from deep inside him, I could tell. It came from deep inside and bubbled out.

"I'm not sure I care about you caring about my tone," I said, feeling suddenly twelve. "The poor guy has been waiting out there going on three-quarters of an hour."

"Does he look like he can pay?" Dex asked.

"He looks like he can manage all right," I said.

"Well, good. Let him ripen a bit more."

"But Dex!"

"Never mind, Kitty," Dex said archly. "Tell him I'm already with a client. He'll be all the more appreciative for it when I'm done. Another half hour or so should do it."

I stood there for a minute just contemplating my boss. This was new. He was disrespectful of almost everyone, but usually in a fairly polite way, especially to their face. And he usually made a show of sobriety, at least while it was still light out.

"I'm sorry, Mr. Sweet," I said when I was back at my desk. "Mr. Theroux's previous appointment has gone far longer than imagined. It's a . . . a very urgent matter." I tried not to think about Dex and Mustard guffawing into their drinks as I said it. Swapping war stories or embellishing tales of skirts they'd both chased, weekends they'd misplaced together, battles won and lost. "However, he doesn't want to inconvenience you unduly and has authorized me to take the details of your case so that I can . . . I can fill him in later."

All of this was, of course, a bald-faced lie. I had never been authorized to do anything besides type and answer the phone. Make coffee when called upon. And I knew Dex would just as soon have me discuss his case as water down his hooch. I was implying—no, *saying*—that I was an associate of Dex's, maybe like a sort of junior detective. But if that were the implication, it was also a lie. I was Dex's secretary, nothing more. Though truth be told, there was nothing more I wanted. The trouble was, it had been a slow month and the end of it was heading towards us fast, plus Dex's fool behavior was making it slower. We needed cash and no one knew that better than me. Apparently, not even Dex.

Matty Sweet had cash. I could practically smell it on him. And he had need of Dex's services, otherwise he wouldn't have subjected himself to going on an hour in the waiting room. So me? I figured I'd make everyone happy and take his money off him. Provided, of course, I could get him to play along. I held my breath while I waited for his reply.

"That sounds sensible," he said when I'd finished my little speech.

I was afraid I'd get him talking and then Dex would finally come waltzing out of his office, just in time to gum up the works. I decided I wasn't going to take a chance on that.

"I'd like to be certain we have absolute privacy." I'd started with a lie and now there seemed to be no stopping them. While I spoke, I took a quarter out of the cash box in my desk, thought about it, and took another one. "There's a coffee shop in the next block. Perhaps the agency can treat you to a cup of coffee and a slice of cherry pie?"

If Matthew Sweet thought there was anything fishy about being asked to tell me his personal business in a busy coffee shop at three in the afternoon when coffee shops are generally busiest, he didn't say anything. I figured I was lucky he was young and didn't know any better. Maybe he figured that's where PIs always did their business, over coffee in places known for their very good cherry pie. My own youth and appearance probably didn't do anything to hex the matter, either. Most of the men I've met are suckers for a well-turned ankle, and it's not bragging for me to say mine do all right, even without especially high heels.

As we headed for the elevator, Sweet helped me settle my light cotton coat over my shoulders. And I—well, I just couldn't help myself when I looked up to thank him and I felt my eyelashes fluttering like they would blow his hat off if given half a chance. Suddenly the whole shebang felt more like a date than a business meeting. I wasn't sure what to do about that. What was worse: I wasn't sure I *wanted* to do anything at all.

Sitting across from Matthew Sweet at Gracie's Café I realized my mistake. His eyes had a slaty-gray quality that made me think of the puddles that would form after a rain when I was away at school in San Francisco. It was a thought that made me sigh. I hated that it made me sigh. And it didn't hurt my eyes any to watch the way the corners of his mouth crinkled up when he grinned or the way his whole face lit up when he smiled.

I didn't see much smiling on that first day because he'd come to see Dex on a serious matter, one that demanded all of his concern and wiped whatever smile he might have handed me clean off his mug. I had to work hard not to show any signs of distress when he revealed that the object of his concern and the reason for his visit to a detective was his fiancée, the unbearably delicate and unspeakably precious Miss Flora Woodruff of West Adams. It took all my strength not to loathe the very sound of her, which I knew even in the moment was unfair. But to see Sweet's tender expression when he talked about her was enough to turn me the most embarrassing shade of green. Suddenly the fact that the rent on the office and the electricity bill at home were both due was the last thing on my mind. For a heartbeat, I felt like walking out the door and leaving Matthew Sweet to his musings on the fair Flora. There were more serious matters at stake than me acting like some smitten schoolgirl, though. I sat where I was and pushed my feelings aside.

"So you feel she's in some danger, then?"

While I fought my own little war, Sweet had been telling me some story about his intended. He felt she was somehow at risk. And I knew that, if I were to pass myself off as a PI's worthy assistant, I'd have to pay closer attention. I'd have to pretend to be the person I'd like Dex to be. That thought made me sit up straighter. I reached for my handbag and pulled out the pad of paper I'd brought along with my fountain pen.

"Forgive me, Mr. Sweet. I was distracted for a moment. Let us order some coffee and perhaps some pie—this place is known for its pie. And then we can begin again."

The coffee, when it came, was good and strong, the way Gracie herself likes it. The pies were flaky and just right—I ordered that famous cherry, while Sweet had a slice of apple—and I enjoyed the thought of Dex's face upon discovering I was treating a potential client on his dime. But then Sweet started talking and I started listening and the rest of everything fell away in his tale.

Sweet's intended, the aforementioned precious and delicate Miss Woodruff, was—according to her fiancé—a horsewoman of some note. She spent all available time at the stables in Griffith Park where she was training herself and an expensive horse that her father had bought for her in Germany the year before.

Miss Woodruff, I was told, according to her admiring but not entirely unbiased fiancé, was quite the paragon. Not only was she beautiful and of sweet disposition, she was deeply talented and had set her sights on competing in the Three-Day Event at the Olympic games that were to be held here in Los Angeles the following year.

"So she's ambitious, then?" I asked, not really needing the answer, but wanting to fill in the space. Sweet had been going on so about his beloved Miss Woodruff. He clearly expected some comment in reply.

"Oh yes! Very much so. Some men might find that off-putting, but I don't. I find it most admirable. Don't you?"

The problem was not with her riding. At least, not entirely. Though the events that had led Sweet to seek Dex out had occurred at the stables. Someone had begun threatening Miss Woodruff. Matthew had taken it upon himself to get something done about it. "And here I am."

"Yes. Quite. Here you are. But the threats were not carried out directly, you say?" I was trying hard to think what sorts of questions Dex might ask. And what sort of information I'd require in order to be able to fill him in properly once I was back at the office and had worked up the courage to tell him what I'd done.

"No, no. See: that's part of the problem. If a direct course had been taken, we would be able to respond in kind. However, the notes have been left in strategic locations—locations where only Flora would find them—making it very difficult to discover the identity of the threatener."

"And it's all been notes, correct? Nothing more."

"Yes. That's right. Thus far. We fear . . . well, we fear escalation."

"And how many notes have there been?"

"Just two."

"Do you have them with you?"

Sweet shook his head. "Flora has them," he said. And then,

almost shyly, "She doesn't know yet I've been to see anyone about it."

I liked him for the admission. Plus it made me feel a little better about my own deception.

"All right," I said, "but can you tell me where the notes were found and what information they contained?"

He nodded his sleek head, clearly pleased that there was something he could answer in the positive. "Flora found the first one about a week ago. She has a locker in the tack room at the stables in Griffith Park. When she's out for a ride she doesn't keep it locked because she has her tack with her. So on this day she returned to put away her saddle and bridle, as she would on any other. When she opened the door, a note fluttered out."

"Fluttered, you say?"

"That's right. She said it struck her that the note was positioned so that it would fall in just that way when she opened the door."

"And the note itself," I was moving him along. "Did you see it?"

"I did. It was very rough. The paper itself was quite coarse. And the writing was large and blocky, as though it were written by a child."

"And is that what you supposed? That it had been written by a child?"

"No, ma'am. Our impression was that it was childishly written, with the intent to deceive."

"I see," I said. "And what did the note say?"

"It was a warning. It warned Flora against competing at the Winter Carnival horse show."

"Warned?"

Sweet hesitated before answering. It seemed that even repeating someone else's words in this regard caused him pain.

"It said . . . it said if she competed, she would die."

I toyed thoughtfully with the bit of crust from my cherry pie still on my plate. I knew I would eat it; I was just prolonging the pie eating time involved in the operation. Gracie's pie was that good.

"Those are strong words to be tied to a horse show," I said. "Is there a lot of money involved?"

"In the show, you mean? No money at all. Ribbons, trophies. That's all. However, in Flora's case the show will be a qualifier towards Olympic competition."

"What are you saying? That if Flora competes successfully in that show, she'll be able to compete at the Olympics next year?"

"Well, not quite. But it would make her that much more difficult to keep out."

"Pardon?"

"Well, there's never been a woman on the equestrian team, you see."

"Never?"

"That's right. And, Flora . . . well, she's just that determined. She's trying to remove any obstacles they have. She has a fantastic horse. And she's a very talented and accomplished rider. And it's not that she's as good as the men on the team . . ."

He let the rest of it go unsaid, perhaps thinking it would sound arrogant. Or boastful. But I heard it anyway: Flora wasn't as good as the men on the team. She was better. She'd have to be, too, if she wanted to find a place among them. She'd have to be a lot better to hope to compete at that level. That could be part of the problem, I thought. Part of what she was facing now. I kept the thought to myself.

"Do you think it's possible? Flora making the team, I mean. Do you think there's actually a chance?"

"She thinks so. She's been working towards Olympic qualification for two years. She's not the only one, of course.

But no one in this region is as likely to make the team as she is. And she's ready: she's got a very good horse, she's in great form, and she's confident. Or, well, she was. You know. Before all of this began."

"And the second warning? Was that also related to horse show competition?"

"No, ma'am," he said, and I had to restrain myself from pointing out that I was younger than him and "ma'am" could scarcely apply. "It happened while Flora and I were at a dance two nights ago at the Midwick Country Club."

"In Pasadena?"

"Alhambra," he corrected.

"All right," I said.

"Someone left a note on the seat of my car while we were inside. On the passenger seat, on her seat. All it said was 'Watch your step.' "

"At a dance? You didn't think it was ironic?"

"No, ma'am."

I had to try even harder to ignore the second "ma'am."

"But you felt the two incidents were related?"

"Well, they had to be, didn't they? Who goes around leaving notes like that?"

"Still, it sounds very different from the first."

"It didn't *feel* different," he said, perhaps a bit huffily. "And the presentation was similar."

"The presentation?"

"The coarse paper. The childish writing. But there was no direct threat this time. Flora made me *swear* I would not tell her family."

"Oh, I see."

"She was afraid that, after the first note, they'd put her under lock and key."

"That might not be a bad idea," I said.

"You don't know Flora," he said, sounding a little feverish. And then, "I imagine it's clear now why I've come to you."

"Well, slightly. But why don't you make it plain and tell me straight out?" Before she had the chance to top off our coffees, I waved the waitress away with a smile. He was talking now. I didn't want anything to slow him down.

"As I said, she made me swear not to tell her folks about the second note. Yet I fear she's in danger and if something should happen to her due to my negligence in this matter, I'd never forgive myself. Do you understand?"

"Quite," I said. "But what are you hoping we can do for you?"

"Isn't that obvious?"

"Not really. On the one hand, I would imagine you want us to discover who's behind the notes."

"That's right," he said passionately. I almost wanted to laugh. But gently. There's just nothing sweeter than a young man in love.

"Of course. But on the *other*, it's possible you want someone to watch Miss Woodruff. If she really *is* in danger, you'll want to take steps to keep her safe. That's another aspect of the service we can provide."

I heard the words play back in my head: *another aspect of the service we can provide . . .*

And I wondered, perhaps somewhat arrogantly, if Dex's little shamus operation had ever been represented with such polish. It was all I could do to keep from slapping my own back. There were still things I needed to learn.

"Well, I . . . I hadn't thought of that," he said, obviously pained by his omission. "I've come here on my own. Without consulting Flora's family. It seemed to me they weren't moving quickly enough. And since Flora hasn't been entirely forthcoming with them in terms of the number of threats she's received,

I thought it imperative to put . . . measures in place before something happened."

"Quite right," I said, trying to sound knowledgeable, in control. Trying also not to let my voice hint at what I was really thinking, which was how I was going to tell all this to Dex without having him blow his top. Not that he usually blew his top. But then I'd never actually shanghaied one of his clients before now. Which reminded me. "And one thing you should consider, Mr. Sweet: are you certain she has also been entirely forthcoming with you?"

"What do you mean?"

"Well, she didn't want you to tell her family about the note you found in your car. Is it also possible that there have been other threats? Ones she didn't want to tell *you* about for fear that you would worry."

He shook his head, but I could tell from his expression that this was something he'd given some thought to. If I was right, though, he didn't follow the thought. He chose, instead, not to be distracted from his original mission.

"Can you help us?" was all he asked.

"Well, based on all you've told me, your needs fall well within the realm of what the Theroux Agency can do for you."

The Theroux Agency. I liked the sound of that. I'd have to tell Dex.

Maybe. Maybe I would tell Dex.

His face cleared instantly. "Why, that's wonderful. Can I engage you right now?"

"Umm . . . yes. Yes of course," I said, madly thinking through logistics. "Mr. Theroux charges twenty-five dollars a day. Plus expenses. Though if you decide on surveillance *and* security, the fee would, of course, be appropriately higher."

"That sounds within the realm of what I expected," Sweet said, calmly taking out a billfold and beginning to peel out some bills. "We'll start with surveillance. If I give you two hundred dollars today, will that be enough for you to begin?"

Would it? I did some fast calculations. Our office rent was one hundred. My pay for the month was sixteen bucks. There was a bookie named Smitty who kept calling for Dex and I knew Dex owed him a C-note. Plus Dex would want some walking around money. This job looked like it was going to go deep, and I could see that though he was extending a couple of hundred-dollar notes to me, the bills had brothers still in his wallet. I swallowed my nervousness so he wouldn't see it and said, "For all of what we're discussing, three hundred would be more appropriate."

I knew it was pushing things, but Sweet had no problem with it. He reached into his wallet and fished out another bill, then handed the three of them over to me, nice as you please.

And here I was with three hundred bucks in my mitts and no receipt book. I was reluctant to have Sweet come back to the office before I'd had the chance to work on Dex. On the other hand, though, the man couldn't be expected to give me that much cash and just trust me. After all, he didn't know me from Eve. I needn't have worried, though, because clearly, the three Cs meant more to me than they did to him.

"I didn't bring a receipt book with me from the office," I began. But he held up his hand and stopped me.

"No problem, Miss Pangborn. You can give it to me next time you see me."

"When would you like us to begin?" I asked.

"As soon as possible. If you come to the stables in the morning, I'll introduce you to Flora. We can go from there."

CHAPTER TWO

Before I got anywhere near Flora Woodruff, I had to set things right with Dex. Once I got back to the office, I realized that was going to have to wait for the following day. When I opened the office door, the strong smell of tavern wafted out. Spent cigarettes and spilled booze struck me as inappropriate scents for a place of business but, judging from the sounds Mustard and Dex were making, they thought it smelled just fine.

". . . And there you were: hat on backwards, standing in the middle of the street, shoes in one hand, and a girl in the other."

"Remember that girl? What the hell was her name?" This was Mustard. The door to Dex's office was open and too much of them was spilling out.

"Was it Celeste?" Dex asked. "No, Celine. She couldn't have been much more than about eighteen."

"I could have fallen for that girl, you know."

Dex hooted at this. "Sure you could have. If she hadn't fallen for *me*."

"Is *that* how you played that whole thing out in your mind? 'Cause me? I came up with a different story."

"Sure, but who was it had their shoes off?"

"And they weren't even your shoes!"

I stuck my head into the office to see if things looked as bad as they sounded. In addition to smelling like the bottom of a barmaid's shoes, the room was a mess so, in that regard, things were worse.

"There you are, Kitty," Dex said, a little thickly I thought. "You've been pretty quiet this last while. I figured you'd come in before now to see if you could shake me loose to see watziizname."

Which meant Dex didn't even know I'd been gone.

I quickly debated if I should tell him that I'd taken the meeting with his client and now had quite a lot of what was actually Dex's money in my handbag, but I could see this wasn't the time.

"Matthew Sweet, Dex."

"Right. Matthew Sweet. Why haven't you been chewin' my ear down to a nub?"

"He left, Dex," I said, glad it wasn't a lie. Matthew *was* gone.

"He left! Imagine. That's not the way you win the services of the top PI in the Southland, that's for sure."

"Wait," Mustard said. "*The* Matthew Sweet."

"He's the only one I know of," I said. "But he didn't look all that impressive to me. He's only about my age. Maybe a little older."

"Ah," said Mustard, "that'll be junior. If I'm right, his old man is in oil. Half the derricks you see between here and Culver City? Sweet Oil has got their hooks in them somehow."

"Well, that makes sense, anyway," I said. "I'd have figured he was from money."

This made Dex sit up a little bit. At least, that was what I thought.

"Well, why didn't you say that before, Kitty? I've always got time for a client with something that jingles in his pocket."

"Ha," I said. "This one has got the stuff that folds, Dex. And I didn't see you punching the clock in an effort to get to him."

"Ah well," he said, slumping back down and taking a sip from the half-empty lowball glass in front of him. "My watch musta stopped."

"Well, good then," I said. Suddenly inspired. "Because I made an appointment for you to meet with him out at the stables at nine tomorrow."

"Well, cancel it."

"What?"

"Look, if that was an appointment I wanted to keep, I would have kept it already. Now you call him up and tell him it's off. Got it, Kitty?" He unfurled himself from behind his desk and popped his hat on his head. Mustard followed his lead. I could see they were preparing to go.

"But, Dex," I said, scrambling for the right words to get him to change his tune. They didn't come to me, so I ended kind of weakly. "You need the . . . *we* need the work."

Dex looked at me close then. He looked me up and down. And he didn't look at me the way you want some bird to look at a dame. No: Dex was looking at me the way you look at a little kid who's pushing you too far. The kind of kid who's going to either get a licking or half an hour alone in the corner, staring at the wall. When he spoke, his voice was level. Quiet. Like he meant business. I haven't heard that voice often; not directed at me. And I knew he wasn't kidding around.

"I ain't going out there in the morning, Kitty. And I'll have you remember: the only one that can decide if I need work is me."

He didn't wait for my reply. And he didn't waste any more words or time. With a curt nod and with Mustard on his heels, he walked down the hall towards the elevator without sparing a glance back over his shoulder. Once there, he pushed the call button. It came half a minute later and carried them away.

CHAPTER THREE

I had three hundred bucks in my pocketbook. I considered feeling guilty about it and started worrying about what the next day would bring, but life is short. And times? They're hard. Dex isn't one to hold a grudge or even remember he'd been upset with me after an afternoon of hard drinking with Mustard. I figured the next day everything would come right. For now, though, a tiny bit of that three hundred clams was burning a hole in my pocketbook. Just a *tiny* portion, mind you. I knew it belonged to Dex.

For example, under the circumstances, it didn't seem right to begrudge myself the nickel it cost to ride Angels Flight up Bunker Hill on my way home. For one thing, walking up all of those two hundred steps with all that loot might just invite trouble. Who knew what sort of mishap could befall a girl?

On Bunker Hill and on my way home, passing the butcher's on Olive gave me an idea. I ducked inside and got a pound of ground round and, almost as an afterthought, I got him to add in a dozen sausage links for good measure.

Back at the house, Marjorie was beside herself when she saw my bounty. "I'm only going to have to decide what to do with it all, aren't I? I was going to make boiled cabbage and potatoes for dinner. Should I throw in some sausage links, you think? Would make for a nice richness. Or maybe a meatloaf on the side and save the sausages for morning?"

I smiled and said it was up to her: I'd happily eat whatever she decided to dish up. Then I escaped to my room, knowing she'd rhapsodize through possibilities until she needed to stop and make dinner.

Beyond the odd chicken or bit of suspicious-looking ground beef that Marjorie was forced to stretch beyond all recognition, meat was a treat we hadn't been seeing often of late. And I knew that no one felt its lack more than Marjorie, who always wished she could somehow do better for the eight or ten people who boarded at the big house I still called home.

Marjorie and her husband, Marcus, were the owners of the house on Bunker Hill that my father built for my mother when they were first married. He'd died suddenly during the stock market crash of 1929, but I always figured he must have seen the writing on the wall because, though he'd lost everything, a few months before he took his own life, he'd left our home to our family retainers. It was maybe the only good and savvy move he made in his last year because he died owing a lot more than he had. Had the house been left to me, his creditors would have managed to get their hooks into it. As things were, Marjorie and Marcus let me stay on, as Father must have known they would. And things went on much as they had before, but for the boarders Marcus and Marjorie took in to help make ends meet. And that state of affairs suited me fine: it had always seemed to me that the house was too big just for Father and me. Too big and too dreary. I'd spent my early childhood knocking around in endless corridors with empty spaces between them. When I thought back to my earliest years, I saw only the shadow of my father and those bleak and lonely rooms.

Things were different now. It seemed disloyal of me to admit it, but with my father gone, it seemed the light shone more brightly through the windows. Or maybe it was just that I'd never been aware of how much light he'd ordered blocked off. He'd not been a happy man and it had surprised no one at all that he'd not ended happily, either. No one was surprised but me, I suppose. Though I was surprised enough for everyone.

I was away at school in San Francisco when he ended his life, so was spared the final days of angst and anxiety followed by the plummet of ruination. Sometimes I wonder if it all would have turned out differently if I'd been home. Could I have helped him make sense of his world, or what was left of it? Could I have convinced him to rely on me? To believe in the strength he hadn't even seen in the both of us?

When thoughts like these come up, I chide myself because, to be honest, I'm not sure I *would* have had the strength, the fortitude required. I was young and inexperienced. I was a child of privilege. A debutante with my life mapped out, though it had proven to be the wrong map. Had I been home to witness his despair, I'm not sure I *would* have known what to do. Not then. That's a different kind of regret.

Now, in the waning months of 1931, my life was different. I had a job, not one that I did because it amused me, but because I needed the money: I needed to eat. Though I had been raised to be a dutiful daughter who would grow into someone's dutiful wife, now my only duty was to myself and to the ones I had chosen to honor—Marjorie and Marcus, in a way.

And Dex. I had to admit that, in our relationship as boss and secretary, he purchased a kind of duty from me. I owed him my honesty and to be the very best I could at the job for which I had been hired. Which was the reason I was now in such a conundrum. Sometimes I felt I understood what was best for Dex more than he himself did. And though I knew that to be a kind of arrogance, I couldn't change how I felt. But I allowed it was possible that, this time, I had taken things too far.

While waiting for the dinner Marjorie was no doubt already concocting, I sat in my room and thought about the three hundred clams currently trying to dig their way out of my handbag. What kind of duty was I showing Dex now? But it wasn't stealing. I had no intention of keeping the money. I just had to figure out how to *explain* it to him: how to let him know I'd not only successfully powwowed with a client, but had settled on a fee *and* taken the dosh. And never mind that it turned out it was a client he'd already decided he didn't want. Dex could be flexible when it came to decisions like this; I'd seen it before. Right now he was adamant about not taking the case but I had the feeling that he'd take it if it were presented in the right light.

On the stairs on my way down to dinner, I got a whiff of a delectable odor I hadn't experienced for too many days: cooking meat. Marjorie had decided on meatloaf after all. My stomach started grumbling and I moved a little faster. And everything but dinner and a peaceful evening at home fell right out of my mind.

CHAPTER FOUR

On the long journey out to the Griffith Park Riding Academy in Burbank in the morning, I forgot all about duty and Dex and instead cursed my lack of foresight. I could have told Matthew Sweet to meet me downtown or someplace easier to get to by streetcar than Riverside Drive. I could have copped everything to Dex and gotten him to get Mustard to arrange a car. I could have confided in Mustard and gotten a car on my own—Dex had taught me how to drive. But none of these easier things had occurred to me in time and I hadn't realized how many Red Cars I'd have to swap to get myself out to the far side of Griffith Park.

I arrived a full half hour late for my appointment with Matthew Sweet and there wasn't a darn thing I could do about it. The last forty-five minutes of traveling had taken it out of me, and I was stressed and steamed by the time the streetcar let me out near the riding academy.

The day was warm and I guessed that the stress had raised my temperature. I could feel my skin grow moist as I went from building to building at the stables, trying to figure out where Flora Woodruff's horses were stabled, then tracking down Miss Woodruff herself. It didn't help my mental condition any when I realized I also had to hope I'd find Matthew Sweet with her and that he'd filled her in because, if he hadn't, she'd probably give herself a wonder as to why I'd tracked her down.

I found the two of them in the small but posh restaurant in

the clubhouse that was part of the riding academy's complex. Uniformed wait staff hovered nearby while the couple cozily enjoyed their morning tea and toast. The place was nice— elegant and beautifully furnished, not exactly the kind of place you figured would be attached to a barn. I hadn't figured on it, anyway. It made me hope that, after all my traipsing around, I smelled better than I felt.

Despite having been left waiting, Sweet was as friendly and forthcoming as he had been the day before. Miss Woodruff, meanwhile, was doing a good impression of someone who didn't need or want rescuing.

She was nineteen or twenty, tops, with a tidy little profile, marcelled hair the color of a shadow, and a steely gray gaze that made one think she could take care of herself, despite her small stature and delicate build.

"So you're the big shamus," she said, looking me up and down. I felt my cheeks color under the intensity of that look. Her frank gaze might have been slightly rude but I could see it wasn't mean and that suited me fine: if I have to have one, I'd rather not have the other. She indicated I should take the empty seat at their table, and when I did she promptly pushed a cup and saucer in front of me and showed that I should help myself to tea from their pot.

"Well, hardly big," I said, smiling, though in truth even though I'm more likely to be called lanky than anything else, and I'm tall—for a girl—I felt like a pony next to the elfin Miss Woodruff. There was something about her that reminded me of a fawn: she was delicately made but you sensed a strength—not deeply hidden—that brought the forest to mind.

"My boss, Dexter Theroux," I said, "he's the big one."

"I'm sorry to see he couldn't make it this morning," Sweet said. "Did his case become even more complicated?"

"Quite," I said nodding. "That's exactly right. Though I can't talk about it. You understand." Sweet nodded, but Flora didn't look impressed. I got the idea she'd be a tough one to knock the socks off of. No melting lipstick. Not on our girl.

"Will he be joining us later?" she asked.

"Not today, I don't think. But soon. And don't worry," I said, crossing my fingers behind my back, "I'll fill him in on all we discuss once I get back to the office."

"Well, you can fill him in all you want," Flora said with an exasperated tone and an affectionately cross look at her fiancé, "but I think Matty is being a big silly."

"Really, Miss Woodruff," I said, aiming for the tone Dex might have taken: the experienced PI. It came out sounding more like stern older sister, but it was all I had. "One shouldn't take such threats lightly. You have to proceed in a serious fashion. At least until we discover who sent the notes and determine the condition of their mind and thoughts."

"You mean until we figure out if it's someone crazy?" Sweet said.

"Yes, of course," I said, "that too."

But Flora was thinking about something else. "Matty, you told her about *both* notes?"

"Why, sure I did, Flora. I figured I had to. All I want is you safe."

"But what about what we discussed?" she said in a stage whisper.

"I agreed not to say anything to your dad, Flora," and I was pleased with him for the bit of steel I heard in his voice. "And I kept my word."

"Why, yes you did, Matty. I can see that. You kept your word by going around it and telling someone altogether different. Is that what being married is going to be like? You sneaking around behind my back?"

I busied myself with my tea while this exchange was going

on. Examining first the bottom of the cup—the china was Beswick and quite lovely. There was a rose pattern on it and it seemed as strong and as delicately made as the bones of a bird. Then the tea. I took a bit of sugar. Then a bit more. Then just a splash of cream, trying to think of the last time I'd had real cream. I couldn't. It made the tea all the more delicious. All the while I hoped they'd settle their little argument quickly and peacefully. Because if it got any more heated, I figured I'd go out into the sunshine and wait for them to finish their argument.

"C'mon Flora, no," Matty was saying. "It wasn't like that at all. Don't you see? I love you. More than anything. And I just couldn't live with myself if something bad happened to you and I'd done nothing to stop it: if I just stood by and watched it happen, when there were things I could have done."

"So you hire *her*? Why, look at her, Matty. I could do a better job of taking care of myself!"

I wanted to point out that I was *sitting right there*, but opted to keep my mouth shut and focus instead on the important business of choosing a nice piece of toast to go with my tea. And it looked like *real* butter in this joint, too, I noted, as I spread it a little feverishly on my toast. That *would* be a treat.

"Her boss is one of the best known PIs in the city, Flora." This was true. Actually, it was once more true than it was at the moment Matty said this, but I thought, again, keeping my mouth filled with buttered toast might be the better part of valor. In any case, the salty/sweet/fat flavor was nearly causing me to swoon. Paradise lost and regained, all on a small triangle of toasted bread. "She's his secretary and she helps him out some. But I hired you the very best."

"And what's Daddy gonna say?"

"What do you mean?"

"Well, he's going to wonder why you got all hot and bothered and hired a private dick—no offense, Miss—over just that single note. He's gonna wonder why, if it's such a hot idea, he didn't think of it himself."

"I don't think we ought to think of any of that."

"You don't, do you?"

"No. I think we ought to just think of your safety. Yours and Fritzy's."

"You think Fritzy might be in danger?"

"Sure. If it *is* someone who doesn't want you to compete, I would imagine the threat might include him. That was always the impression I got, anyway."

"You did?" There was real horror on her face now. As though having her own safety in danger was one thing. But Fritzy? That was something altogether different.

"Who's Fritzy?" I asked. My toast was done and I was unable to contain myself any longer. *Fritzy.* I imagined a child—perhaps a young nephew. Or some other person of small stature who required protection. The heat of the argument had died down at the mention of his name, in any case. I could see Flora re-evaluating the situation in light of this new information: she was weighing everything she had and looking for dangers she might have missed. I recognized the expression. She'd been brave before, careless with her own safety. But she was scared in the face of what Matthew had opened up to the air.

"Fritzy is my Hanoverian," she said.

I just looked at her, waiting for the words to organize themselves into some kind of sense.

"My horse," she said, a little more insistently, as though wondering if I was hard of hearing. "Fritzy is my horse."

"Ah," I said. This actually added up. I could see I should have figured it out on my own. "And fill me in on something, please. Because I really don't know very much about horses."

At this Flora shot Matty one of those couples' looks they

never think anyone else can see. This one said, "See!" The look he returned was just tired. But all she said was, "Shoot."

"There was something in your tone that made me think you're quite attached to Fritzy."

"Of course," she said immediately.

"But also, in terms of competition: if something should happen to . . . Fritzy, would you be able to replace him?"

"Not easily. He's a very special horse. We're a team! It would certainly take me a long time to be competing at anywhere near the same level, even if I were able to acquire a horse of equal caliber."

"But Fritzy came from Germany," Matty reminded me. "Flora's dad paid a small fortune for him . . ."

"Matthew!"

"Well, he *did*. I just want Miss Pangborn to know: she has to have all the details. Fritzy is a very special animal. And it's true: not realizing that he might also be at risk could be a terrible mistake."

I sighed deeply, quickly thinking this through. Now we had to watch the girl and make sure nothing happened to her *and* watch the horse and make sure he was okay, too. Plus we had to figure who was up to all these shenanigans. The way I figured things, that was going to be job one because, with that sorted out, all this other stuff would go away. We had to find out who wanted to do Flora Woodruff some harm. To that end, I asked a series of gentle questions: who, if anyone, would want to hurt her? Had she had any altercations with anyone at all recently? And since the threat had mentioned a specific horse show, who would benefit if she weren't able to compete in that show?

She claimed that there was no one she could think of, so I tried a different approach. "What about the Olympics?" I prompted.

"What about them?"

"Matthew told me you were trying to qualify."

She looked away. "It's a little more complicated than that."

"Tell me."

She met my eyes then and I could see something deep inside them. It took me a moment to place what it was. When I did, it was so intense it put me back on my haunches. It was something like desire. I knew I was looking at an idea Flora wanted so badly, if Matthew had understood the depth of it, he would have gotten up and walked out the door. There was no way a mortal man could compete with what I saw—just for a second—in those beautiful eyes.

"No woman has ever been allowed to compete in the equestrian events at the Olympics." When she spoke, her voice was calm and walked on a single note. It didn't betray any of what I'd seen. "But I shall. I'm that good. Tell her, Matthew. Tell her I'm not boasting."

Matthew smiled, perhaps slightly embarrassed, but when he spoke there was no hesitation. He meant what he said.

"She's that good," he said with a nod. Then to Flora, "I already told Miss Pangborn that anyway."

"And Fritzy. He's that good, too. We *have* to be that good if we're going to make the team." Her quiet confidence impressed me. I hadn't seen her ride, but looking into those eyes and feeling all that confidence, I didn't doubt her words.

There wasn't a lot to say on top of that. We were finished with our tea anyway and they took me out to the barn to meet Fritzy and to see the tack room where the first note had been found.

The tack room was not exciting. As the name implied, it was just a room. Filled with lockers, two couches, a smattering of scarred wooden chairs, a battered coffee table, a radio—some of the more flighty horses were apparently soothed by the sound of it—and a whole lot of saddles and bridles and piles of other stuff apparently necessary for well-to-do horses. All of this pile of stuff, Flora explained to me, was blanketed by that word: tack.

Fritzy himself was impressive. Greeting us over the top of his stall door, he seemed to me to be impossibly tall, though Flora was quick to tell me he was sixteen-one. When I looked blank, Matty offered actual information.

"He's sixteen-point-one hands. And there are four inches to each hand."

"To the tips of his ears?" I asked.

"No," Flora said, "to his withers," and she pointed to the bumpy bit where his neck met his shoulders. Withers. I had a lot to learn.

But he was a very handsome animal, even I could see that. A beautiful brown so dark it was almost black. They informed me the color was called chestnut. (And I did not ask why horse stuff all had to have special names.) The color of his mane and tail were similar to that of his body, but all four of his legs were a crisp white, almost all the way up past his knees.

"They look like stockings," I said.

"That's what they're called," Flora said.

"No kidding," I said.

When he first recognized Flora coming towards him, he rumbled deep in his throat and though it sounded a bit threatening, I could tell it was not. It was a whickery equine welcome. She rubbed his neck and tickled his velvety pink nose as she made the introductions. I was a little touched by how much she obviously cared about the horse, though it did strike me as ironic that she seemed more tender with Fritzy than I'd seen her be with Matthew, who I figured was every bit as handsome as her Teutonic equine.

"*Meine liebchen,*" she crooned to him when he extended his neck for more petting. "*Meine suisse Fritzl.*"

"What are you saying to him?" I asked.

"German," Matty supplied. "The horse has only been here for a few months."

"Right," said Flora. "He still mostly only understands German. *Ist das nicht richtig, Fritzy?*" This last, obviously, was directed at the horse. And I could hear it was a question and was glad she hadn't left a space for him to answer.

"Uh . . . when . . . when will he learn English? Don't the other horses find it confusing?"

Flora cast a look at me, I could tell she was checking to see if I was teasing and, bizarre though I found the situation to be, I was actually serious. After all, he was in America now. Shouldn't he understand the lingo?

"Why, he's learning all the time. Not everyone speaks German to him. I just learned a few words so I could bond with him when we first started working together."

"I think that, with other horses, he speaks . . . em . . . horse," Matty said, earning himself another one of Flora's looks.

The stall was near the center of a large barn with two wide aisles of sixteen stalls on each side. Considering the location in the busy barn, in his stall and during the day, Fritzy was about as well located as one could wish. I said as much to Flora and Matty, then asked about what happened in the barn at night.

"What do you mean?" Flora asked.

"For safety. I imagine there's a lot of coming and going during the day? Horses in and out? People coming and going?"

"I suppose so," Flora said vaguely. "I really hadn't thought about it."

"What about at night?" I asked. "Is the barn locked? Is there a security guard? Or . . ."

"I honestly don't know," Flora said, looking slightly embarrassed at the admission. "I'm so seldom here until dark, let alone after it. I've never given it the slightest thought. I can't imagine they guard it, though. These are *horses*, Miss Pangborn. Not motorcars."

"Still," I said quietly, not wanting to argue but understanding what needed to be done, "we'll need to find out for sure."

After a bit more of a look around the facility, I told them I would do that research, then give some thought on how to proceed.

"I won't give you my assessment now because I'm sure Mr. Theroux will have recommendations and ideas." I did not add that I hoped fervently that my words were true, though I *did* suggest we meet again the following day—with Dex. I crossed my fingers behind my back as I said it. Flora requested the meeting take place at her house.

"My parents are in Carlsbad for a few days," she said, and I understood the comment to mean that, for the moment at least, she didn't want her parents worried by the possibility that she might be in danger. I thought that, if she *was* in danger, her parents ought to be informed. After all, the more eyes that kept a careful watch, the less likely something would slip by. But we could worry about that up the road if necessary. For now I had other concerns. Concerns that seemed larger to me. Like, for instance, where—oh where!—I was ever going to begin this story when relating it to Dex.

Back on the streetcar I had plenty of time to ponder. And then something else gave me reason to think: I saw Matty Sweet stream by me in a white-on-cream convertible. The passenger side was empty. He had a dreamy expression on his face and I could see the wind ruffle his hair. He was heading towards the city, which meant, with a bit of forethought, I could have begged a ride.

I sighed deeply, then took it as penance, settling back into the worn seat on the public conveyance and trying hard to ignore the slight stench of the man near me who was perspiring heavily into a heavy woolen suit that was too hot for the day. Sweat seemed to ooze even from under the brim of his bowler hat. I imagined a job interview somewhere and the only suit he owned. A figure in a tragicomedy. Sad. If only he didn't have to sit so close to me.

I tried not to think of Matty, now far ahead and gone in his creamy car. If not for my willful ways, I wouldn't have needed a ride home. Dex would have had one less client but I would have been light at least that much guilt.

CHAPTER FIVE

By the time I got to the office, I had worked up my nerve to tell Dex everything. He wasn't there.

The sign said, "Back in a half hour," which made me smile. For a PI, Dex had a funny streak of ambiguity. Sometimes you got the feeling that Dex thought this: why walk a straight line when half a dozen squiggly ones would get you there all right?

The fact that he wasn't in the office annoyed me, though. I'd spent most of the long Red Car trip back from meeting with Matty and Flora dreaming up how I was going to tell Dex how far all of this had gotten. I'd tried out various phrases in my mind and thought about the best way to approach the whole matter. Most of all, I'd bolstered my courage so I'd be able to talk to him. Not finding him there sucked the wind right out of my sails.

I took the sign off the door and settled in at my desk, still musing on what to tell my boss. Inevitably, he'd come waltzing in the door in whatever condition the day dictated and I'd have to tell him about the case I'd taken on in his name. For the first time ever, I found myself hoping Dex would turn up half-cut. He's a gentle drunk, is Dex. Never a mean one. Drink makes him more affable. I figured I could use some of that when the time came.

When he arrived though, he was stone-cold sober. More, his suit was pressed and his hat was brushed and there was a brightness to his face that told me he hadn't suffered any ill effects from the previous evening's activities. It had looked to me like he and Mustard were ready for an evening filled with nothing but serious drinking and the swapping of soggy tales. I figured inebriation of some type would be a factor. Yet here he was, all bright-eyed and bushy-tailed. I wasn't quite sure what to do.

"Well, there she is," he boomed to no one at all when he caught sight of me. "There's the secretary who thinks it's just the thing to come breezing in after noon." Despite the words, there was no rancor in what he was saying. I'd been Dex's secretary for a couple of years. I was dependable. I was usually even punctual. He might be curious about why I'd come in so late, but he didn't look steamed. Rather, he stood in front of my desk with a big grin on his face as though he knew something he shouldn't.

"Oh, Dex," I said, blushing when I caught his meaning. "It's nothing like that."

"No?"

"Nothing at all! In fact, it's got to do with work."

"Really," he said, not sounding at all convinced. "How so?"

"Well, you remember Matthew Sweet?"

"I may have been drinking yesterday, kiddo, but I can remember that far back. He was the client you got so riled up about me blowing off."

I just looked at him then, the import of what he was saying not coming quite clear, yet I knew I was hearing something I hadn't heard before.

"What do you mean, you blew him off? You didn't."

"I didn't?" Dex said, looking amused. "Actually, Kitty, I believe that's exactly what I did."

"You didn't *want* to see him?"

"That's right. I don't trust him. I've had doings with his old man. Left me feeling like I'd just rather not have truck with the lot of the Sweets. See, the old man? He's got more money than

God. Figures that gives him the right to treat a man like he's worse than the dirt under his feet. I got no use for people like that, Kitty. I don't ever need the work that bad."

"So you and Mustard . . ."

"Yeah: we waited him out. Luckily I had a fresh bottle of bourbon in there because he hung around for a real long time."

I didn't know if I should be mortified or angered by this revelation.

"Why didn't you just tell me that you never intended to see him? Why didn't you let me know you wanted him to skedaddle? You gave me the idea you and Mustard were just passing the time."

"Ah, well, Kitty, you're a sweet kid. It's one of the reasons I like having you around. You're always on the up and up with everyone." I blushed a bit at this, but I didn't think Dex noticed because he went on without missing a beat. "If I'd told you he woulda seen it on your face. And I wanted him waiting and optimistic."

"You wanted to punish him?" I said. "For something his dad did? That doesn't seem quite fair."

"Fair? What the hell is fair? I guess I hadn't considered it that way, though," Dex said, not looking particularly remorseful. "Ah, well. The kid is gonna have to learn sometime he can't have everything he wants. He may as well start here."

"Well, actually, Dex, that . . . um . . . reminds me. There's something I need to talk to you about."

He plunked himself down in the chair opposite my desk, stretched out his long legs, tidily crossed his ankles, and shook a cigarette out of the crisp, new pack of smokes he pulled out of his pocket.

"Shoot," he said as he bent his head to light the cigarette. I found myself only slightly annoyed that he was being very agreeable as well as abnormally sunny. My little confession would

41

have been easier if there was a cloud over his head, and not just of smoke.

"It's about Matthew Sweet."

"Ah," he said thoughtfully. "You're not sweet on Sweet, are you?" Dex grinned, clearly pleased with his own joke.

"Oh. *No.* It's nothing like that."

"That's good," Dex said and I was surprised that he sounded genuinely relieved.

"It's just that, when you wouldn't see him yesterday . . . well, I feared we might lose a client we needed. The money, that is. And I . . . well, I took him on myself. For the agency. For *your* agency."

Dex looked at me blankly, the smoke forgotten for the moment at the corner of his mouth. I knew I wasn't explaining things very well. I could see the result of that on Dex's face. And his smile had been wiped clean away.

"I don't get what you're saying, Kitty. That is, I have a hint that I do, but I'm hoping I'm wrong."

"Well . . . that is . . ." I took a deep breath and decided to get it over with, like jumping in a lake on a cool day. A plunge into icy water, then everything is fine. "The thing is . . . when you wouldn't see him, I took him for pie and coffee. At Gracie's?"

I looked at Dex and he was just looking back, not smiling. Not nodding encouragingly. Just a flat, hard look.

"And . . . and he told me about the case. And . . . well, I took it."

"You. Took. What?"

I gulped a bit at his tone. He was about as mad as I'd ever seen him. At me, that is. As mad as he'd ever been. At me.

"The case," I said, my voice lacking the strength to lift very far beyond a whisper.

"But how could that be, Kitty?" His voice was casual now. Too casual. Almost light. But I knew him better than that. I knew we weren't yet out the other side. "You're not a shamus, are you? When I wasn't looking, did you hang out a shingle: Katherine Pangborn, PI?"

"Oh no, Dex. Not at all. I meant . . . only . . . that is . . . I took him on as a client *for you.*"

Dex was quiet a moment before he spoke again. When he did, his voice still held that reasonable tone.

"But, Kitty: if I wanted him for a client, don't you think I would have taken him on myself?"

My previous confidence in the wisdom of my actions was gone. What, really, had I been thinking? I suddenly had no clue.

"I . . . I guess you would have. It's just that, well, you and Mustard were drinking and . . . well . . . I got the idea that . . ."

"You got the idea that I was having such a good time with Mustard I couldn't be bothered with a client?" His tone let me know just what he thought of that. For my part, I didn't even nod my agreement. When put that way, it really *did* sound ridiculous. "What the hell do you think of me, Kitty? Am I such a boozehound I wouldn't even bother with a client?"

"Well, I wouldn't have said *that,* Dex . . ."

"After all this time together, Kitty, when have you ever seen me too far out on the roof to deal with someone's paying troubles?"

I actually thought about this one before I answered. Because, though it was true that I'd seen Dex plenty drunk during business hours, he had never been too far lit to take a meeting. Sometimes it had been a close matter; that was true, as well. Sometimes he'd needed me to bring him coffee and maybe a cloth to wash his face, but he'd always managed to pull it together enough to do a credible job representing his company.

"Never, Dex," I said now, not quite meeting his eyes.

"So what gave you the harebrained idea I was doing it yesterday?"

And now, with this question, I actually felt as though I had a leg to stand on.

"Why, you did, Dex! You and Mustard just sat in here and dipped the bill and laughed and told stories. What did you think I'd think?"

"Honestly, Kitty? I don't know. But that's not the point, sister. You're my secretary, remember? You're not supposed to take on clients. You're not supposed to decide things at all. You're supposed to sit at this desk. Answer the phone. Type. Get coffee when I ask. That's what I pay you for. And suddenly you're off taking meetings and what-not and I guess that means you're not doing your job."

As he spoke his voice had filled his lungs so much that, by the time he finished, he was standing in front of my desk with his arms crossed and his voice raised to a level that was so close to a shout you could barely tell the difference.

"I was trying to help," I said, my voice dipping as his rose. "You don't sit here eight, ten hours a day. You don't have to answer the phone and listen to people call who want their money. We've been a little short around here, Dex. You had to have noticed. And then a guy walks in and offers us money? What do you think I do, Dex? I take it. Sure I do. And I'm sorry: if I'd known you had some kind of . . . what? Some kind of beef with the kid, I most certainly wouldn't have taken his case. But you didn't tell me."

"You took money?" Apparently, out of all the words I'd said, those were the only ones that had registered. I felt my shoulders slump and I sighed. We were getting no place fast.

"Yeah, Dex. Yeah. I did."

"How much?"

"Three hundred. I told him fifty bucks a day. Plus expenses. And three bills up front. He didn't bat an eye."

"Well, he wouldn't, would he? He's too busy scraping the tar sands off his shoes. You gonna give me the money, or are you waiting for me to beg?"

I hauled out my purse, and handed over the three hundred clams, minus the bit I'd spent on sausages and streetcars.

"I nearly left it at home," I told him. "I was scared to drag it all the way out to Burbank on the streetcar."

"Burbank?"

"It's a long story. Before I tell it, I wanna figure where we are."

"What do you mean?"

"Are we going to take the case? Or not?"

"What are you talking about, Kitty? I thought you said you already did?"

CHAPTER SIX

I do not understand Dex. Most of the time, I know better than to try. There were moments there, after I told him that I'd taken on the case, where I honestly thought he was going to fire me. He looked so unspeakably angry. Once all the facts were laid down, though—and once they were all added up—Dex seemed happy enough with the way things were turning out. And while I got the idea he was pleased the case had to do with an oilman's son's girlfriend and not the oilman himself, he didn't tell me that, so I didn't know it for sure. But I think that may have been how he rationalized the whole business: how he made working for this client not break his personal code. Bottom line: we had a case and it meant we would eat. However it had come about, I got the idea he had decided not to examine the history of how we'd gotten the case too closely.

Dex didn't have any appointments booked for the afternoon, so I made some coffee and brought it into his office along with a cup for myself. Dex seemed to like the coffee well enough, though he chased it with a couple fingers of bourbon that he poured into a lowball glass alongside.

"These tastes go great together, Kitty," he said over his second double sip. "You oughta try it." I wrinkled my nose and shook my head. I don't, as a rule, drink spirits. And I certainly didn't feel like getting mixed up with the hair of Dex's dog.

And then I filled him in. Everything I could remember: that first fluttering note. Then the one that had been left in Matty

Sweet's car. The fact that Flora didn't want her parents to know how serious the matter had become. Which reminded me of my own observation: that Flora herself didn't seem to be taking the matter seriously at all.

"Is it the boyfriend?" Dex said.

"The boyfriend, what?"

"The boyfriend trying to protect her? Doesn't want to see her get messed up?"

"Right."

"Or *is it* the boyfriend?"

"Leaving the notes?"

"Right."

"I don't think so, Dex. He looked like he was more afraid than Flora."

"Hmm," Dex said. And I didn't know if that single syllable meant never trust an oilman's son, or if it meant we always hurt the ones closest to us. Either way, I *did* know Dex well enough to understand that he intended to keep an eye on Matty Sweet. I didn't think it was necessary, but I also understood his reasoning. In cases like this, closest was the first place we tended to look.

I was pleased that Dex asked me a lot of the same questions I'd asked Matty and Flora and so I was able to supply him with some of the information he needed. I guess I actually *had* been paying attention at least part of the time while I'd been sitting in Dex's outer office, answering his phones and listening to parts of conversations in our tiny waiting room. Or while I was making coffee, or ordering up booze for Dex, or cars. But Dex was not as confident that Flora needed a bodyguard. "It doesn't sound like a professional thing to me," Dex said. "You know: some rival of her father's or someone who *really* hates her. If they wanted her dead, they'd've thunked her on the noodle with a baseball bat . . ."

"Dex!"

". . . or fed her some poison scones."

"Poison scones?"

"You get what I mean. But this kind of thing? Someone's try-ing to scare her, that's all. And, from what you say, it doesn't sound like they're doin' a real good job."

I thought about Flora's confident little face and the way she'd laughed at Matty for worrying.

"Well, you're right about that, anyway. She's not scared. But that doesn't mean she doesn't have a reason to be."

Dex thought the horse was a different matter. "The threats have been about a horse show, right? So it seems to me it's pos-sible it's a competitor; someone who maybe thinks our girl is a threat and wants her out of the picture. You kill someone under those circumstances? It's murder. But the horse . . ."

"I see what you're getting at. You think Fritzy might be in danger?"

"Aside from the other horses laughing at his moniker? Yeah. I'd say. And the horse is valuable, you say?"

"I don't have a number, but her dad bought the horse for her in Germany. Had it shipped here." I decided not to mention for the moment that Flora apparently thought the horse was German-speaking. I already had enough to deal with. "And she figures she can compete on him in the Olympics and that it wouldn't be possible for her to train another horse in time."

"Well, that's the key, then: we need to protect that horse."

"The other thing is this: there's never been a woman on the Olympic equestrian team."

"No kiddin'?"

"It seemed to me it was possible someone was maybe trying to keep her off the team."

Dex laced his hands behind his head and leaned back in his chair, considering.

"Sounds far-fetched to me," he said finally.

"Me too. But, look: no one has actually done anything. Just left a couple notes. Could it be someone who doesn't want to see a girl compete in the Olympics?"

"Someone like who?"

"I don't know. Someone on the local Olympic committee, maybe? Or someone else on the team."

Dex shook his head doubtfully. "That might be too big a field to mow, Kitty. But we can try. Even in that case, though, the horse might be key. We need to keep a close eye on him."

I was skeptical of that. But it turned out I was wrong. Problem was, by the time we figured that out, it was too late.

CHAPTER SEVEN

West Adams wasn't far from downtown, but it was far enough. Walking was out of the question. I might have tried it, but I knew better than to suggest it to my boss. I *did* suggest we take the streetcar, but he pretended not to hear. He got me to call Mustard to have him send over a car and a bottle of bourbon. When I got him on the phone, Mustard said he wouldn't have trouble with either. Then he asked about my boss.

"How's Dex's head today, Kitty Cat?"

"Don't *call* me that. How many times do I have to tell you?"

"Two million," Mustard said. And then, like a mischievous little kid, and before I could say anything else, he hung up. I wondered idly how many more it was going to take to get us to the number he had mentioned. The way I was feeling, we'd get there in under a week.

The next day, the car showed up just when Mustard had said it would. It was long and black and it made me mad to ride in it: the journey took all of ten minutes. I figured we could have walked the distance without too much trouble, but I kept my mouth shut. I was already steamed. If I said anything, Dex would get mad. I figured I should cut my losses and just have one of us steamed. Better it was me.

The Woodruff pile was an alabaster monolith, and not in a good way. It was difficult to determine the style, but the towering white columns made me think Greek revival, while the turrets and huge mullioned windows added a look that was decidedly rococo. I figured that, whatever style the Woodruffs told their friends it was, what it shouted was: money lived here. They might as well have made a big sign: the people who lived here had more money than they knew what to do with, but they'd made it recently enough that they still liked the idea of throwing it around.

As he pulled the car through the porte-cochere, I looked at Dex and he looked at me and we both knew what was on the other's mind: if money was getting tossed around, we were putting on catchers' mitts. It was just as simple as that. We weren't greedy, just that times were hard. If we didn't catch it, someone else sure would.

Before we'd set ourselves to knock, the double-height front door was pulled open and a uniformed maid ushered us in. I had an impression of overstuffed, overwaxed, and probably overpriced furniture as we were led through the house and out to the garden where we found Flora on a chaise lounging next to the pool, red-tipped nails wrapped around a tropical-looking drink. Matty was in the pool doing laps, streaking through the water as efficiently as a seal. When he saw us, he pulled himself out of the water and came towards us, hand extended, oblivious to the rivulets that poured off his well-muscled form.

"Mr. Theroux," he said. "So good of you to come."

I tested his voice for sarcasm but didn't hear any. I was relieved. A thing like that with Dex, well, it could just go either way.

"Not at all, Mr. Sweet. Not at all. Miss Pangborn here has filled me in on the details."

Flora rose out of the lounge chair and headed towards us. When we got a load of her, both me and Dex's eyes almost bugged out, but for different reasons. Well, maybe it was the same reason, but it came from a different place.

Flora's swim costume was . . . well, it was shocking. It appeared to be made from a single piece of some clingy orange fabric and it was fitted to her body like a second skin. Her arms were exposed, all the way to the shoulders. You could see every inch of her legs, all the way to her torso. The neckline plunged to expose a wide expanse of white flesh over her small breast line, and there was a similar plunge behind. Very little was left to the imagination. You could tell that the athletic young woman carried not a single ounce of extra fat on her frame.

I couldn't imagine swimming in such a get-up, without the protection of skirts around my legs and sleeves over my arms. Why, in the ocean, it was possible a fish could actually touch you and never mind what it would do to the men who looked at you: though if Dex was any indication, it would make them insane.

She came towards us, hand extended.

"How do you do," she said, as though it was Sunday afternoon and she was the queen. "I'm Flora Woodruff. And you are . . ."

"I'm Katherine Pangborn, Miss Woodruff. We met yesterday morning."

"Oh. Yes. Of course we did. But I meant who . . . ?" And she looked up at Dex with an endearing simper. I don't hold it against him, but Dex tends to have that effect on most women. It's just something in the cloth from which he's cut, I guess.

"This is Mr. Theroux, Flora," Matty supplied. "Miss Pangborn's partner. Remember? We asked them to join us today."

"Remember!" she said. "Of *course* I remember. I quite remember. Please, both of you, have a seat."

She called for the maid to bring out lemonade, then sat down at a patio table next to the pool. Dex fairly melted into the chair opposite hers. Matty and I selected chairs as well. If Dex's tongue was any further out he could have used it as a necktie, though, truth be told, I could understand why.

Flora sat there, across from us, as comfortable as you please. As though she were at some high society luncheon, or maybe the kind of tea that serves sandwiches with the crusts sawed off; yet for all of that, she was as close to naked as anyone I'd ever seen in my whole life. I had a hunch that the same could not be true of Dex—I figured he'd seen a naked person or two in his time—but he seemed entranced or mesmerized by her just the same. Maybe both at once.

She started to talk, but I'm pretty sure Dex wasn't listening. I could tell by his eyes: all he was hearing was a lot of "blah, blah, blah." I was wondering how to fix matters, when Dex took the whole thing into his own hands.

"Miss Woodruff," he said, interrupting her gently, but she turned an attentive face towards him and didn't seem to mind. "I trust you won't think me rude," Dex went on, "but I'd like to ask you something."

"Oh, Mr. Theroux. I'm a modern girl! You can ask me anything you like."

"You will forgive me? And, understand, I mean no disrespect. However, I would be most appreciative if you would find some sort of robe or covering."

"Excuse me?"

"Your bathing costume? It's most revealing. I'm finding it difficult to concentrate on the business at hand."

I was oddly pleased to see Flora blush at Dex's words. And she complied, disappearing into the cabana without further ado and returning moments later wrapped in a silky turquoise robe.

"Better?" she asked, a bit of the coquette returned to her face.

Dex smiled and said, "Much."

I glanced at Matty Sweet to see how he was taking all of this, but he kept his face neutral and I couldn't read a thing.

"Right," Dex said, picking up his lemonade and sipping. I'm

probably the only one that would have recognized the grimace. And I covered my mouth with my hand to hide the smile; Dex was probably thinking a shot of bourbon would sweeten things up considerably. "Miss Pangborn has filled me in and, in most regards, we are agreed."

"Most?"

"Right. It's certainly not a casual matter," he said to Flora sternly. "Any time there is a threat involved, one must weigh the possibility of someone aiming to carry it out."

"You see, Flora?" Matty sounded vindicated. "That's just what I told her, Mr. Theroux."

"Quite," Dex said and, again, I detected a sneer, but I didn't think they would. Nor would they have reason to know he usually didn't sound quite so much like a character out of an Agatha Christie novel. I wondered what he was thinking but knew I was unlikely to really ever find out. "Based on what I've been told, we're going to go with a three-pronged approach."

"Pronged?" Matty said.

"I myself will do the investigation," Dex said, holding up his right hand and ticking off one finger with his left. "We'll put a man at the barn," another finger, "and Miss Pangborn here will act as Miss Woodruff's companion."

Both our heads shot up. "What!" we said in the same moment.

Dex was unruffled by our reaction; he'd probably been expecting it and was ready. "It makes the most sense," he offered casually, though from where I was sitting right then, it made no sense at all. "Two young women, gadding about together, filling in their days as young women will. Nothing could be more natural. And it will allow Miss Pangborn the opportunity to keep an eye on Miss Woodruff and see to it that nothing untoward befalls her."

Flora and I eyed each other up and down and neither of us said anything.

"What about my work, Dex?" I said finally.

Dex smiled, not unkindly, and said, "I think we'll manage in the office for a bit, Kitty. And this is more important." He did not add—at least not in front of clients—that he would also save a bundle doing it this way. I'd be doing surveillance for the pittance of a secretary's wage. He would have had to pay serious muscle much more serious money. It did not escape me that it was also possible he was punishing me for sticking my nose in and taking the case.

"Do you at least ride?" Flora said, sounding more like a petulant child than I'd yet heard her.

I shook my head. I had studied many skills required by young women before my father died when he lost his fortune, but I'd never taken to horses or riding in a serious way. I'd learned the basics, of course. I'd been taught to ride well enough to sit a horse if pressed into an excursion. But anything beyond that . . .

Flora didn't say anything, but her disapproval was a live thing.

"What can *I* do?" Matty Sweet wanted to know.

"Just keep your eyes and ears open for any funny business," Dex said, not adding that he himself would be watching Sweet for business that was funny. "And if you see anything at all, report to either me or Miss Pangborn."

"Okay," he said. "And when will we begin?"

"No time like the present, right Kitty?"

I bit back the retort of protest I felt forming, caught my lower lip between my teeth, and nodded.

"Good," Dex said, rising. "That's settled then. I'll head back to the office and set up something for the horse. Someone to watch him, as we discussed. I'll make some phone calls as well. Flora, I'll need to reach you later today to make sure my man will have access to the barns. And he'll need to know where to go. Will you be here all day?"

"I'll be here at home until around two. If you don't get me by then, have your man meet me at the stables. My animals are stabled in Barn Twelve. Well, Miss Pangborn knows, she was there, so she'll be able to tell you."

Dex shook his head. "No, remember? She'll be with you."

"At the barn?" I said.

"Right. Listen, Kitty, I want you to be Miss Woodruff's house guest for a while."

"I beg your pardon?" said Flora.

"A big old pile like this," Dex said. I didn't like the shape of his smile. "I wouldn't imagine you'd have trouble finding a corner where Miss Pangborn could stay. She doesn't take up much room."

"It's not that," Flora said, "it's just . . ."

Dex didn't wait for her to finish. "And it would be best if no one knew the truth. I think Kitty is maybe a few years older than Flora." I glared at Dex. He smiled back. "But you should maybe tell people she's a friend from school."

Flora looked me up and down, then said dismissively. "No one will believe *that*."

I could feel my face redden and tears sting my eyes. I wanted to look away, but I didn't know where to look. I could suddenly feel how thin my dress had become in spots. How worn. I could feel every repair Marjorie had done so lovingly. And my shoes felt suddenly very down at the heel.

Dex smiled at her. Only I could have detected that his smile did not reach his eyes.

"Oh, but I think they will," he said evenly. "Miss Pangborn's blood is quite blue. At a guess, I'd say it's somewhat bluer than yours."

Flora blanched a bit at that, but Dex went on. She wasn't used to people talking to her like that. With Dex, no one ever was. The other thing she would have had no way of knowing:

56

Dex's show of not caring really was no show. At a word from Flora—the wrong word—he'd pick up his hat and head for the door and never give Flora Woodruff another thought. Maybe she suspected it, though, because her next words were more conciliatory and she aimed them at me.

"Forgive me," she said. "I forget myself."

I nodded at her, perhaps somewhat coldly. The words had stung.

"Miss Pangborn's father was a wealthy man." Dex just couldn't seem to let it go. I squirmed a bit in my seat. Uncomfortable.

"*That* Pangborn?" Matty said. "I'd wondered."

"What Pangborn?" Flora said.

"The Pangborn Building Pangborns?" Matty said.

Dex just nodded. I studied my lap. Mortified. When my father was wiped out after the crash of '29, he jumped from his office window. He'd lost everything. Even the Pangborn Building was renamed when his creditors took it over. Flora was just nineteen now. This would all be ancient history to her. At sixteen or seventeen her biggest concern would have been how much tulle to include in the design for her coming-out dress, not what boring financier had lost everything on a bad bet. And rightly so. Sixteen isn't meant for such concerns. Matty knew, though. Matty remembered the name. I flushed again, but for a different reason. I could see that the way he looked at me had changed.

"I'll leave Miss Pangborn with you now and head back to the office. Kitty, I'll figure some way to collect you later."

"It's all right Dex," I said, and I noticed he looked relieved. "I'll take the Red Car."

Once he was gone, I felt curiously alone, not to mention out of place. One of the things my reduced circumstance had created was a dip in the quality of my wardrobe. It was something

I hadn't thought about much before. In fact, I could scarcely remember the time when I put aside an item of clothing because it was too worn. It hadn't been so long ago that I'd either outgrown things or, as I got older, I simply grew tired of them or they fell out of fashion. It hadn't been long, and yet it felt like a different life. It was easy to feel that the carefree girl I remembered being, the one who never wore out her clothes, hadn't existed at all.

And where did these perfectly good clothes go when I put them aside? I now had no idea. I had a hunch Marjorie had made certain they got into the hands of young women who needed them. Fashions changed more quickly then than I acknowledged now. That was, at least, until I sat at Flora Woodruff's polished side. Even her robe was more fashionable than the dress I wore.

"Until we get used to each other," Flora said, "I'd rather not sit here like lumps. I have to train this afternoon. Let's go to the stables early, all right? You said you didn't ride, but you're not afraid of horses, are you?"

I shook my head.

"Well then," she said, "do you like them?"

I had to think about the question. Did I like horses? It was something I'd never considered before. They were pretty, certainly. Pleasing to look at, from a distance, when they were in a field. What girl does not *like* horses? That said, I'd never considered starting up a friendship with one. I'd just as soon have befriended a motorcar or a bicycle and, in some ways, those things felt less foreign.

I said none of this.

"Sure," I said. "I like them well enough."

"Well, that's good then. Maybe we can outfit you for the barns with some of my stuff. You're taller than me, so my jodhpurs would come up short, but if we can find you a pair of riding boots, the tops of them will cover the lack of length."

I sat in a gold brocade chair in Flora's suite of rooms and watched while she went to work putting together my first equestrienne ensemble. While she scurried around, I tried hard not to feel like the poor country cousin or the hired help, though I supposed under the circumstances, the latter was just what I was. She got a couple of the maids involved, checking old trunks and her father and stepmother's closets, and I sat there feeling dispirited, knowing that no matter what they came up with, there was no way I was going to feel any worse.

As it turned out, I was wrong.

CHAPTER EIGHT

I ended up in camel-colored jodhpurs from Flora and a dark green hunt jacket she said belonged to her stepmother. To my humiliation, the boots I wore were her father's, but I had to wear two extra pairs of socks to fit them out. I was told they were paddock boots, not proper riding boots. I figured it was just as well that I didn't have the eye to tell the difference.

"You'll do," Flora said, eyeing me critically.

"For heaven's sake, Flora," Matty said when he saw me. "You could have stopped at the tack shop at the Academy, picked something out."

"I know," Flora said impishly. "I thought of it. But this was much more fun." And she said it with such simple delight, I found myself liking her for the first time.

Matty drove us out to Burbank in a different car than the one I'd seen him in before. It was a vehicle so outlandish, my eyes widened when I saw it.

"It's called a Hispano-Suiza H6," he said when he caught my look. "I just picked it up this morning."

"And he's ridiculously proud of it," Flora said, getting in the passenger side of a car as orange as a West Coast sunset. "He has been since he ordered it four months ago!"

"And why shouldn't I be?" he asked, helping me into the backseat before settling himself behind the wheel. "D.W. Griffith himself has one of these babies . . ."

"So you say," she said tartly.

"He does. And I had to special order it from Spain."

"Spain!" I repeated, happier than ever that I'd asked him for more money than he'd initially offered. Anyone who special ordered a car from Spain could afford Dex's very highest day rate. These days, I'd have a tough time choking up enough cash for a jar of Spanish olives.

As I'd suspected, the trek out to the stables went by much more quickly than it had when I'd been on an endless series of Red Cars. It was one of those gorgeous late fall days: not too hot, not too cool and the balmy air as well as the pastures zipping past us along the way soothed my soul. I reclined in the luxury of the backseat of Matty's pride and joy, where there was enough noise that all I could really hear clearly were my own thoughts. It wasn't unpleasant.

When we got to the stables, Matty pulled right up to the clubhouse, but didn't park. "I'll see you ladies later," he said, doffing his hat. "Watch your step, Flora. And do what Miss Pangborn says, all right?"

She didn't answer, but shot him a bright white smile as she closed the door in his earnest face.

At the barn, there was no sign of whatever muscle Dex was looking to hire to keep an eye on Fritzy, but the horse was fine and greeted his mistress with a warm whicker.

"Hey, old son," she said, rubbing his face affectionately. "There's a good boy, *meine suisse.*" And then, to me, "You really don't ride at all?"

"I've been on a horse," I said. "And I had basic lessons at school. But I've not really done enough of it to say I ride."

"Well, Fritzl and I were planning on riding the park today." My eyes widened with concern and Flora laughed. "I *know.* And I *am* going, Miss Pangborn."

"Katherine," I said. "Please."

"All right then, call me Flora. But you're going to be calling to the *back* of me if you decide not to come along because I *am* going."

"Right," I said. "I got that already. But I don't . . . I don't have a horse."

Flora laughed at that. I found I was liking her better by the minute. "I know that, you goose. But now that we've determined that—forgive me?—you're really not much of an equestrienne, I know that none of the horses my family keeps will do for you. From what you've said, though, I know what type of horse I'll have to borrow for you."

As she went out the big double doors, she assured me over her shoulder that she was fine; she was just running to the next barn. True to her word, she was back in under ten minutes with a horse whose white coat was shot through with black speckles. He seemed very tall and regal to me, though Flora laughed when I said so.

"This is Blinky. He's about a hundred years old and has taught almost every kid in Los Angeles how to ride."

Blinky.

"Is he really a hundred?"

Flora graced me with an astonished look before she burst out laughing. "He's a horse, not a turtle. I was *kidding*. He'd old, though. For a horse. Somewhere near thirty, I would guess."

She told me that his color was called flea-bitten gray, which didn't sound very distinguished to me, and I thought the speckles looked nothing at all like flea bites. I thought he was beautiful. But for the name. Blinky. I thought he deserved a much more elevated moniker.

By the time the horses had been tacked up and Flora had made me take a few practice runs around the arena and then the four of us—Fritzy, Blinky, Flora, and me—headed out into the park, I was in something a bit like love.

There really is something magical about horses, about riding.

All that strength and speed. Freedom that you control with a bit of pressure from your legs and frail bits of leather in your hands. I was an instant convert. Flora could see it in my face—I must have looked either rapt or insane. Perhaps both—but she caught my eye at one point and she smiled, the way a mother smiles at a child who's understood something not readily apparent.

"It can come on you like that," she said, when we hit a bit of the trail wide enough for the horses to move along side by side. "I've seen it before. You go through your life without horses, wondering what all the fuss is about and then the first time you're within close proximity—boom!"

Yes, boom, I thought. That's just how it was.

I was clearly a neophyte, though. And if I'd forgotten, my body would have reminded me before long. I was using muscles I hadn't even known I had a few hours before.

"Your body gets used to it after a while," Flora said, perhaps noticing me grimace.

"But not today," I said.

"No. That's right." She smiled, though not unkindly. "Not today."

Fritzy was taller than Blinky and seemed to require more adjustments. He floated along on legs that wanted to go faster than Flora was letting him go; you didn't need to be any kind of expert to see that. He reminded me of something alight, yet barely contained. Something that would explode if not watched carefully. She had her hands full keeping him to the speed she was asking for, yet I would have said she was enjoying every second.

Flora told me when we were coming up on the hunt course, "You'll not want to follow me. Neither you nor Blinky are quite ready for this." It suited me fine to sit it out. I pulled Blinky up on the side of the course, and he and I stood aside and watched the young athletes at their training. I opted to stay in the saddle, simply because I was fairly certain that if I got off at this point, my muscles would give me hell if I tried to get back on.

It was astonishing to watch Flora and the big chestnut Hanoverian. I felt as though I were witness to a transformation. The spoiled little rich girl was at her very best on the back of a horse, I'd seen that already. But here, training to do the thing she wanted to do more than any other—compete for her country—I saw her collect herself and focus. Each time Fritzy headed for a jump, I saw the two merge into one, a beautiful centaur with the determination to jump any obstacle. I knew nothing of the sport, but I've got eyes: anyone could have seen that these two together were powerful contenders. Had I been uncertain, the applause from the other side of the course would have set me straight.

As it was, that applause startled me. I had thought we were alone in this sheltered woodland arena. I was wrong. Flora and Fritzy's audience was a tall blond man standing next to a tall, pale horse. They must have arrived while I was watching, but I hadn't noticed them. The horse was saddled, and the man was leaning on him, a cigarette dangling easily from his left hand. Both horse and master looked comfortable and relaxed.

"James!" Flora called when she saw him, then she cantered Fritzy across the arena and towards them before I could stop her. As I put Blinky inelegantly into motion in their direction, I made a mental note to have a talk with Flora later. If I was to keep an eye on her, galloping off towards strange men would have to cease, immediately.

Up close, Flora's audience was younger than he had appeared from a distance. Younger and paler. In fact, up close I could see that his hair was so pale, it was almost transparent. With that hair and skin, he'd have to keep covered up most days or risk burning to an absolute crisp.

"And who have we here," he said as I clumsily reined Blinky in.

"This is my . . . cousin. Katherine. Katie, this is James Stroud."

Cousin. *Katie.* I looked at Flora, but she just blinked at me and smiled. I realized I'd have to watch her even more carefully. Anyone who lied that smoothly . . .

"Hello, James," I said.

"Hi, Katie," he said. "I can see that good looks run in the family."

"Oh, James!" Flora said cheerfully, "just stop it."

"Apparently however," I said, "the ability to ride well is not inherited."

"I'll say," James said. "You should see my dad in the saddle. Scary sight, eh Flora?"

Flora nodded. "Quite," she said with a smile.

"You and Fritz were looking splendid out there today, Flora," James said. "Just splendid. You're going to have to make room for some new hardware after the Winter Carnival. You and Fritzy *are* planning on competing, aren't you?"

"Of course we are, James. Why ever would we not be?" Again, I looked at her carefully and could see no trace of the lie she was telling. Flora Woodruff lied just about as well as anyone I'd ever seen.

"Oh, no reason," James said, and I noticed that he, too, looked cool. As though the answer couldn't possibly matter. "Just asking."

"You'll be there, of course," Flora said. "You and Cedar."

"Of course," he said, giving the pale horse's neck an affectionate slap.

"Of course."

"What about the hardware?" I asked. Both of them looked at me questioningly. "James said something about needing room for hardware."

Both of them laughed. It was such a new world to me, but I was getting tired of being the butt of every joke.

"Trophies is what he meant," Flora said. "We call trophies 'hardware' for some inexplicable reason. Do you know why, James?"

"I do not. Because they're heavy?"

"There you go," Flora said, nodding, "because they're heavy. Where are you heading, James?"

"Back to the barn," he said. "Cedar and I had a big workout yesterday. I just wanted today to be light."

"And it was, too. All that sitting around and watching me and poor Fritzl doing all the work."

"It's true," he said. "Watching you made me feel totally rested." He gave a theatrical yawn and Flora laughed.

By tacit agreement, James swung up and the three of us moved out together. I decided to hang back a bit and watch carefully. Honestly, Blinky made that decision for me and I decided to go along. That and my nonexistent ability in the saddle. But I told myself I was falling back to give Flora and James a chance to talk. Flora seemed a bright enough girl. If something were amiss with James, she would likely notice.

But Flora didn't seem to find anything wrong with James Stroud at all. He was a tall man on a tall horse, and the combination was one she had to tilt her pert little nose up towards, despite Fritzy's towering Teutonic height.

I wondered at the flirtatious way she interacted with James. From back where I was riding—just out of easy earshot—her behavior was even more marked. The way her little gloved hands fluttered when she spoke, the impish way she tilted her head, the gentle pink stain on a perfect cheek: I could see all of this much more clearly out of earshot than I think I would have had I heard the words.

As we approached a fork in the trail, James said his good-byes.

"I'm supposed to meet some fellas over by the polo ring," he told us. "Lovely to have met you, Katie. Maybe we'll see you again?" And then he doffed his hat and was gone.

After the fork, the trail widened and Flora and I rode along companionably, side by side.

"He seems nice," I said.

"Oh, he's lovely," Flora said. "We've known each other since we were kids. He's *very* dependable."

I didn't know what she meant by that and I wanted to ask, but the words reminded me of something she'd said before: something I'd wanted to ask about but couldn't in James's presence.

"Why did you introduce me as your cousin?"

I'd begun liking her a while ago, but now her answer made me rethink that feeling.

"Why, I just thought he might believe cousin. I don't think he would have bought that you were my *friend*, do you?"

The words were said without malice. Maybe that made them hurt all the more. She said it as though it were the most natural, the most obvious, the most irrefutable thing in the world.

I was about to ask Flora what she meant by that when Fritzy sprang forward, without warning. As green as I was, it was all I could do to keep Blinky from lurching ahead when Fritzy bolted. Even so, I could see that Flora had her hands full. Something had frightened the big German horse terribly, and as Flora managed to calm him not far up the trail, I noticed a rivulet of blood running down his haunch.

"Oh my God, Flora. Look, he's hurt. What happened?"

Flora swung down and I watched her face as confusion turned to concern turned to anger.

"Did you see it?" she asked as she ran her hands up and

down his legs, checking for heat and other injury.

I shook my head. "I don't know. I didn't see anything."

"Go back and check, will you? I don't," her voice faltered. She pushed on. "I don't want to leave him."

Blinky and I didn't have to go far to find what I was looking for. Perhaps twenty feet back on the trail, the rock was the size of a large man's fist, and there was no doubt that this was the offending object: the sharp-edged rock was easy to see, as was the sheet of white paper tied to it with coarse twine.

Though I was reluctant to push my muscles enough to leave the relative safety of Blinky's back, circumstances forced me down. Every part below my neck protested as I slid to the ground. I steadied myself for a moment on Binky's patient side before looping an arm through his reins and bending down painfully to retrieve the rock.

"He seems to be all right," Flora said when she saw me leading Blinky back down the trail towards her. I'd walked the short distance because I was afraid I wouldn't be able to remount unaided. "It could have been much more serious quite easily: a little to the left and just a bit deeper, it might have hit a tendon. What's that you have?"

I held the rock and its cargo towards her. "Looks like it might have been a message," I said.

She pointed to the note. "In more ways than one."

She took the rock from me and slid the note out from under its binding before it even occurred to me to wait for Dex.

"Maybe we shouldn't open it right away," I said hurriedly. "There could be fingerprints, right? Or . . . well, something like that."

"Fingerprints on a rock?" she said. "Anyway, it's too late." She'd untied the package and was peeling off the note, dropping the binding on the trail beside her. "It's mine and it's open."

"Well, it is now."

Her face fell as she read.

"More of the same," she said, handing it over.

Once again the writing was crude, and what looked to me to be deliberately childish. The warning was equally unsophisticated.

Did this warning hurt the horse? Ignoring it would make things so much worse.

I turned the note over. It didn't seem to be enough.

"But they're not really saying anything," I protested.

"Don't you see, Kitty? They hurt him. He's *bleeding*. And they've said much more is possible."

I saw her scanning the empty trail, looking for someone, or at least a spot where someone could hide. I looked, too, but there was nothing to see.

"Let's get back to the barn," I said. "I'll feel better away from here. And I need to call Dex. Can you ride him?"

"I don't think I'd better," Flora said. "I don't want to take any chances until I get Doc to look at him."

"Doc is the veterinarian?"

"No. Doc is one of the stableboys, but he knows everything about horses. You can ride ahead, though."

I shook my head, secretly relieved my muscles were going to get a tiny break. I wasn't sure I'd ever be able to sit again, much less climb up on the back of a horse.

I retrieved the binding and made sure all the pieces of the deadly message were in our hands, and then we set off to hike the last half mile back to the barn.

CHAPTER NINE

When we got back to the barn, there was a young man in a poorly pressed suit and a slightly too large fedora smoking outside of Fritzy's stall.

"You can't smoke in here," Flora said, pointing to a sign practically right over his head.

"What?" he said, raising a watery gaze and exhaling a blue-gray column towards the ceiling.

"Smoking." She pointed again. "It's against the rules. This is a *barn*," she said, as though this final bit of information had been overlooked and would add clarity, but it didn't seem to.

"You want I should put it out?" he asked.

"Yes," Flora said tightly. "That would be very nice."

"Is one of you dames Kitty?" the kid asked once his Chesterfield had been ground under his heel.

"That would be me," I said, surprised. Even though Dex had said he'd arrange someone to watch Fritzy, I hadn't been expecting anyone yet. And certainly no one who looked like this. I'd have thought Dex would try to find someone who would fit in hanging around outside a horse's stall at a tony riding academy. But the only place this guy could hang around un-noticed was a speakeasy, if it was one of the rougher ones.

"Calloway," he said, making no effort to take my hand. The suit fit him uneasily, I noticed, as though the clothes he usually wore were rougher. The ill-tied knot in his tie confirmed my guess. "This the nag I'm s'posed to keep my eyeballs peeled for?"

I saw Flora's head go up a bit at the word "nag," but she didn't say anything, just sucked on her lower lip hard enough to make it turn bright pink.

"Yes," I said. "This would be him. Calloway, meet Fritzy."

"Fritzy, eh," Calloway said, "that's a funny name for a horse."

"Yeah," I said. "Funny."

"Sounds Kraut," he said.

"It is. He's from Germany," Flora said.

"A Kraut horse," he said with a snort. "How do you like that? So what's the plan?"

"Plan?" I said.

"Yeah. What you want me to do?"

"We have reason to believe the horse might be in some danger."

"What'd he do?"

"Do?"

"Yeah. Like, what? Did he croak another horse or somethin'?"

"That's funny," I said. "You're a funny guy. But I don't need funny. I need you to watch this stall. The funny you look for is business."

"Huh?"

"As in 'funny business.' You see any of *that*, well, you call me or you call Mr. Theroux or you get hold of Mustard. Got it?"

"Sure. Sure I got it." I could see by the look on his face that he was surprised at my tone, and perhaps the approach I was taking. I didn't care. I'd done my best to draw myself up to speak to him as I thought Dex might. From the kid's reaction, I was doing all right at it, too.

"I don't think this is going to work," Flora said.

"Sure it is. You heard him; he knows just what to look for now."

"No. I mean, look at him." She said it as though he might be a piece of furniture. It made me realize that, to her, he was. I guessed I was, too. "He doesn't fit in here in the least."

I gave the kid the okay sign, but led Flora out of earshot.

"I agree he's less than perfect for this, but he's all we've got."

"But just *look* at him. He can't hang around the barn looking like that. I mean, honestly, he really does look little more than a thug. What will people think?"

"Flora," I said, leaning in very close so that only she could hear, "he doesn't look little more than a thug at all. He *is* a thug. But that's just what we need. Maybe we could get him some different clothes? So he looks a bit more like . . . like a stable boy. Or a groom."

"No. I say . . . *no*. There's nothing we can do to him that will make him right. I aim to let him go."

There was more I wanted to say to her, but she didn't hang around to hear me say it. Instead she stomped right back to Calloway and started to give him the bum's rush.

"Your services are no longer required," she told him imperiously.

"You can't fire me, lady. Mustard hired me."

"I can and I will. And I am," she said.

"But I'm s'posed to get five dollars."

"How long have you been here?"

"About a half hour."

"Well then, you can have two, and you should count yourself well compensated."

"Flora, that's enough," I said. "Put your money away. How can you do this after what just happened out there? We need him. Now, please: get him some different clothes if you must, but if you care about Fritz's safety at all, you'll stop worrying about what people think and just help me do what we need to do now in order to get through this all right."

Flora drew herself up and turned on me then. At her most outraged, she was no taller, but her presence seemed to fill all available space. "I'll not argue this with you, Katherine Pangborn. I have to go find Doc now, to see to my horse. When I return, I want him gone from here." She indicated Calloway, who was regarding her with an unconcerned smirk. "Do I make myself clear?"

"But Flora, what about the . . ."

But she didn't let me finish. In a way, I'd never thought she would.

"No buts. *No.* I want him gone." With that she turned on the heel of her boot and headed more deeply into the barn. I knew what a last word looked like when I saw it.

"So who's gonna give me the two bucks?" Calloway asked.

"No one. Not now, anyway. You'll get paid when you're done."

"But what about what she said?" He indicated Flora's retreating form.

"Never mind what she said. Mustard hired you, right? She can't fire you."

"Listen, lady, I can see you've got some kinda argument going on here and I'm with you. I didn't make the trip for biscuits. But I don't got to stay here and get hollered at by some society dolly, okey? Now gimme my spinach and I'll skedaddle."

I looked at his tough-but-boyish face and could see he meant business. Since I seldom carried more than a quarter, I told him apologetically to collect from Dex or Mustard. Then I watched his back regretfully as he walked towards the parking lot. I didn't have a good feeling about this at all.

CHAPTER TEN

"Here he is, Doc. Thanks so much for agreeing to see him."

"No problem, Miss Flora. Your Fritzy's a nice hoss." A stable-boy, Flora had said. Yet the person she'd brought with her looked more as though he might be a grandfather than a child.

He was old—I wouldn't have dared to guess just how many summers he'd seen—and his voice was infused with the warmth of the South. He wasn't tall, but his back was straight and his eyes, when they met mine, were clear and kind. I imagined there was a time when his skin would have been dark but age had lightened it to an ashy gray. His tightly curled hair was gray, as well. The entire picture he presented was one of healthy old age.

"Doc, this is Miss Pangborn. She's helping me look after Fritzy."

"Af'noon, Mizz Pangborn," Doc said with a smile, but his eyes skipped along quickly. It was clear that the injured horse was his main concern. When Doc entered his stall, the highly strung horse seemed to settle slightly, just at his presence.

Though I might have spoken, Flora shushed me with a look and we watched together while Doc ran his hands knowledge-ably over the big horse. I got the idea that no veterinary instru-ments could have done a more thorough examination.

"You was right, Mizz Flora," he said when he was done. "There's no harm done, but he was lucky. It wouldn't have taken but a few inches to have done s'real damage. What you say it was? A rock?"

74

"That's right. Someone threw it. And there was another note."

Doc looked at Flora with interest, though my own glance was one of surprise that she was confiding in him.

"What it say?"

Flora reached in her pocket and thrust it at him.

He handed it back with barely a glance. "I cain't read, Mizz Flora," he said, as though this were the most natural thing in the world. But Flora flushed with embarrassment.

"Of course, Doc. Forgive me? That was thoughtless of me."

I looked at her closely as she said this, surprised by her tone and trying to place it. And then I did: respect and humility. That wasn't a combination I'd heard from Flora before. I suspected there weren't a lot of people who had.

"Oh, that's all right, Mizz Flora. You jes' tell me what it says."

And Flora did. I saw Doc's face harden and darken at the words.

"You hear that, Fritzy?" he said, slapping the horse's neck with affection. "They is all talkin' 'bout you. We'll have to keep a big watch out, hey boy?" Doc continued talking and I realized that he was choosing the words not for their import, but for the soothing effect they might have on the horse. I knew I was right when, not long after, Fritzy sighed, took some of his weight off the injured leg, and cocked that foot, then seemed to settle down into something like sleep.

"That was amazing," I said some time later when Doc emerged quietly from the stall, leaving Fritzy still dozing behind him.

"Ah, that," the old man said, shrugging. "It's not anything really. Horses like me fo' some reason."

Flora smiled at him with affection. "That's putting it mildly, Doc. And you know it."

The old man shrugged, but did nothing more to discourage her praise.

"Doc, is anyone in the barn overnight?" I asked.

"How you mean?"

"From the Academy. Is there a night watchman or anything?"

"No, ma'am. Nothin' like that." He looked as though he might say something further, so I pressed a bit.

"What is it, Doc? I don't think Flora told you, but I'm a private investigator."

"A shamus?" he asked. And I couldn't tell if it was incredulity or respect I saw on his face. I suspected the former but hoped for the latter. It was a forgivable conceit.

"That's right. And Flora is my client. Anything you say to me will be in confidence." I saw him waver, so I pressed on. "You can trust me not to repeat it."

"Why you hirin' a shamus, Miss Flora? On account of the notes? The rock?"

"That's right. So whatever you can tell Miss Pangborn might be important."

"Right," I said. "And you were telling us about a night watchman . . ."

"Well, there ain't no night watchman," he said with confidence. "But . . . if you're sure they won't get in trouble?"

"Whatever you tell us will be in confidence, Doc," I said.

"Well, some of the boys—the younger ones don't got anywheres else to go?—they sleep in the feed room. Sometimes. I don't think any of them sleep there all the time. But there always at least a couple of them there."

"It's against the rules?" I asked.

"That's right," he said. "But they don't hurt nuthin'."

"No, of course, you're right," I said. "In fact, it's probably a good thing. Someone should talk to management. You might be surprised, they might welcome the fact that they've got people here, watching things, overnight."

Doc nodded politely but didn't say anything. I could see

what he thought of my idea.

"Well, thanks for looking Fritzy over, Doc," Flora said. "And you don't figure it'll hurt to ride him?"

"No ma'am," he said, clearly relieved to have the conversation back on horses. "Let him rest today, maybe. Jes' get over his fright. You go home now and don't fret yourself. You come back tomorrow and ol' Fritzy be right as rain."

But he was wrong. Of course he was wrong. Because by the time we came back to the barn in the morning, everything had all gone painfully awry.

But first, we still had to get through the evening together. And whatever Dex was doing, I hoped he was getting some results.

CHAPTER ELEVEN

Flora had one of the Academy cars bring us back to her house. That simple act reminded me of something I'd forgotten: the casual entitlement of the wealthy. I hadn't thought to miss it when it had been mine. But when Flora walked into the clubhouse and everyone who worked there doffed hats and offered help, she accepted it all with the quiet calm I'd even forgotten how to generate.

"Yes, Reeves," and "Thank you, Anderson," and "Please have a car brought round for me, McPherson."

And when the car showed up, we hopped right in and allowed it to take us where we were going, without thought for the lives of those who were making it all happen. I didn't think about the Red Car even once.

While we drove, I tried to sort out who might have been cooking up the notes. Being present for the delivery of one of them had made the whole thing more real, somehow. I didn't much like it.

"Penny," Flora said, breaking into my thoughts.

"Hmmm?" We were in the back of the well-upholstered limo. It was surprisingly quiet; quiet enough, in fact, for reflective thought. There weren't a lot of cars that could be said about.

"You looked so far away just now. I wondered what you were thinking about. Your father? A boy? What?"

I laughed, partly out of shyness and partly out of just how far off she'd been.

"None of those things, no. I was thinking about you, actually. Well, your situation, really. And trying to make a list of people who might be trying to scare you. What about you, Flora: have you been giving it any thought?"

"Well, honestly? Considering the nature of the threats and the fact that they've all been somehow related to competition, my own best guess is someone on the Olympic committee or the equestrian team."

"Really, Flora? To be honest, that sounds far-fetched to me. After all, Olympic committees: don't they thrive on doing things right and above-board?"

"Well, you'd think so. But there's been an awful lot of resistance to having me join the team."

"Not just you though, right? Any woman."

"No, that's right. And see, if *ever* a woman should be considered for the team, it's for this upcoming Olympics."

"Why this one?"

"Well, money being what it is, Daddy heard that they won't even be having a full equestrian team here next year. None of the countries will."

"But this is an American Olympics. You'd think they'd field a full team?"

"Still: we're a long way from the East Coast where the team is mostly based. And it's an expensive trip. So I've been saying, since I was old enough to want it, that I'd compete. And I think they might have let me, too. But Doak blocked me six ways from Sunday."

"Wait: Doak. That's not a name you've mentioned to me before."

"I haven't? Well, I should have, because if anyone wants to keep me out, it's him."

"Who is he?"

"Major Sloan Doak," she said, drawing his name out as

though it were made of caterpillars. "He's director of the U.S. Olympic team."

"Equestrian team?" I said, but Flora shut me down with a look.

"We're not talking field hockey, that's for sure. No, I would have made the team by now, but for him."

"How would one get in touch with him?" I asked.

"Well, I'm not sure about that. But the team is stabled at the Riviera Country Club, so you could find him there."

"The Riviera? In Pacific Palisades?"

She nodded. "It's the only one I know of. The Olympic equestrian events will be held out there next year. The team has been training since spring."

"He's on the team?"

"Not this year, though he was in previous Olympics. No: Doak is team director, as I said. And there are cottages out there, as well. They're staying there—at the Riviera—while they train. You going to go see him?"

"Hmmm? No, probably not me: I have to stay with you, remember? But I'll tell Dex and he can go."

Flora nodded in a satisfied way. I didn't know what she was thinking, but I had a hunch she wasn't wishing Doak well.

CHAPTER TWELVE

Back at Flora's place, as soon as we were in the door, I could sense something different. And I was right: Flora sensed it, too, but she knew what it was.

"Daddy!" Flora said with a child's delight, rushing through the house to meet him. I followed behind at a more sedate pace, wondering who I would be introduced as this time. Surely not a cousin: presumably Flora's father would remember all of his nieces.

Cedric Woodruff was a surprise. For some reason, I'd expected someone charming and elegant, like his daughter. But he was a rotund little man with a thick mustache, a dark fringe of hair, and a way of speaking that put me more in mind of the docks than the Ivy League.

"Flory!" he said when he saw her. "There's my girl," and he gave her a big hug. "What have you been up to, dear child? Keeping busy with that big bruiser of a horse of yours?"

"Yes, Daddy, Fritzl is splendid. We're working very well together."

"That's grand, my pet. And who have we here," he said, as I arrived belatedly in the room.

"This is . . . this is my friend Katherine. Katherine Pangborn."

I saw the name register. "Pangborn?"

"Yes sir," I said. "*That* Pangborn."

"Ah. My sympathies, Miss Pangborn. I knew your father,

though only slightly. He seemed . . . he seemed a decent sort. I was . . . well, I was sorry to hear."

"Thank you, sir." It had been good of him to reach for something, even though I'd seen him stretch. I liked him for it. In fact, I liked him overall.

"Cedric, what's all the fuss?" The woman who followed the voice into the room looked only a shade older than Flora, though I felt certain skillfully applied cosmetics and generous doses of beauty sleep aided with that. Flora's stepmother didn't look thirty. She was beautiful in some darkly exotic way, taller than her husband and reed thin.

"No fuss, dearest. Flora has a friend over."

"A friend?" the woman said, as though this were an isolated occurrence. And then, once we'd been introduced, "I don't think I've ever heard Flora mention you, Miss Pangborn."

"Katherine, please," I said.

"It's not as if I talk to you about *any* of my friends, Carmella," Flora said.

"That's true, dear girl. We should rectify that. A girl *should* have friends. Ones who aren't horses, I mean."

Carmella's voice had a singsong quality. I wondered if it was for my benefit or if she talked like that all the time. If she did, it might explain why Flora seemed so ready to be irritated with her: there was a grating note to the woman's voice when she spoke to Flora. I put it down to the inexplicable dynamic between stepmothers and the young women who end up in their charge. I'd never experienced it firsthand—my father never remarried after my mother died when I was born. But I'd attended a private girl's school in San Francisco for many years. Among the daughters of the wealthy, stepmothers were not entirely uncommon. I couldn't recall ever seeing a healthy relationship in the whole bunch.

"How was Carlsbad?" Flora asked. I got the feeling that she

didn't much care, but wanted to divert attention from herself.

"Oh!" said Carmella, "so sad. Wasn't it sad, dear?"

"Yes," her husband replied, a touch of the parrot to his tone, "very sad."

"What was so sad?" Flora asked.

"Oh, that beautiful new hotel. And everything just *so*, you understand? Everything just as anyone could ever want it. It reminded me of *Europe*, in a way, didn't it dear?"

"Europe, Carmella. Yes. Quite."

"Everything," she said again, "just *so*. But the place was empty, wasn't it dear?"

"Yes," he said, "quite empty."

"Why, it was positively a *tomb*. And we were there for several days and not once during our stay did we see more than a handful of people in any of the dining rooms, on the strand, taking the waters. Anywhere. Dreadful."

"Why was it empty?" I asked.

Carmella dropped her voice to a conspiratorial whisper, "It's *money*, you understand? No one has it anymore. Why, they just finished building the place at the beginning of '30 and by then—boom. And we try to go, really we do. But there's only so much one can *do*, you know."

"Yes, actually. I do."

It amused me a little—it amused the part of me that did not feel sad—that Carmella Woodruff's idea of doing her part was staying at a luxury hotel on the ocean. And she'd said no one had money anymore, but I could see that wasn't true. The Woodruffs had money. They had heaps of it; you could feel it all around. And there were others like them, as well. Cedric Woodruff was a real estate developer. Lots of his kind had gone under, but he didn't look lean in the least. What was the difference, I wondered? My father had been a man of action, a man of vision. And look where it had led him. And Cedric Woodruff?

He looked as though he'd always taken the safe course. Was that the difference, then? Slow and steady, as they say. Would the meek inherit? Somehow this was not a reassuring thought.

These thoughts consumed me as I sat there, in the bosom of Flora Woodruff's family. Her doting father. Her lovely, if slightly unnatural, stepmother. Her beautiful horses, her stunning home, her adoring fiancé. Her enviable life. This could have been me. So easily. It *should* have been me. I wasn't jealous, though I could have been. But I felt suddenly empty, and the sadness that fell on me then was inexplicable, unexpected. I couldn't shake it and, all at once, all I wanted was to be away.

"Flora, dear," I said when I'd tried to divert my thoughts but they would not stray, "I think I'll go home now. It's been a long day. You're not going out tonight?" Dex had told me to stay but I found that I really hadn't the spirit for it. I wanted to be back in my own threadbare room with leftover meatloaf in my tummy and watered-down coffee with dessert. I wanted *normal*, I realized, and what had become normal to me.

Flora looked at me from under her lashes and I could see that, if she *was* going out, she wasn't planning on telling me.

"Let's talk in the morning," Flora said, and I noticed she hadn't answered my question. "We'll make our plans for the day then, all right?"

"Did you have a car, Miss Pangborn?" Cedric Woodruff said. "No? Let me have Schuster drive you home."

And so Schuster did. The Woodruffs' limousine was big enough for an Okie family of six to live inside. I sat in the back quietly for a little while, just letting the soft shocks cushion us along. I kept my face neutral and I didn't say a word. But I was schooling myself as I sat there. And I was wishing bad thoughts away. Because it seemed to me I'd spoiled all my chances and somehow I'd never even known they were right there, in front of me, all along.

Chapter Thirteen

Schuster had me about halfway home before I fought my way through the grayness and marshaled my thoughts.

"Listen Schuster," I said, winding down the glass barricade that kept our air from getting mixed up, "if the family doesn't need you tonight, any chance you could drop me off in the Palisades?"

"Certainly, Miss," he said in exactly the tone I'd known he would. The Woodruffs had looked settled in for the night: at least the elder Woodruffs, so to speak. And Flora? At least taking the car might keep her honest, keep her home. Though I knew I wasn't kidding anyone, even myself. If Flora *really* wanted to go somewhere, not having the car at home seemed unlikely to stop her. She could always call Matty, or even a cab. For all I knew, she might even have her own car; such things weren't unthinkable anymore, especially for someone as athletic and daring as Flora.

As we took the long sweep of Sunset Boulevard towards the sea, I saw fingers of pink and purple light reaching up from the horizon. It was beautiful. By the time we reached San Vincente, it was dusk and the light that hit the white board fencing on either side of the long curving drive created a prism that bathed everything in a dreamy end-of-day glow: the horses in their paddocks; the fairways; and then, rounding the final bend in the club's private road, the huge clubhouse, which stood framed magnificently in the cleavage of the foothills of the Santa Monica mountains. It dominated the acres of perfectly tended greens, the gleaming stables and polo fields, and even the distant ocean.

Schuster pulled the limo into the porte-cochere in front of the clubhouse. It did not look the least out of place.

"Shall I wait, Miss?" he asked.

"Tell me honestly, Schuster: would you mind very much if I asked you to? That is, I have no business asking if you would . . . but it would be ever so helpful if you did."

Schuster smiled at me then. I could tell he was not much used to consultation. "That's all right, Miss." He indicated a newspaper on the seat next to him. "I've got company for the next half hour. I'll wait for you here, take you home."

I smiled my thanks and slipped out of the enormous car, feeling less silly than I might have thought. It was the venue, I supposed. And, for one thing, the car made my clothes seem less dowdy. That is, if you commanded a car like that one, it really didn't much matter what you wore.

A doorman pulled the door aside and directed me to the concierge.

"I'm looking for Sloan Doak, please. He's staying here, I believe."

"That's right, Miss," the tidy desk clerk replied. I noticed that his tie was in the colors I saw all around me—club colors, I imagined—and that his hair was so firmly pomaded, it did not move even a fraction of an inch. "Major Doak is currently a guest of the hotel. However, this time of day he tends to be down in the stables."

"Can you direct me, please?"

He did, and by the time I reached my destination and saw all of the club's beautiful accoutrements along the way—the fountains, terraced walks, and perfectly coifed gardens—I was prepared to be astonished by whatever I found at the stables, and I was.

Though they were designed to look just like the buildings all around them, once inside you noticed right away that the temperature was several degrees cooler. On closer inspection it was apparent that the stable buildings were made entirely of concrete and built in such a way that it seemed likely they would survive any type of fire or attack.

Scent of hay and the warm, musky smell of horses, well cared for. A neatly attired young cavalryman sweeping the wide aisle.

"Can you tell me where I might find Major Doak, please?" I asked.

He pointed and grunted at about the same time, indicating a door at the side of the long, low building.

"Hot walker," was all he said.

I might have asked him what he meant, but opted instead to head off in the direction he'd indicated.

On the other side of that door, I found a small courtyard. A large apparatus dominated the space. It looked very much like a giant four-armed contraption for drying clothes. On the end of each arm a horse was tethered. As the horses walked in a sedate circle, the contraption rotated with them.

I was so entranced by the spectacle that I stood rooted for a full minute before looking around to see who else might be there. When I did, I saw a handsome man in a uniform regarding me with amusement.

"What are they doing?" I breathed, forgetting myself.

"Cooling down from their workouts," he said in a voice that was touched by the South.

"It's amazing," I replied.

He grinned. "Not really. Hot walkers are getting to be pretty common. But it does save us a lot of work, cooling them down."

I recalled myself then and felt color stain my cheeks in embarrassment.

"I'm sorry," I said, "I'm not usually so . . ." I struggled for words.

"Adorably childlike?" he supplied with a grin, and I felt my color deepen still further.

"I was actually going to say 'at a loss for words.' "

For some reason he laughed at that. "But I imagine you're out here for something other than marveling over our hot walker?"

"I'm looking for Major Doak," I said quickly, trying to recover. "Major Sloan Doak."

"Well then, you're in luck: Major Doak, U.S. Cavalry, at your service," he said with a shallow bow and a mock salute, and though the greeting was hearty, I could see he was wondering what someone like me might be doing looking up someone like him. Though he didn't look particularly put out at the prospect.

"My name is Katherine Pangborn." I was relieved when he didn't ask if I was *that* one. Also, I was surprised. I'd expected an ogre and Sloan Doak was anything but. "I wanted to ask you about Flora Woodruff," I said.

"Oh yes," he said guardedly. The temperature had cooled a few degrees at the mention of her name, though there'd been no change in his tone. "What did you want to ask about?" He stood in front of me, with his arms crossed. I was aware, too, that while his full attention was on me, he kept one eye on the horses in the hot walker.

"She told me she's a contender for a spot on the U.S. Olympic team . . ."

"She did, did she?" he said with no visible discomfort.

"Yes, and that you're really the only thing standing in her way."

"That's a lot of hooey," he said without heat.

"Pardon?"

"Hooey, is what that is. Miss Woodruff being on the team. We've been very clear about that with her. *Very*. But she won't take what we say at face value."

"I'm sorry," I said, genuinely confused, "I don't understand what you're saying."

"Well, that Woodruff gal has got the idea that all she has to do is ride well enough on a good enough horse and she'll be invited to join the team. That we won't be able to *not* invite her."

"Well, yes, I suppose she does. But isn't that right?"

"It may be right, but it ain't how it's done. Why, next year's Olympics is going to be the first time the whole team is going to have half-decent horses. And we're here, training, months in advance. We're doing it up right this time—my recommendation. We've got a chance to make a decent showing this time."

"My understanding, though, is that Miss Woodruff is very accomplished and that her horse is one of the top competition animals in the world, so neither of those things should be a problem."

He looked at me long and hard for a moment. I had no doubt that, for the moment at least, I had his full attention. Finally he spoke.

"You do know why that's not possible, don't you?"

"I don't understand."

"I mean, it's not possible for Miss Woodruff to be on the team."

"Because she's a woman," I said.

"Well, it comes to that in the end, I guess. But, no: it's because she's not in the service."

Chapter Fourteen

I looked at him for a full half minute trying to make sense of what he'd said. "Wait," I said finally, "are you telling me that everyone—your whole team—is made up of people in the service?"

"The cavalry, that's right. And not just our team; all of the teams are military men."

"No kidding?"

He just raised his eyebrows. And then he shrugged. "No kidding at all. I don't really know what to tell you. Poor little rich girl, she has some idea that if she hollers loudly enough, we'll let her play. The thing is, we did so bad in '28, she'd probably have a shot of making the team if she had a shot, if you follow."

"So it's an international rule or something?"

"Far as I know. The competing members of the equestrian teams are all military. And not ex-military, either: all active duty."

"So there's no way . . ."

He shook his head adamantly. I believed him. "None. Like I said, last time out, in equestrian sports, the U.S. came in eighth place out of sixteen competing countries. That ain't good, ma'am. We'd do just about anything to change it. And I've seen Miss Woodruff ride . . ."

"You have?"

"Sure. She insisted I come to some horse show a few months back: right after the team came out here to train. Sent a car for me and everything. Wouldn't take no for an answer. And I had a nice time and all and I sure was impressed with her ride and with her mount. Afterwards I told her the same thing I'm telling you; if there was a way she could ride for us—and if it was up to me?—hell, I'd let her. Pardon the language, ma'am, but she's that good an' so's that big horse of hers. But it ain't up to me: it's up to the Olympic committee and they're not about to change their own rules for one little rich gal, now are they?"

CHAPTER FIFTEEN

Major Doak went on in this vein for a while. I let him, too. Truth be told, I could have listened to his soft accent all day. West Texas, that's what he told me and he almost hadn't had to; I could hear the sun there. Almost taste the dust.

Before I left, he asked me to join him in the clubhouse for a drink. I turned him down, of course. Schuster was there waiting for me, for one thing. But also, it didn't seem right somehow. He was a lot older than me, sure. But the uniform, the accent, and his natural good looks pretty much cancelled that out. More importantly, though, he was the enemy as far as my client was concerned. It just wouldn't have seemed right to spend any more time with him than was strictly necessary. Plus, I wanted to get back to the office before I ran out of day. As late as it was, I didn't think there was much chance I'd catch up with Dex, but at least I could leave him some notes that he'd see the following day.

The office was locked when I got there, so I knew right away Dex had gone for the evening. I rolled a blank piece of paper into the typewriter and started writing up a list of things for Dex. Just things I thought he should know about: the way things had worked out with the kid—or rather, not worked out—and the things I'd learned from Sloan Doak. I'd always figured the Olympic connection was a long shot, but it was good to have it confirmed. That, at least, seemed like one angle we could put to rest.

I must have been sitting there, typing on and off, for close to an hour when Dex came in. He was surprised to see me.

"Hey kiddo," he said. "I heard the typewriter, but I figured I must be hearing things because I know for sure you're not supposed to be here."

I smiled at him thinly but I could see that he was only half kidding.

"She was in for the night and I just couldn't stand the thought of being there all evening."

"So you left," he said.

"So I left," I agreed. "There was stuff I wanted to do."

"But I thought I told you . . ."

"Listen, Dex, playing nursemaid to a rich girl was never part of our deal."

"No, you listen, kiddo; no one is taking this whole thing very seriously. Least of all you. When I tell you to stay put, you hafta stay put. It's part of our trust, Kitty. What if something happens to her? While you're not there?"

"Nothing's gonna happen, Dex. She's home with her folks and about a thousand maids and stuff. And, listen, one of the things I wanted to do was check out the Olympic angle."

"And you did?"

"I did. The Olympic team is training out at the Riviera Country Club."

"In the Palisades?"

I nodded.

"Nice," he said.

"Yeah, pretty nice. Anyway, Flora had told me that the team was already out there and assembled. Training. And she gave me the name of the guy that calls the shots."

"No kidding?"

"Right. So I went out there and chinwagged with this guy and—guess what?"

"I ain't guessing, Kitty."

"There was never any chance of Flora making the Olympic team, Dex. You have to be in the military to compete on horses at the Olympics."

"And you're sure he's on the up and up?" Dex asked.

"Yeah, I am, actually. It didn't seem like the kind of thing you could lie about. Easy enough to check, anyway."

"Good point. I'll do that tomorrow."

I started to protest, but he stopped me. "See," he said, "you *can't* do that, on account of you'll be busy with Miss Woodruff."

"Right," I said, trying to keep sour out of my voice. "What are you doing here anyway? It's after seven."

"I've been out chasing my own leads down. Just wanted to come back here and sort things through before I went home. Just like you, I guess." It wasn't something I'd known that he did. And the fact that I'd instinctively followed a similar pattern was a surprise. "Plus, usually it's quiet here in the evening." He looked pointedly at the typewriter and I smiled, despite myself.

"How did your day go?"

"It went all right," he said. "A few good leads. A few not so good. You know how it goes."

"Tell me."

"All right. Let's move into my office, though. You know I'm always happiest with a bottle in front of me."

"Not a frontal lobotomy?" I tried, but neither of us laughed when the quip fell flat.

So we moved into his office without laughter. I curled into the big chair opposite his desk and didn't even protest when he poured me a drink. I had no intention of drinking it—as I say, I don't care much for spirits—but I also know Dex doesn't like to bend an elbow solo when it can be avoided, and I was right there.

"You find anything good?" I asked when Dex was done fussing with booze and glasses and had tucked the bottle back in its spot in his desk.

"Good I don't know. But I found some stuff. Maybe tomorrow I'll find out if any of it is good."

He told me he'd spent some time on one of Woodruff Development's construction sites. "You know, Kitty, they're one of the last companies still building things. That alone made me kinda suspicious. Most of the others have put all their projects on hold."

"Kinda things?"

"Well, get this: Woodruff's company has the contract to build most of the housing for the athletes next year."

"For the Olympics? I thought they put them in hotels."

"Well, that's what they're doing with the women. But the men will be staying in a kind of village up in Baldwin Hills."

"A village?"

"Yeah. There's going to be training facilities up there, and places to eat and even get out a bit. A movie house where they'll be able to see Hollywood movies *and* see moving pictures of their performances of that day. And there's going to be housing for over a thousand athletes. That's what Woodruff's outfit is doing: construction of the village itself. That contract has to have been one of the most lucrative of the games."

"So the contract was hotly contested?"

"I don't really know, Kitty. That's what I've been trying to find out, because there could be some hurt feelings there. More than hurt; we're talking about a contract worth over a million dollars. That's enough loot to do more than hurt feelings. Say, did the guy Mustard sent out get there okay?"

"He got there all right," I said. "Flora sent him away, though."

"What? Why'd she do that?"

"Well, in fairness, he really *did* have the wrong look for the Academy, Dex. He looked more likely to throw down at a poker

95

table than hang around at a horse barn. And he kept smoking in the stable. I thought Flora's head was gonna unbutton."

"Now *that* would have been something."

"Anyway, she took one look at him—with his high-crowned fedora and his double-breasted suit—and she sent him packing. Maybe we can find her someone who looks a little bit more like he belongs in a barn."

Dex snickered a bit. "That's the ticket though, ain't it Kitty? You want someone who looks right at a riding academy *and* knows how to handle himself; protect someone else. That might be a tall order."

"Well, Dex, if you want someone out there, you'd best do it 'cause Flora didn't look too vexed about having to send this one away. I've no doubt she'd do it again. Even though we had trouble on the trail, I couldn't talk her into keeping him."

Dex's ears pricked up at that. "Sort of trouble?" he wanted to know.

"Another note. This one attached to the business end of a rock. Hurt the horse, too. When it landed. Out on the trail."

"Ouch. Hit him in the noggin?"

"Naw. Other end."

"Still," he looked sympathetic. "That can smart. What did the note say?"

"More of the same," I said.

"Well, crikey, that's no good. I'll call Mustard, see if we can get a replacement for the kid Flora sent away. I don't think it'll happen tonight, though. Even Mustard can't always work that fast."

"Well, whenever we get someone out there, it'll have to do. The horse has been all right this long, he'll probably be all right another night."

We talked some more about the investigation thus far. He told me that he'd gotten further with information on the

Olympic construction than he had with the line of questioning he'd wanted to put to someone—anyone—connected to the equestrian team.

"But then you got that covered, you said."

"I did. Anything else I can do?"

"Sure, kiddo," Dex said, looking at me with a knowing grin. "Sure, plenty."

I sighed when I caught his meaning. "Flora?"

"Right. In fact, isn't that where you're supposed to be to-night?"

"I know, I know. But listen, Buster; I know this ain't no union, but asking me to work 'round the clock is a little much, even for you." I was so anxious to make my point, I found myself sitting at the very edge of my seat and not breathing any more than was necessary.

"She started getting to you, huh?"

At his words I exhaled and sat back. "Shows?"

"A little bit," Dex replied with a gentle smirk. "Sorry, kiddo. I shoulda seen it comin'. I was just thinking about me: you know their world. You can be useful there and keep an eye out while fitting in. I didn't let myself think about the fact that, well, I saw her be kinda awful to you myself earlier today, didn't I? And I could see what she said hurt your feelings pretty much. I guess I just think of you as being made of tougher stuff than that."

This was Dex at his most empathetic, and I appreciated the effort. "It'll be okay, Dex. *I'll* be okay."

"That's good, kiddo, because your eyes and ears out there mean a lot to me. Take this new note, for instance. This clan is so closed-mouthed, it seems possible we might not have heard about it if you weren't there."

"True enough. I'm sorry, though. Flora insisted they wouldn't be able to get fingerprints from a rock, and I let her bowl me over and just handed the whole bundle over to her, then thought about what I should have done later."

"Well, you know, she probably doesn't realize it, but she's right enough about one thing: they would have had a helluva time lifting prints off paper and rock, Kitty. Even if our perp forgot gloves, which he probably didn't do anyway. You said there was twine, too?"

"Yeah. Almost like ribbon."

"Well, let's try to retrieve the whole package from Flora tomorrow. Get it to the police lab and let them spend a lot of time comin' up with nothing."

"Huh," I said, "that's some attitude."

Dex grinned. "I'm a realist, Kitty. You know that. Saves me from disappointment."

Dex still had a car and when he offered to give me a lift home, I took him up on it. And gladly. I was tired from a long day and sore from spending unaccustomed time in the saddle. All I wanted to do was get home, maybe find a bowl of soup, and climb into a hot bath. Just the thought of walking the few blocks to Angels Flight had almost undone me, and then I'd still have to spend the nickel or hike up two hundred steps.

I said good-night to Dex at the curb, then trudged up the walk and into the house, too tired even to be mouse-quiet. Hearing me come in, Marjorie met me in the foyer. She took one look at my tired face and limp hair and was glad to rustle me up a bowl of soup and a thick piece of her homemade bread smeared with lard. While I ate, she made tea and ran me a bath, which I sank into gratefully as soon as I was upstairs.

From the warmth and comfort of the scented water, I could see the dark paneling in my room, the leaded windows, the rich wood floors. All remnants of my childhood luxury.

My stomach was full, and good food it had been, too. It hadn't been made with the most expensive ingredients, but it had certainly been made with love. The lavender that scented my bath was from the garden. Another luxury, but one that cost us nothing at all. I had a job I enjoyed, at least most of the time. And, again, most of the time, I had enough to eat. And, yes: my plans had changed. I'd always miss my father. And I hadn't hadthe chance to go to Vassar as I'd planned. My life was different than it would have been, it was true. But would it have been better? I wasn't convinced it would have been.

These thoughts carried me from the bath to my bed. I slept with the conviction of someone who has done a good day's work, though also like someone who had given more to the physical than was her wont. Full stomach. Warm bath. Pleasantly sore muscles. The prospect of restful sleep. It made me think, for a while anyway, that success—affluence—is entirely in the eye and heart of the beholder. Most of the time that's still what I believe.

In the morning I got up. I got dressed. I breakfasted. I took the Red Car the not great distance to Flora's. I changed into my loaner jodhpurs and boots. She had Schuster drive us out to Burbank. On the journey there was laughter involved. I don't remember what about. Only that we were enjoying the sunny, fragrant morning. And truly enjoying each other's company, perhaps for the first time.

As Schuster stopped the car in front of the Academy, it had all the signs of being a very good day.

Then we got to the barn. And all hell broke loose.

CHAPTER SIXTEEN

I will spare you the carryings on. The cursing followed by swooning followed by still more cursing. I will spare you both the threats and the promises to a vengeful God. The tears. None of it matters in any case. None of it changes the outcome. We were there and the horse was not; it was just as simple as that.

There was no note, not this time. No indication at all of what might have happened. As we walked up the wide aisle, I could feel Flora collect herself when Fritzy didn't stick his head above the half-door and greet her with his customary whicker. Perhaps she feared illness at first, I don't know. But by the time we reached his stall, she was running. Me, hard on her heels.

The stall was empty. As though to reassure herself that this was the case, Flora hastily opened the wrought iron horseshoe-shaped slide bolt and moved deep inside the stall. Once she was in the center of it she stopped and turned around, her hands spread wide. I didn't know what to say.

When she'd collected herself enough to move again she came out of the stall and did an inventory. Fritzy's halter was missing from its peg outside the stall. Flora said it was leather with a wide brass band engraved with his name. A lead shank was missing as well. Neither of these missing things told us anything but the obvious: the horse had neither dematerialized nor wandered off on his own.

I followed as Flora scurried around the Academy, asking anyone if they'd seen him. No one had or, at least, not so they'd noticed. A big chestnut horse being led across a riding academy, out to the trails or even into a trailer, would hardly have attracted attention: not here, where you couldn't turn your head without having yet another horse enter your line of vision.

"What do we do?" she asked when we'd spoken with everyone we could think of. Her little face was pale and there were signs of strain around her eyes and mouth. It seemed to me it wouldn't take much to set her off either crying or screaming. She looked close to her edge. "Should we call the police?"

"Probably," I said. "First, let me call Dex. He'll know our best course of action."

Dex wasn't happy to hear from me, not in the least.

"Christ on a crutch, Kitty!" he bellowed into the phone. "The horse is *gone*? Of course you have to call the cops. You have to call them first. Now get off the phone and do that."

"I will. But what'll the cops *do*, Dex?" I was suspecting they wouldn't do much. "The horse is *gone*."

"Yeah, Kitty. I got that part. But you go ahead and call them, all right? And get Flora to talk to 'em. Make sure she tells them just who she is; they're more likely to treat it all seriously if they know she's a swell."

"Great."

"I know. Just the way things work in our fair city. Never mind, though. I'll come down there myself so I can have a look around. Keep her away from the area as much as you can. There's probably nothing, but if whoever took the horse left some type of evidence behind, it would be better if she didn't mess it up, okay?"

Keeping Flora away from the barn proved more difficult than I'd imagined. She was like a distraught mother whose child had been taken. She was climbing the walls.

While we waited for Dex, I took her to the clubhouse and ordered her some tea, and then, as much to keep her calm as for any help she might be able to offer, I asked her to think what she figured the best way to take a horse might be.

"Depends on where they were going, I guess."

"Well, sure," I said. "But, well . . . let me put that another way. Would it be reasonable to ride a horse through the park in the dark?"

Flora cringed at the thought. "Oh my God," she said, as though playing through all the possibilities for disaster in her mind. "If anything has happened to him, I'll just die."

"I know, Flora. But you'll see, we'll get him back." I didn't even know why I would say such a thing. It wasn't a promise I could make. She just seemed so close to coming unglued. And I . . . well, I couldn't imagine a world where I would have allowed this to happen.

She didn't respond, in any case. Just looked at me hopefully.

"So," I went on, "let's say someone *did* take him into the park. In the dark or very early in the morning. Any idea where someone might aim in a case like that?"

"Kitty," she said, "do you have any *idea* how big the park is?"

I shook my head. With various bequests and acquisitions, I knew the park had been growing of late, but I couldn't even hazard a guess.

"It's big. *Very* big. There are a lot of places someone could take a horse and either hide him—right in the park—or load him onto a trailer and take him right away without anyone ever seeing."

She looked even more stricken at this new thought. I knew I wasn't helping her state of mind. Still, I couldn't help feeling there might be something in the answers she gave. Something that would be meaningful and valuable to Dex when he arrived.

"So, okay: let's work this out together. Let's say that's the goal. Taking a horse through the park in order to take him somewhere. Where could you do that?"

"Oh, Kitty." Her eyes, when they met mine, were twin pools of distress. "So many places. I couldn't begin to say."

"Try, please." It was information I wanted. But I also knew that the effort it cost her would help keep her together until the police arrived to take an official statement. For my part, I tried to pay close attention to every little thing she said, knowing from experience watching Dex that the very smallest thing could prove to be a clue.

"Well, there are a number of stables that ring the park," she said, and I could see both the effort it took and the fact that it was a good effort. "There's Pickwick Stables, you know of it? And also Sunset. That might be a good one, because it's fairly new and so not as established as some of the others, you see? People don't know each other as well. Also, you could take trails practically straight across the park to get from here to there . . ." Flora's words trailed off, and as bright and hopeful as her mien had been moments before, her face now fell with a new thought.

"What?" I asked, seeing the transformation.

"Well, I was just thinking: he's a big chestnut horse. All of these stables are *full* of big chestnut horses, Katherine. I mean, I'd know him in an instant if I saw him. But other people looking?" She shook her head doubtfully. "Whoever took him could even hide him in plain sight. They could have made boarding arrangements with one of the other stables, ride him over, and just tuck him in while no one was around and no one any the wiser."

"But see? That's something to hope for then, Flora. We'd be able to find him then. Ultimately. He'd be *safe*."

"Another thing," she seemed brighter with the thought, but also a little more distraught, "there are lots of places in the park where you could *hide* a horse. There are old farms and farm buildings from when the parkland used to belong to people.

Some of them have been torn down, but some of them are just empty and ramshackle. Heck, Kitty: he could be in someone's old *bedroom* right now."

There were other, even worse, possibilities. I didn't want to remind her of any of them. It was a big, wide world. And there were a lot of horses in it. And a lot of places to hide a horse, even a German one. I was relieved when I saw Dex arrive, bringing with him the air of confidence he can only manage early in the day before he's done very much drinking. Mustard was with him, which I figured was even better. Flora would have two slightly sodden knights. That had to be better than one.

Dex poked his head into the clubhouse and I waved him and Mustard over.

"Cops not here yet?" Dex asked.

I shook my head.

"Now don't look so glum, Miss Woodruff," Dex said. He and Mustard had sat themselves at our table and had a disapproving waiter bring both of them cups of tea with empty lowball glasses on the side. "With the situation we're dealing with here—with the threats you've been getting and all—I wouldn't be the least surprised if a ransom note or some such shows up."

"In fact," Mustard interjected in an easy way that made me think this had probably been their topic of conversation on the way over, "it's possible this whole thing—the notes, the threats, and so on—have all been a somewhat elaborate run-up to this very moment."

"You think so?" Flora said, looking hopefully from one man to the other.

"Could be," Dex said.

"I . . . I don't think so," I said quietly.

Flora looked stricken. Dex looked irritated. Mustard looked like he was at someone else's party.

"Why the hell not?" Dex said.

"Well, it doesn't fit," I said. "Not really. They've done a lot of silly back and forth if all they ever wanted to do was to . . . to horse-nap him."

"Back and forth?" Dex said.

"Well, notes and nightclubs and so on. If all you wanted to do was take the horse for ransom, why not take the horse in the first place?"

"So, Miss Smartypants, what do you think happened?"

"Well, in one way, it seems fairly obvious," I said.

"Someone who doesn't want me to ride in the winter horse show," Flora said.

"I'd say that's a good guess."

"Well, we'll keep that all in mind as we move forward, certainly," said Dex. "But it seems like an awful lot of trouble to go through to accomplish something fairly simple."

"How do you mean, simple?" I asked.

"Well, if you *really* don't want someone somewhere, there are ways to make them play ball."

Mustard was nodding his head. "Lots of ways," he agreed.

"Easier ways than all this mucking about with horses."

"Like what?" Flora wanted to know.

"Well, a bullet to the back of the head, for one," Mustard offered affably.

"Mustard!" I said.

Flora paled.

"Well, it's the truth, ain't it?"

"Or a broken leg maybe or broken arm," Dex offered.

"Yeah. Broken limb," Mustard agreed in a professional tone, "that's a good one. Always gets someone's attention."

"You two stop it," I said. "Clearly, those aren't the kinds of tactics being used here. Instead of sitting there like a couple of lumps and frightening the poor girl, maybe you could give some thought to just who would use the tactics actually being used rather than the ones you're so helpfully cataloging."

"What do you mean?" said Mustard.

"It seems to me that the . . . the *methods* you mentioned would be used by a certain type of operator."

"Yeah," Dex said. "So?"

"Well, that's *not* the methods being used here. Obviously. So I'm guessing that should tell you something about who *is* doing it. Or who isn't."

"Like what?" Mustard said.

"I think I see what Kitty is getting at," Dex said. I was relieved to be understood. "She means that she's thinking maybe whoever is doing it ain't a pro."

"That is what I mean," I said, relieved to have Dex put my thoughts into words. "Yes. Or, at least, for whatever reason, doesn't want us to think they're a pro."

"Which would put us back where we started," Dex said.

"I guess it would, yeah," I admitted.

"Still, if they ain't a pro, well . . . who are they?" Dex added. "And if we can figure *that* part out . . ."

"We find the lost hoss," Mustard said.

"He isn't lost," Flora said fretfully.

"He is right now," Dex said, "but don't worry. We'll find him."

CHAPTER SEVENTEEN

Dex and Mustard left and the police arrived not long after. I was a little astonished: it had taken a long time, even for Los Angeles cops. Then I thought about where we were and who Flora was and where she lived and realized there might have been jurisdictional battles going on behind the scenes before the cops ever came out to help us. It wouldn't have been the first time I'd heard a story like that. L.A. was so big and sprawling and was changing so quickly, sometimes it was difficult for them to figure out who was in charge of what and where.

I was less forthcoming with the police than I had been with Dex and Mustard. Flora was too. For my part I could see no reason for it other than my growing suspicion of flatfoots since I'd come to work for Dex. With few exceptions, L.A. lawmen were a breed unto themselves. Between keeping the Okies out of the county and the payouts coming from the bootleggers and mobsters, they had their hands full. Dealing with actual crime on an everyday level didn't seem high on their lists. And a kidnapped horse? I would have bet good money the only reason they'd even bothered to show up at all was because Flora was Cedric Woodruff's kid. Everyone knew there was a lot of money there. Some of it might rub off on them; that's just how things work.

The flatfoots were named Burns and McPhee. I didn't catch their first names, but I could tell they were detectives because they were in their own clothes, not uniforms. Burns was neat and tidy, right down to the buttons on his jacket stretched tight across his waist. McPhee looked oddly unwashed to me, as though he gave water a wide berth when encountered. They acted sweetly solicitous of Flora and even asked her for a description of the animal.

"He's a big brown horse," I said before Flora could answer. One thing I've learned from Dex: there's no sense wasting a bunch of polite on L.A. cops.

"He's chestnut," Flora added a little more helpfully.

"What's that?" said Burns.

"It means he's brown," I said.

"How big?" said McPhee.

"Sixteen-one," Flora said.

"How's that?" said Burns.

"Means he's big," said I.

"So, we've got a big, brown horse," Burns said. I rolled my eyes. It was what I'd been afraid of.

"Any distinguishing marks?" This was McPhee.

I started to say something smart, because I knew McPhee was trying one on, but Flora beat me to the reply.

"Yes, in fact," she said. "He has a brand. On his haunch. His left hind haunch."

The two flatfoots just stared at Flora for a minute. Maybe they didn't know what a haunch was. Or maybe they only knew where it was on venison—in the pot—not on a living, walking-around horse.

"Now you mentioned it," I said, "I *did* notice that. Yesterday. On the trail. I thought I must be seeing things because, a big, beautiful horse like that. It didn't seem quite logical."

"Well, normally you'd be right. But Fritzl is Hanoverian and they do that at the Verband, in Germany, when they're just foals. That way there's no mistaking them; throughout their lifetimes, you can tell a true Hanoverian by that brand."

"Verband?" I asked.

"It's like a stud—a breeding facility—but it's also a school. After Daddy bought him for me, I spent three months there training with him, before I could bring him home."

At this thought her face clouded and I understood. This was one of the reasons she'd said he was irreplaceable. The bond forged between them had been professionally created by top trainers and experts in the breed. And somewhere in there, Flora had come to love the big chestnut horse. Her grief right now was naked on her face. It was too big to contain and anyone could have seen it. Anyone. Even a big, dumb flatfoot.

"I don't know, Miss Woodruff," said McPhee, shuffling those flat feet a bit now. "I don't know if we've ever dealt successfully with a horse-napping at the department."

"That's right," said Burns. "Seems likely he's on his way to be made into hamburgers by now."

Flora's face when they said this, I can't describe it to you. Deep and awful pain and an anger so intense, if she had a gun, she probably would have put a brace of bullets—Bang! Bang!— right into their cardboard hearts. I understood the feeling. I felt it myself just then. I settled for a complete reversion to the birthright of my childhood.

"That will be all, officers," I said, rising from the table with the composure of a duchess. "And, while we're about it, I think that will be quite enough."

"What's that?" McPhee said. He wasn't being sarcastic, either. I could hear it in his voice. He honestly wasn't quite sure what to do. I helped him out.

"You've made it clear what you feel your . . . success rate might be. Now, understand, we feel . . . that is, Flora's father, Cedric Woodruff, will feel, that it is your job to find this animal. A horse, I might add, who was so expensive, he is probably worth three or even four times the amount of the new car you might be coveting. He might even be worth more than your *house*. Make no mistake: this is an *extremely* valuable animal. Miss Woodruff will anticipate hearing from you *when* you have any news."

They looked a bit fazed at this dismissal, but I figured they were probably used to being spoken to that way; they were used to following orders.

"Should we look at where the horse was stolen from?" McPhee asked.

"What do *you* think?" I said.

They shuffled off. I considered going with them, showing them Fritzy's stall, then decided to stay where I was. They were detectives, after all. And they were big boys. They'd figure it out.

When they were gone, Flora turned her stricken face to me.

"Did you hear what they said? They said Fritzl might be . . . that is, he *could* be . . ."

"No, Flora. I mean, yes I heard. But that *isn't* what this is about. You know that yourself. It's tied in to the notes you got. It has to be. Someone wants to get to you."

"Well, it's worked, hasn't it?" She made no effort to stop the tears from falling now that the cops were gone. The busboys in the clubhouse noticed, but left us alone. "They've got Fritzl. I won't be competing in the winter horse show, that's for sure." And then her voice dropped to a whisper. It was as though it was too heavy for her to make it any louder. "And I won't be competing at the Olympics next year, either."

"Flora, stop it," I commanded. "Those two? They're just full of a lot of hot air. Anyone can see that Fritzy is a wonderful horse. And he's very well trained. Even if what they said *was* true—and it's not—no one would let that horse go for . . . for what they said. He's too fine an animal. Why, he's worth more alive than he is . . . in any other condition. And imagine: your dad would pay a lot, just for ransom. Much more than they'd get for him in the . . . in the way they said. Anyone would know that; anyone with an eye in their head could see."

"You really think so?"

"Of course I do," I said with confidence. And I believed what I was saying, too. Even while I prayed that I was right. "No, don't give up hope. Those two lame ducks will have a poke around. And Dex and Mustard are already out looking for something. And you and I, well, we'll figure out something so we're not just sitting around here twiddling our thumbs; we'll figure something to do to help. And we'll *find* him, Flora. You'll see. I just know we'll find him."

CHAPTER EIGHTEEN

But we did not find him. At least, not right away.

After a while I left Flora in the clubhouse and joined the cops in the barn. I wanted to be sure they'd found their way all right. They had, but they didn't like what they discovered any better than I had.

"You know, there's not going to be anything to find here," Burns said with an expert's tone when I joined them.

"What do you mean?" I asked.

"Well, look around: we got straw an' hay and other soft materials that don't take so well to finger-printin'."

"Yeah," McPhee added. "Just what the hell are we supposed to be looking for?"

"How do I know?" I said. "You're the cops; *you're* supposed to do the finding and the figuring out."

"You're a pretty lippy broad," Burns said, a little huffily.

"Yeah?" I drew myself up to my full height. "That's 'cause I know more than eleven letters of the alphabet and my times tables past three. Like I told you: Miss Woodruff's dad is Cedric Woodruff. Does that name really not mean anything to you?"

They both shook their heads.

"Maybe you should be using a newspaper for more than just wrapping fish."

"Hey!" said McPhee.

". . . you just tell your boss that name: Cedric Woodruff. And then see what new dance steps he makes you learn."

"Why, we could run you to the station, talkin' to us like that."

"I'm surprised you knew what most of those words meant." I could feel my temperature rising at his words. There are people who are frightened by empty threats like this. And it made me mad that these two galoots would consider even trying it. Better to bite 'em hard this time and let them think twice the next time they tried it on, that's what I was figuring, anyway. "And while you're at it, why don't you try stringin' more than two thoughts together? You might find an idea inside your head to keep 'em company. Just remember: if you know what's good for you, you'll do a thorough job on your investigation and you'll find Miss Woodruff's horse."

"Yeah?" said Burns, recognizing the threat. "Or else what?"

"Don't ask *me* that," I said, already moving towards the big double doors, "like I said: ask your boss. If your captain finds out that one of the city's most prominent citizens' case was handled by a couple of apes who would rather investigate their sock drawer for orphans than do a real job, the next time you have any kind of business with a horse will be shoveling the horse's business."

All the two of them could do was look down to see if their socks matched.

Despite my bravado with the cops, the search did not, initially, go well, though a lot of effort was expended on it, from every quarter. Dex and Mustard checked every stable they could find within a ten mile radius of Griffith Park. They looked and looked and reported nothing doing.

Flora and I rode out to several canyons and valleys right in the park where she figured it might be possible to hide a horse if you staked him out. I got a look at parts of the park few visitors had ever seen and were unlikely to see: remote nooks and crannies and mostly deserted trails. We saw many things—deer and white-tailed hawks, an eagle, and a purple finch—but we didn't see a sign of Fritzy or anything that might lead us to him.

McPhee and Burns presumably did something, though what it was we did not hear. It brought no results in any case because none of the attempts turned up even a single chestnut hair.

Halfway into that first day of our search for the missing horse, Matthew showed up. I'd gotten so involved in our quest, I'd forgotten all about him. Flora and I had been out on the trail, me on Blinky, Flora on her father's horse: a great brown lump of a brute called Sven, of all things. We hadn't found anything. We were back and Flora was overseeing the unsaddling and grooming of our borrowed mounts, when Matthew came up behind Flora and put his arms around her.

"I came as soon as I heard," he said. I envied the way she settled into him, just relaxing her back in a way she had not seemed able to all day.

"I'm glad you're here," she said.

I was too, but I kept my mouth shut. It had been a lot of work keeping Flora from going over the edge in her loss. I was glad Matthew was there to give me a hand with keeping her from falling apart.

We went back to the clubhouse and she filled him in on all that had been happening. When we came in, the staff all looked at Flora with concern. I gathered that word had spread through their ranks. This idea was confirmed a few minutes later when the Academy's manager joined us at what I was coming to think of as "our" table.

"Miss Woodruff, the entire staff would like to convey their concern about your lovely gelding," and he really did look concerned. The man's jowly face was fairly aquiver with it.

"Thank you, Mr. Biedermeier. I appreciate it."

"We feel awful . . . that is to say *I* feel awful that it . . . well, that it should happen anywhere but especially—*especially*—that Fritzy should disappear from the Academy . . ." He pulled a handkerchief from his breast pocket and began to mop at the damp that had sprung up on his brow. "Please, might I join you for a moment?"

I was relieved when Flora nodded. Biedermeier was very large and very flustered. I'd rather he sat than have a stroke. "Please, of course," she said. "Join us."

"We . . ." he said as he pulled out a chair and sat down, "that is *I* . . . I mean, really, all of us here would like you to know that if there is *anything* we can do, anyone at any time in any *way*, that you must just say the word. Just a single word. Please. Is that quite clear?"

"Yes. Thank you. The . . . well, the sentiment is appreciated."

"And it's *not just* because you and your family are wonderful . . . patrons of the Academy. Like many here, we are looking forward to you *and* Fritzy representing us at the winter horse show. We would be . . . that is to say *I* and really, all of us here, would be very disappointed . . ." His voice trailed off at that, clearly aware he was saying too much of the wrong thing. Especially when Flora began to cry again. This time Matthew came to her aid.

"Mr. Biedermeier, thank you so much for your time," he said, rising and gently helping the distraught man to his feet. "And thank you for your concern. It's much appreciated. I will convey your regards to Mr. Woodruff personally."

"Oh, would you?" Biedermeier looked frankly relieved. "That would be *most* appreciated."

"Now, if it's all right with you, I think Miss Woodruff is overstimulated just now. It might be best if she were just to sit here quietly. With her friends. You understand."

"Yes, yes. Of course," Biedermeier said. He began backing away from the table. "I just wanted her to know we were . . . well . . . deeply troubled by her . . . concerns."

"Thank you. We all . . . thank you."

When he sat down again, I thought Matty looked a bit taut. And pale. "Sorry I couldn't get rid of him more quickly."

Flora made a sort of shooing motion with her hand. "It's all right," she said. "He means well."

Before we even really got settled, a waiter arrived at our table with three glasses on a tray.

"Brandy," the man said quietly. "Compliments of Mr. Biedermeier. He asked me to tell you it's meant to be medicinal. Under the circumstances."

"Prohibition is in tatters," Matty said, raising his glass. "But Biedermeier is right, Flora; a taste of this might be just what you need. Let's drink to Fritzy, all right? We'll drink to his safe return."

And so we drank, Flora and I sipping carefully, Matty taking his in one neat gulp. I could see that Flora had taken Matty's words at face value; she seemed deep in thought as she sipped. I imagined her summoning a mental picture of her horse, wishing him well and wishing him home. I didn't point out to her that wishes were never horses. In fact, I shared Flora's hopeful wishes and drank to Fritzy's return as well.

"I think you should go home, Flora," Matty said after we'd quietly consumed our brandy. "I don't think there's anything more you can do here just now, wouldn't you agree, Miss Pangborn?"

"Actually, I would. And Flora, if we learn anything, I could have you notified right away. Why, I could come over myself and do it."

"Oh, would you Kitty? That would be wonderful. Maybe I *will* go home. Just for a while. It's funny, I feel all in."

"It's all the emotion you've been expending," I told her. "It gets to you. After a while." This was a thing I knew. From experience.

Flora seemed to take my words to heart, however, and let

Matty pack her off into the Hispano-Suiza.

After she was gone, I wondered what about her was different because she didn't seem the same girl I'd met just a few days before. It took me a while to figure it out and, when I did, I was sad. The girl I'd met had been full of fight and fire. Unafraid of anything at all and ready to take on the world. Today she was . . . diminished. She even seemed a bit smaller, which I knew to be impossible unless, of course, her spirit was taking up slightly less space.

And I realized something else. Much as I'd found that girl to be overbearing and certainly spoiled, today I missed her easy confidence and the stalwart way she approached her world: as though she knew and understood that everything required would fall right at her feet. I missed that confident girl and hoped like hell we'd be able to find her again. And soon.

Chapter Nineteen

After Matty had taken Flora home there really wasn't any reason for me to hang around the stable. I knew that if I were following the assignment Dex had given me right to the letter, I'd have gone back to the house with Flora and Matty. But I figured that, in her present mental condition, Flora was unlikely to get into any trouble. Plus, Matty showed every sign of staying glued to her side.

I thought about heading back to the office in the Red Car, but found I just didn't have the stomach for the necessarily long ride. And I thought slightly longingly of borrowing Blinky and going off on my own, but though I'd mastered the controls well enough, I'd never tacked a horse up before and wasn't even sure I'd get all the straps in the right spot. It seemed a better—and safer—idea for me to stay on the ground.

I decided to go back to the tack room and have another look around. I knew it was unlikely I'd find anything; Dex and the police had both had a good snoop. Still, I needed something to occupy my time until I figured out what I really ought to be doing. I knew that I should be on a Red Car—and likely would be within the half hour—but I could put it off a little longer just by hanging—and perhaps asking—around.

In the tack room I encountered a girl of about Flora's age soaping her saddle. Her short gold hair framed a horsey face. She was a big-boned girl who I suspected only avoided fat by dint of larger than normal applications of exercise. She was

118

tidily dressed for the stables: fawn-colored jodhpurs, good black riding boots, and a tailored white blouse that barely contained the full figure she tried so hard to conceal. Hers was not the elfin, boyish frame currently popular. She barely hid the fact that she was Rubenesque at a time when it was unfashionable to be so.

"You're Flora's friend, aren't you?" she said when I came in. There wasn't an ounce of welcome in her voice.

"I am," I said, "but I fear you have me at a disadvantage."

"Excuse me?" she said, pulling her attention away from her saddle.

"I mean to say, we have not been introduced." I extended my hand and she wiped the saddle soap off hers so she could meet it. "I'm Katherine Pangborn."

"How do you do?" she said, "I'm Willamina Huffle."

"Your name is familiar to me," I said, considering.

"The Baltimore Huffles," she replied as though I'd asked. "Perhaps we met during the season?"

"Perhaps," I replied, not telling her at the same time that, these days, the only meaning I took from "the season" was that I might need a different coat and that we could expect our electric bills to fluctuate. But I had no need to tell her that and, even if I had, I was not convinced she'd understand.

"I heard about Flora's horse," Willamina said. "Kidnapped. That's just an awful thing. Poor Flora." But, oddly enough, she didn't sound sorry at all. "It's all such a shame."

"What do you mean?"

"Well, a shame, you know. They've been very strong competitors, Fritzy and Flora. And now . . . well . . ." She let her voice drop in order, I gathered, that my imagination might fill in the blanks.

"Actually, we don't know for certain that the horse has been kidnapped," I pointed out. "Only that he's missing."

"Hmmmm," she said, as though I hadn't said anything. "Kidnapping seems most likely, a horse like that, wouldn't you say? Nothing else really makes sense."

"We're hoping you're right. In the meantime, tell me: are you and Flora friends? She's never mentioned you."

"Friends? I wouldn't go so far as to say *that*. But I've certainly made her acquaintance and on more than one occasion." There was something dry and inexplicable in her tone. "Now, if you'll excuse me," she said, turning away from her cleaned saddle and quickly stashing the saddle soap and cloths and brushes in her own locker. "I want to get an hour or so in the arena before it gets too late. Good day, Miss Pangborn. Perhaps we'll see you another time?"

And with that, she was gone, her saddle glowing over one arm, the reins on the bridle on a big bay horse over the other.

As the substantial Miss Huffle led her horse away, I noticed something. Willamina's horse wore a brand in the same place that Fritzy did: only it was a different one. It probably didn't mean anything, I told myself.

It probably didn't mean anything at all.

CHAPTER TWENTY

I was going to follow Willamina Huffle and ask about her horse's brand but, just as I left the tack room, I saw James Stroud and Cedar head in her direction. James intercepted her; they spoke for a moment, then went off together.

I told myself there was nothing to it. Why would there be? Two riders who happen to stable their horses at the same barn going off to ride together; it hardly seemed significant. On the other hand, as soon as I'd seen them in the same place, alarm bells had gone off in my head. I told myself to stop being silly, to stop clutching at straws. After all, we'd had few enough breaks in the case thus far. Was it possible I wanted a lead so badly I was wishing things to be so?

I turned back to the barn, intending to return to the tack room and have that look around I'd promised myself earlier. Before I turned away, though, I made a mental note of the direction Stroud and Willamina had headed, even while I chided myself for doing so.

The tack room, predictably, turned up nothing new at all. If there had ever been anything like a clue, there wasn't one now. Between the previous searchers and all the usual hands that used the room, there was nothing of the past left to talk to me.

"It's a bad business." The voice startled me and I jumped but was relieved to see it was Doc, his grayish face perhaps slightly more ashen today. I understood it. He had seemed to like both Flora and Fritzy very much.

"It is," I agreed. "Say, Doc: no one's mentioned anything to you about seeing anything, have they? I mean, seeing someone leaving with Fritzy in the night?"

"No ma'am," Doc said, "but I can ask around if you like."

"Thanks. That would be much appreciated."

After that I spent some time wandering around the various barns and other outbuildings at the stable, holding onto the unlikely hope that I'd see something that would fit the other pieces I held. But though I saw horsemen and grooms brushing and saddling and riding out and though I saw platoons of staff and even someone who looked as though they were planning a wedding, I didn't see anything at all that seemed amiss or ajar or in any way off or wrong.

By mid-afternoon I could see there was no reason for me to stay out at the stables, and I began my lengthy Red Car trip back to the office. When I got there, Dex was out but, anticipating me, he'd left a note on my desk. "If you're here," read the note in his strong, clear hand, "and Miss Flora is not with you, you should not be. Perhaps I was not clear? Don't let her out of your sight."

I sighed deeply, rolled my eyes, and gathered my stuff once more. Though I would have liked half an hour of normalcy and peace at my desk, perhaps answering phones and drinking coffee, there was nothing at all ambiguous about Dex's note. I put on my coat and hat and walked right back out the door.

CHAPTER TWENTY-ONE

Approaching on foot, the West Adams house seemed even larger than it had on my previous visits. Something about walking past the manicured lawns, admiring the flower beds and seeing those graceful, creamy columns from a distance. From my vantage, it looked less like a private home and more like the headquarters of some manufacturing giant or maybe a small hospital. Or maybe not so small. It was a very large, impressive house, but it had an empty look, for all that. It did not have a welcoming façade.

I felt ridiculous tapping at the giant door: like a mouse come to beg cheese from a cat. The door swung open almost instantly and the maid peeped out. I recognized her from previous visits.

"Hullo, Macy," I greeted her, "is Miss Flora about?"

"She's by the pool, Miss Katherine," the woman said. "Shall I announce you?"

"No, that's fine. I remember the way."

Though the day was fine, Flora was bundled up on the chaise looking as though she'd rather be anywhere else. Matty was nowhere to be seen.

"He left you alone?" I said by way of greeting. "I thought I gave him strict instructions to keep an eye on you."

This raised the faintest ghost of a smile. "I sent him packing. He was being so solicitous. He was driving me *mad*. Anything?"

"Sorry, no. I met a friend of yours, though. Willamina Huffle."

"Hardly a friend. In fact, when I found the first note, it was her face that jumped to mind."

"Really? Why didn't you tell me that?"

"It seemed childish of me to say, I guess. I mean, just because I don't *like* her is no reason to go about accusing her of things."

"True enough. But if you've got reason to think it might be her, she might bear watching."

"Reason? Well, she loathes me. Is that reason enough?"

"I'm sure she doesn't *loathe* you," I said, amused despite myself. Very few years separated us, though at times like this it felt like decades. I felt sophisticated and worldly to her youth and relative naiveté. " 'Loathe' is, after all, such a strong word."

"It's precisely the right one, though. That's why I chose it. She hates everything about me. Well, you met her. She hates that . . . well, she hates that I'm a sparrow to her robin." I smiled appreciatively at the picture and at Flora's wit. "And I'm lighter in the saddle, as well. Oh, not because of my size, either. I'm just . . . well, I'll say it: I'm a better rider than she is. And she's always been in love with James, yet I think he's a little in love with me—well, I think you saw that. And Fritzy is a much better horse . . ." Her voice trailed off as she realized what she'd said.

"We *will* find him, Flora. Dex is out there right now looking for him. We'll turn something up. Fritzy didn't just disappear into thin air. He's out there; we just have to figure out where."

We lapsed into silence. It wasn't uncomfortable. I ran through possibilities for Fritzy's disappearance in my mind. Flora likely did the same in hers. After a while, a maid brought out a tray with tea and tiny sandwiches. I noticed right away that their little crusts had been cut off, and I smiled in anticipation. It was one of the many luxuries I missed: these days, food was dear. I was compelled to eat every bite, crusts and all. Some people might think caviar was a luxury. Or turtle meat, rare and exotic. But to me, this was it: bread without crust. That seemed like luxury out of mind.

"I want to tell you something else," I said, after I'd doctored my tea and eaten one of the tiny sandwiches, relishing butter blended with carrot and ginger. A wonderful, extravagant *mélange*.

"What?"

"After our talk, after she left the barn, Willamina ran into James Stroud."

"How do you mean she ran into him?"

"They met. With their horses. And they rode off together."

"That's not that odd," Flora said, but I'd felt her hesitation.

"They looked pretty chummy."

"Really? Willamina and *James*? *My* James?"

"How can he be your James?"

"What do you mean?"

"Well, you already have Matty."

"Oh," she said. And then, "That. Well. Yes, yes. I guess I do. So you think Willamina and James . . ."

"I didn't say that. I didn't say anything. I just thought it was funny, that's all, that they should go off together. And I guess I wanted you to think about . . . about what it might mean."

She shook her head. "I really can't imagine James would have anything to do with this. He . . . why, he *dotes* on me."

I made a mental note. It had come to my attention that a man could go from doting to wanting revenge for doting in fairly short order. Dex and I had paid our rents on that very idea more than a couple of times.

"Something else I noted: Willamina's horse? It had a brand, something like Fritzy's, only different."

"He's a Dutch Warmblood. The brand you saw: it's called the lion rampant. As soon as I brought Fritzl home from Germany, Willamina went running to daddy for a European horse. Obviously, I think the Hanoverian is better. And she could have gotten one, too. But she wanted something different. Something European *and* different. So they went to Holland for her horse. To be honest, her Alfie probably cost a bit more than Fritz. I'm almost sure of it, actually. I don't think she would have wanted him if he didn't."

"You sound as though you don't approve. I must be missing something. Like you said, you got the German horse."

"Right. Sure I did. But I chose the Hanoverian breed because I honestly felt it would be the best horse for my needs. Willamina chose her horse because—for whatever reason—she felt a Dutch Warmblood would be better than whatever I had. You see what I'm saying? I wanted the best horse for the competition I anticipated. She just wanted to beat me."

Now it was my turn to stop and stare. "Do you realize what you're saying?"

"I guess . . . I guess I do."

"Because what you're describing, Flora, it doesn't sound good."

"It doesn't, does it?"

"No. It makes her sound very much like someone who would have been capable of at least some of this."

Chapter Twenty-Two

We sat there in silence for two fat minutes, each of us lost in our own thoughts. Carmella joined us poolside in the densest part of this lull.

"Hello, girls. Are you having a nice visit?"

Flora raised her eyes to her stepmother but didn't say anything. Carmella shifted uncomfortably under the glance while waiting for Flora to respond. When she didn't, Carmella pushed ahead. Flora and I had both known she would; you could taste it in the air. It was easy to see that, right then, Carmella was someone with an agenda. And Flora? She looked like she was prepared to wait it out.

"I wanted to let you know that a few reporters are coming to the house today," Carmella finally announced bluntly.

"Reporters," Flora said, surprised. "What for?"

"I gather this proves to be quite the story, Flora: a connection between the coming Olympics, you know, and your fantastic horse. And, of course, your father."

Flora had told her stepmother about Fritzy, of course. With the police knowing, and everyone at the Academy, it hadn't been something she could keep from her. I could only assume that Carmella would later tell her husband, or Flora would tell him herself. Either way, she had to be done protecting them, now that the worst had happened. The worst, anyway, that Flora could imagine.

"I don't want to talk to reporters, Carmella. Can't you put them off?"

"No, dear. That is, I suppose I could. But it will be the right thing to talk to them," Carmella said with confidence.

"I don't know." The teensiest bit of whine had crept into Flora's voice.

In response, Carmella's voice grew more cajoling. I could see this was a two-step they'd danced before: what Carmella wanted slowly coming to outweigh what Flora needed, then back again.

"Come now, Flora. It will be for the good of all, you'll see. Your father's name in the news, that won't be bad for him. Why, who knows? It might even help them find your horse." Carmella could see Flora's ears go forward at that, and she pressed the advantage she had planted and watched it grow. It didn't take much more wheedling before Flora agreed, just as both Carmella and I had known she would. After that mention of possible benefit to her horse, it had been etched right there, on her face.

Carmella told us the reporters were waiting in the front sitting room.

"They're already here?" Flora said. "You said they were coming later."

Carmella made a very ladylike moue—I wouldn't go so far as to call it a shrug—but she didn't say anything. I heard it, in any case. Would Flora have agreed to cooperate had she been told the reporters were already there and waiting? She would not. And now? She had agreed and what was done was done. Hence that moue.

On the way to meet with the waiting reporters, Carmella made us detour to Flora's room where she had clothing laid out. There was a well-cut, dark two-piece suit for Flora. Simple jewelry. A creamy silk blouse. The outfit struck me as something a young widow might wear. I looked at Carmella, at her slightly hungry face, her perfectly coiffed head, and decided the look she'd chosen for her stepdaughter's press appearance was no accident.

"I thought you said reporters were waiting," Flora said.

"Oh, they are, dear. But they'll wait a bit longer. You have to look just right."

Flora looked as though she might argue, but then quelled the response. With a resigned sigh, she slipped behind a screen in her room and started changing.

"Now Miss Pangborn, if you would be so kind." Carmella indicated a simple but well-tailored dress that looked to be about my size.

"You want *me* to change, too, Mrs. Woodruff?"

"Quite. If you could be so kind," she repeated, but some of the sweetness of the first request had drained from her voice. "You're currently attached to the household, and you're in jodhpurs, so . . ."

"But I haven't shoes to go with that dress. Not here."

Carmella smiled and pointed and I felt silly: of *course* she would have thought of that as well. And they were only about a half size too small, which would be fine to manage the trek between Flora's room and the room where she would receive the press, but only just. If the house had been much bigger, the hike would have caused blisters.

Before we left Flora's room, Carmella looked us over, as I imagined a drill sergeant might survey her troops. "You'll do," she said with a smile perhaps intended to take the sting from her words. But then she added to the sting by pinching our cheeks to bring out the color.

"Harlots have things easier, don't you think? They can use rouge for that purpose."

"Flora Woodruff! That *will* be enough," Carmella said before leading us into the main part of the house.

I had expected a couple of reporters but when Carmella flung the door open dramatically so that Flora stood framed in the doorway, she and I both blinked to see that the room was full of journalists and photographers, perhaps thirty-five people in all, mostly men, a few of them holding fat microphones, making it obvious they were from various radio stations and prepared to broadcast their reports live.

"My goodness," I heard Flora say under her breath and then again, "My goodness."

When the door opened, the room had fallen silent. And it remained silent for about thirty seconds before the sound of hungry reporters swelled into every refined nook and cranny.

"Miss Woodruff!" someone shouted, "Over here. Frank Larson, *L.A. Banner.* We understand your horse has been kidnapped. How much ransom is being asked?"

"Miss Woodruff! Miss Woodruff!" This was someone else. "Clint Feeny, *Sacramento Bee.* Is it true you will be unable to compete for a spot on the Olympic team if the horse is not returned?"

I wondered about this reference to the Olympics. Where had the press gotten this information? Then I looked at Carmella, standing just at the sidelines looking pleased with herself. Had there been some kind of briefing with the press beforehand? I thought there must have been.

"Miss Woodruff, here please! Reston Martin, KMTR News. Are you fearful for the life of your animal?"

Flora just stood, still framed in the doorway, her head going back and forth as though trying to take it all in. I found my voice before Flora did. Since none of the fuss was aimed at me, and since Flora looked so overwhelmed, it seemed a simple thing for me to step forward and fill the void being created by the deer-in-the-headlights position Flora had taken up.

"Miss Woodruff will be happy to answer your questions," I

said in a voice that pleased and surprised me in its clarity. "Just give her a moment, please. As you can understand, this is a difficult time."

Heads and camera turned, as though I'd waved a bloody garment right under the noses of a dozen sharks. They turned on me almost as a single unit. Light bulbs and questions flashed through the air. I chose not to answer a single reporter, instead addressing my answer to the air.

"I'm Katherine Pangborn and I'm a friend of the family."

The next question took me by surprise, though I suppose I should have been expecting it.

"Are you *that* Katherine Pangborn?"

"Excuse me?"

"Daughter of John Pangborn? The Pangborn of the Pangborn Building Pangborns."

Would it never be forgotten? Is this how he was to be remembered always? How I would be forced to remember? *That* Pangborn?

"Yes, yes, I am. He was. But that has nothing to do with why I'm here."

"Were your fathers friends?" one reporter shouted.

"Whose fathers?" I asked.

"Yours and Miss Woodruff's."

"No. Not to my knowledge."

"But didn't they have a deal together on the land in the Baldwin Hills where Olympic housing is currently being built?"

If they had, it was news to me. "I don't . . . I don't believe so," I said honestly. "Actually, I have no way of knowing and it wouldn't affect me now if they did."

The same reporter looked as though he might have more questions along those lines, but Carmella had clearly had enough and she waded in to take control.

"We will *not* be taking questions on my husband's business

dealings today. That is clearly outside our area of interest and expertise, nor is it the reason we've assembled you here. As you've been told, my stepdaughter, Flora Woodruff, has had her competition horse stolen. He was taken from the Griffith Park Riding Academy last night or early today. We felt that, with your combined talents as well as the considerable audiences you collectively command, you might be of help to us in getting him back."

She beamed a smile around the room. Some of the reporters smiled back. She was a beautiful woman and she knew how to use it. Some reporters aren't immune to that. The first reporter to break that silence clearly *was* immune.

"I'm Arlene DeSoto, *Los Angeles Courier*. Have the police been called?" Arlene was a redhead whose hair tended towards curls, despite the close cropping she'd given it.

"They have," Carmella said. "Flora, can you tell us about that?"

Flora shook her head, clearly overwhelmed by it all.

"Miss Pangborn," Miss DeSoto said to me. "You were there, weren't you? With the police. Can you tell us anything?" I could see by the fact that she had effectively turned the spotlight over to me, she was desperate. And I certainly didn't want that spotlight, but I'd help out where I could. And, when I thought about it, this might actually prove to be a useful exercise after all. If the case was getting media attention, the police would have to notice and those darn flatfoots might actually be forced to accomplish something.

"Um . . . yes. Detectives Burns and McPhee of the Los Angeles Police Department interviewed Miss Woodruff this morning. It is my understanding that they're currently conducting an investigation."

"Any leads?" another reporter shouted.

I looked at Flora. She shook her head quickly but still didn't say anything.

"Not that we're aware of," I said to the room.

"Has there been a ransom note?"

I looked at Flora again. I knew the answer, but this was her show and I wanted her to have the chance to speak if she wanted to. But she just shook her head, still struck dumb.

"No note and no suspects, as yet," I said. "We're hopeful on both counts."

"Miss Woodruff," it was the *Sacramento Bee* reporter again. "If the animal is not recovered, will you be able to replace him at a level suitable for international competition?"

Flora spoke for the first time and, when she did, her voice sounded rusty, as though she hadn't used it for while. "Fritzy cannot be replaced," she said. I saw a single tear slide down her cheek but I didn't know if anyone else could. They heard her all right, though. The room fell silent, and we could clearly hear the scratching of a half score of pencils. It was a quietly eerie sound. And it was over all too soon.

"Miss Woodruff: Gwen Clark, *Los Angeles Register.* You said the animal's name is Fritzy? Can you tell us about him, please? What he looks like? What kind of horse he is?"

I was glad to see Flora prepare to answer. She was on solid ground here: these were the kinds of questions she knew might actually help get the animal back. And it was, after all, a topic close to her heart.

"He is . . ." she cleared her throat, began again, "he is a wonderful horse. Very lovely, too. You don't have to know much about horses to see that he's very special. He is a purebred Hanoverian. My father bought him for me at the Hanoverian Verband in Germany a year ago, as a graduation present."

"High school graduation?" someone shouted out.

"That's right," Flora replied. Then, having warmed to her topic, she went on. "He's sixteen-one hands, and I know you'll do your homework on how big that actually is, but keep in mind there are four inches to the hand. If you don't feel like doing the math, understand only this part: he's tall, dark, and Hanoverian." The crowd chuckled appreciatively at her small joke, then settled down because they could tell she would go on. "In color, he's what's called a very dark chestnut. He's a brown so dark that in certain lights, he looks black. He has a long white strip on his nose that ends in a snip, which is just a dash of white on the end of his nose. And four white stockings."

"We've prepared photographs," Carmella interjected.

"We have?" Flora said. I was surprised as well. Carmella seemed to have thought of everything. I looked at her more carefully. She hadn't struck me as the altruistic type. What had she to gain?

"Yes. Each of you will get one on your way out. It's a photo of Flora and Fritzy taken not long after the horse arrived in Los Angeles from Germany."

"Miss Woodruff, over here please. It's me, Clint Feeny again. *Sacramento Bee.*"

"Yes, Mr. Feeny."

I could see that Flora was a quick study.

"Just so we're clear: had you in fact planned on qualifying for the Olympics next year?"

"I had Mr. Feeny, yes. In fact, we've already attended some qualifying events over the last twelve months. And held our own, I might add."

"And it's true that, if you *did* qualify, you'd be the first woman ever to do that?"

"That is correct."

"And now?"

"Now, Mr. Feeny?"

"Yes, what are your plans now?"

"I don't . . . I don't know. I just . . . please . . . I just want my horse back."

And that was the undoing. Maybe Feeny had been pushing for it, because as Flora's brave face crumbled, I saw him signal his photographer who documented the moment. A dozen others followed suit. And in the morning edition of newspapers across the state—and even around the country—that's what was seen on the front page: the beautiful girl in an immaculate suit, tasteful furnishings behind her. Her face is stricken and tears trace down her lovely cheeks. And then there's me. Standing just behind her and to her left and I've got a sour look on my face: preserved there in ink for all time. I look, well, I look out of sorts I suppose. I look as though I'm in a bad mood. But I was not. I was sad, of course. And I was concerned, both for Flora and her horse. But, most of all, I was giving Clint Feeny the evil eye.

CHAPTER TWENTY-THREE

"You're not supposed to be the news, hot stuff." I couldn't tell if Dex was truly annoyed or if he was amused. I decided he was a bit of both.

"I know, Dex. I know."

"How the hell'd you manage to get in the paper, anyway?" We were sitting at his desk, the day after Flora's impromptu press conference. The day after Fritzy disappeared.

"I didn't *manage,* Dex. It was Flora's stepmother. She called all these reporters together, there at the house, and sort of sprang them on us."

"Sprang them on you, eh?" Dex said. He shoved the paper across the desk towards me. "Is that why you're wearing a new frock?"

"It's not a 'new frock,' Dex. Carmella Woodruff. She made me wear it. Because I was wearing jodhpurs."

"Just like you always do," he said sarcastically.

"Oh stop it. You're just teasing and I know you are. Only I'm not finding any of it very funny."

He laughed some more but he also relented. We did have business to do, after all.

"So okay," he said. "Where are we now?"

I pulled my notebook towards me, looked over the things I'd written. I didn't really need to: I knew what was there. Still, it gave me focus.

"Well, cops first, I guess. Anything there?"

Dex gave me a grin that was almost a sneer. I knew it wasn't directed at me.

"What do *you* think?" he said.

I made a careful note in my book: "Nothing from cops."

"What about the construction connection? Yesterday you felt maybe you had something interesting."

"Well, to be honest, that was more Mustard's hunch than mine. And he followed it up. Today he played golf with some guys at the Riviera Country Club out in the Palisades."

"He's getting to be a regular swell. I still can't get over Mustard playing golf, you know. Was he wearing his plus fours again?"

"He was. It's a swank course. Anyway, these three guys were full of sour grapes."

"This is leading up to something we care about, right?"

"It is."

"Okay," I said. "Go on."

"Thank you," Dex said sarcastically. "Well, Mustard sez these guys spent most of eighteen holes nattering on about what sort of lowdown stuff Cedric Woodruff had to do to get that Baldwin Hills contract."

"Really?"

"Really. After their game, Mustard offered to buy them a round. He called me and got me down there so I could hear this griping for myself. Truth to tell though, Kitty, I was disappointed when I heard it."

"Why?"

"Well, like I said, it just sounded like a lot of sour grapes. A lot of 'he said, she said' and 'Cedric Woodruff is treating the Olympic Village like his private country club' kind of stuff. What I figure is this: any time you do a business deal, someone gets the short end, or feels like they have. That's what this seemed like to me. Maybe these guys made a deal and maybe they weren't too happy with it. That doesn't necessarily mean that Cedric Woodruff did anything shady. You follow?"

"I do," I said. "But his shadiness was never the question."

"It wasn't?" Dex asked.

"It was not," I said. "What we wanted to know was who threatened Flora and who stole the big horse? Did these guys seem good for it?"

"Nope," Dex said without hesitation. "They seemed like your regular run of the mill, kinda riled businessmen. Nothing special."

"Okay, then. That leaves us where?"

"Well, I'm not quite done with this story yet."

"You're not?" I said. "What more can there be?"

"Well, as I think you know, Riviera is a golf club, but it's also a country club."

"All right," I said.

"They've got a great course, but they also have a polo club. In fact, the equestrian events for the Olympics are being held out there. Did you know that?"

I looked at him for a good half minute before I said anything. "Do you not listen to me *at all?*" I said. "Major Doak, remember? That's where I met him."

He went on as though I hadn't spoken. "Paddocks line one side of the drive at the Riviera. It's pretty swank. Long driveway, coming and going. The course is on one side. Grazing horses on the other."

"Sounds peachy," I said tersely.

"It is, really. It's about the most beautiful place I've ever seen. Only when I was leaving today, a horse caught my eye. Under normal circumstances, I would have sworn it was Flora Woodruff's Fritzy. But then I thought, naw. Couldn't be. I mean, what would he be doing there?"

"You were mistaken, right? It wasn't Fritzy?"

"Was I?" He pulled the paper back towards himself again. Opened it to the next page, where they'd printed the photo of the girl and her horse. It was a good shot. They looked like competitors in that photo. They looked sharp. Flora in the saddle, Fritzy's ears ahead, and both of them looking ready to take all comers. "I wasn't so sure until I saw this photo." He pointed to the brand you could see plainly in the large black and white image. "It's pretty distinctive."

"It is," I agreed.

"And in L.A.? I think you'd have to go a couple miles to see that, don't you?"

"I guess. Are you saying the horse you saw had that brand?"

"I think so, Kitty. I think it had some kind of brand in that position, anyway. Though I wouldn't want to swear what one."

"What do you aim to do?"

"Guess I'll go back there today, with this paper. See if I can spot that horse again. If I do, I'll try and figure out how he got there. 'Cause I doubt he would have taken it into his head to just trot down the road on his own steam."

"Trouble is, if it *is* him, we're not the only ones that will have seen the paper. Whoever took him might have seen it too and taken it into their heads to stash him somewhere more private."

"I'd best not lose any time then," Dex said, half-rising. "Anything else?"

"Well, Flora did say one thing kind of interesting, about a girl I met out at the Academy yesterday named Willamina Huffle. Know her?"

Dex shook his head. "A girl, you said? Sounds more like a slow dance. Should I know her?"

"Probably not. Just thought I'd check. The way she said it, 'Of the Baltimore Huffles,' gave me the idea maybe I was the only one who hadn't a clue."

"Nope." Dex grinned, "I'm clueless too. Who is she?"

"Well, she's someone Flora knows. I gather they know each other from both their social milieu and the Academy."

"Social milieu," Dex said as though trying it out on his tongue.

"Willamina is also an equestrienne though, according to Flora, she's not as accomplished as our girl. Also, Miss Huffle is in love with James Stroud . . ."

"There's that name again."

"Right. And young Master Stroud looks at least a little in love with Flora."

"Aha. The plot. It thickens."

"Right."

"Well, all of this is interesting, but it sounds like it's in your department."

"My department? When did I ever get one of those?"

"Well, you can't expect me to run down those leads, Kitty. I have to get back to the Palisades . . ."

"Poor baby."

". . . and check to see if that was, in fact, our boy Fritz I saw in a paddock down there. Which reminds me, Mustard asked me if I figured you'd ever want to live in the Palisades."

"He *what?*"

"That's right. I thought I'd mention it in case it meant anything to you." And Dex was looking at me speculatively enough that I knew I was being detected on. But my conscience was clear.

"It doesn't mean anything to me at all. I'm pretty sure I've never even *thought* about the Pacific Palisades in his presence." I hesitated. "So what did you say?"

Dex looked at me blandly. "About what?"

I stifled a sigh. "About the Palisades. And me. What did you say?"

Dex grinned. It made him look something like a Cheshire

cat, which was not a pleasant image. "What do you *think* I said? I told him I had no idea if you'd ever consider living in the Palisades but that I figured you'd like Pasadena all right."

"You *what?*"

"Just pullin' your leg. I told him I had no idea and I let it go at that."

"Why do you figure he asked?"

He looked at me consideringly for a moment, and then: "My story is, I have no idea. It's a good story and I'll keep tellin' it 'til someone believes me."

I shook my head and turned away. When Dex gets it in his mind to be mysterious, there's just no shaking him.

"So what do you want me to do?" I said finally.

"Do?" he said.

"About Willamina Huffle."

"You kidding? You're all on your own there, kiddo," but he looked relieved to be back to business. "With a handle like Willamina Huffle it's a fair guess you'll have a better idea of what to do with her than I would."

CHAPTER TWENTY-FOUR

It was not difficult to track the Huffles down. As Willamina herself had made clear, they were well known in certain circles in the city. In fact, had Willamina been a few years older, or I a few years younger, our circles would have overlapped. For one thing, her father was a financier, as mine had been. Judging from where the both of us had ended up, though, her old man was a damn sight better at it than mine had been. I moved on from that thought. That's just life. It ain't always fair, but it keeps going around. If you don't want your head or your heart in too much trouble, sometimes it's best to just keep moving along. Which is what I did.

There was a woman at the *Los Angeles Register* who had been sniffing around Dex for as long as I'd known him. It was an unlikely attraction. Mavis Bentley wrote the paper's society column and never missed an opportunity to put herself in Dex's path, scarcely noticing when he scarcely noticed. To me it looked like a significantly unsatisfactory arrangement from both ends; even so, I figured she might help me on the off chance that it would get her near Dex.

I couldn't get Mavis on the phone. The guy on the city desk who picked up told me she'd gone down to the library to do some research. The day was fine and I had a hankering to talk to her, so I figured I'd venture the few blocks down to Fifth Street and see what could be seen.

I don't need much excuse to go to the library. From the time

I was small, something about the building—and the whole well-kept grounds—just took my breath away. There's a Hopi Indian legend about the land on which the library is built. They say that the whole shebang is right on top of thirteen underground cities built by the lizard people. I don't know about any of that, but it's certainly a magical place, designed to look Egyptian—not Hopi. A massive limestone building nestled among gardens and fountains. A place designed to make Angelenos proud. And it does.

I figured I'd find Mavis somewhere in one of the big main rooms, so I was relieved to be spared searching through all the possible places she might be when I spotted her on my way to the lower entrance. She was perched on a stone bench in the sunshine, the play of a fountain's water casting a pleasant ghost over the book in which she seemed utterly engrossed.

"What are you reading?" I asked when I drew near. She lifted her head at the sound of my voice and, when she recognized me, fixed me with an attractive yet feral smile. I wasn't sure why she'd never made all the time with Dex that she would have liked to; she was good-looking enough, in a cat-like way. Especially when she smiled, as she was doing now. Then you could see her teeth—ultra white and somewhat sharp. Between those teeth and her black hair and long limbs, she had a dangerous look that would not have escaped Dex's notice. Because of her job, though, she was one of Dex's best sources at the newspapers. That is, there were other reporters more connected, but none as willing to please Dex for an intangible. It was a relationship he seemed determined to leave intact, and so he left her alone.

In answer to my question, she tilted the cover so I could see the title. "*Fish Preferred*," I read aloud. "Is it about fish?"

Mavis smiled as she put the book aside, languor touching her limbs. "It is not about fish. More like pork," she said. "It's

Wodehouse, do you know his work? And it's part of an ongoing tale that just goes on and on and on. I just can't get enough. Speaking of which," her tongue darted out, pink and quick, moistening her lips, "how's your boss?"

"Dex is good enough, I guess. We're working on a case. That's why I came down here to find you . . ."

"To find *me*? How'd you even know I was here?"

"Your city desk told me." I perched next to her on the bench. "Do you mind?" I asked as I settled in.

"Not at all," she said. "Please join me. Where's Dex today?" she asked, looking around as though she figured he might pop out from around the other side of the fountain at any moment.

"Out on a case. The same case I'm poking around on, actually. Dex . . . well, Dex told me to ask you a few things."

"He did?" she said. And, of course, he hadn't, but it seemed a harmless lie. Sometimes you get started on such a thing and there's just no turning back.

"He did. We're trying to find out a bit more about the Huffles."

"The Baltimore Huffles?" Mavis said somewhat predictably. She'd pushed the book a little farther away at the name, as though to distance herself from what she'd been reading. I wondered if she even knew she'd done it. Now she was a cat on the hunt; she'd caught the scent of a story, and would play along until the why came out clear.

"Well, the L.A. branch of that clan."

"Sure, I know them. Why are you asking? Something to do with a case, you said."

"That's right. Do you know who I'm talking about?"

" 'Course I do," Mavis said scornfully. She pushed off her shoes and stretched her stocking-clad legs out in front of her, letting the sun warm their considerable length. Meanwhile she looked at me as though gauging how much she'd have to give before she got what she wanted. And then she started to talk.

She told me that the Huffles owned an impressive neo-classic pile in Hancock Park and that Willamina had gone to the Marlborough School, which I knew to be the most exclusive all-girls day school in the city. She also told me that, in addition to being a serious equestrienne, Willamina played tennis twice a week at the Los Angeles Tennis Club, which was not far from either her home or her former school.

"That's just swell, Mavis," I told her. "That's gonna help a lot."

"And you'll tell Dex where you heard it?" I saw the tips of her teeth again as she said it.

"Of *course* I will. Say, while I've got you, did Flora Woodruff go to the Marlborough School as well?"

"That upstart," Mavis breathed scornfully. "I should think not."

"What do you mean?" But I had an idea. Like many of her breed, Mavis had adopted the preferences of the upper classes. Something she obviously considered herself to be and which she clearly considered Willamina to be. And judging by her tone now, it was a club I suspected excluded Flora and her family. Of course, none of this explained why Mavis had set her cap on Dex, but I've found there are some things in life it pays not to look at too closely.

"Well, the *family*, Katherine. Flora herself is just fine. Have you met her? I've nothing against the girl, understand?"

"Sure," I said.

"But the *father*. Have you met *him*?" I didn't answer, because I figured the question was rhetorical. When Mavis went right on, I knew I'd been right. "He's quite odious."

"Odious?"

"Yes. Ill-bred. It's obvious, don't you think? And his family! Come to think of it, I don't even know what *they* did. But all his

145

money? He made it himself!" It was clear Mavis could think of little more reprehensible.

"You don't say."

"And his wife!"

"Flora's mother?"

"No! Flora's mother was lovely. And the only reason they got as far as they did—socially, of course. No, I mean the *new* wife. Can't think of her name . . ."

"Carmella?"

"Carmella! Yes, that's it. Imagine! *Carmella.*" Mavis practically spat it out.

"I've met her. She seems okay." I thought of her laying out all those clothes. Making sure there were shoes around to match. But I didn't mention any of that.

"Are you kidding? Think of it: *Carmella.*" And here she lowered her voice, about to relay something impossibly secret. "She's *Italian.* Imagine!"

"Italian?" I said, not really understanding the significance. Sure: I'd never known many Italian people, but the pope was also Italian and quite socially acceptable, judging from the papers, so I wasn't quite sure what she was getting at.

"Yes!" It was almost a screech. "*Italian. Who* do they think they're kidding?"

"Well . . . um . . ." Clearly Mavis was fishing for something here. Her eyes fairly glittered with it. I felt around for the right answer. Took a stab. "Not you. Obviously."

Judging from Mavis's response, it had been the right stab. "Obviously!" Mavis said sharply. "And the rumor is," and here Mavis lowered her voice and scanned the area around us carefully with her eyes as though the bushes—or perhaps even the fountain—might be listening, "that she's somehow connected to Tony the Hat."

"Connected?"

"I don't know," she said blandly. "I'm just saying."

"Who's Tony the Hat?" It was an uncommon enough moniker that it could stick in your head, but it hadn't stuck in mine.

"Oh Kitty, please; don't tell me you don't know who that is."

"Mavis . . ." I began, irritated. She must have heard something in my voice because she continued without prompting.

"But he's a gangster, Kitty. Of the Italian family persuasion."

"Are you sure? About Carmella Woodruff's connection to all of this, I mean. Because that's a hell of an accusation. I mean, don't take offense, but . . ."

"No, no; you're right. It *is* quite an accusation. That's why I could never print any of this. But, between you and me . . ." She stretched, cat-like, in the sun. It glinted off her long limbs, reflected off her prominent teeth. I thought again of a prey animal and tried not to look afraid. The end of her sentence was apparently lost. I made no attempt to find it.

"Well . . . um . . . thanks, Mavis." It seemed to me that Mavis was *growing* in a way. Taking all the venom she could spew and turning it inwards. I found I suddenly couldn't get away quickly enough. "You've . . . you've been a big help."

"*Glad* to be of assistance, Kitty. Any time. And don't forget to tell Dex."

"Oh, I won't forget," I said as I got up. "And thanks so much for your time."

CHAPTER TWENTY-FIVE

While I was talking with Mavis, I'd caught my stomach grumbling a few times. It was getting to be lunchtime and after I'd left the columnist behind with her book, I decided to walk over to the Grand Central Market to treat myself to something to eat.

It wasn't quite noon so I knew the market wouldn't be as full as it would be in another half hour or so and I'd be able to get around quickly. There was a deli on the Fourth Street side that I especially liked. Their rolls were crusty and chewy, and the pickles they used were bigger and greener and crisper than any others I'd ever eaten. I aimed myself in that direction and, as I walked, I thought about what I'd learned.

The picture Mavis had helped me build, while somewhat distasteful, also clarified things. I'd been looking at Flora and Willamina as social equals. They were about the same age; they both lived in impossibly big houses; and their interests—through their horses—were not incompatible. By rights they should have been friends. But I'd forgotten something vital; while a lot of the world had moved on from the seldom acknowledged class structure that had played such an important part of life in America up until quite recently, some people had not changed their views or their minds. Encountering these old thoughts now startled me but, once I'd let them out, it all started making an odd kind of sense.

In their world, Willamina was clearly superior. She was a

blueblood, untainted by anything. It was right—proper—that she should do better—*be* better—than her thinner, more beautiful, and perhaps more talented rival.

But life had not been playing along. Flora consistently bested Willamina in . . . well, in everything. She had the adoration of two of the most eligible men in their circle. Flora was prettier and probably more popular. And, to make things even worse, not only was Flora a better rider, even her horse—her expensive German horse—was better.

It wasn't very difficult for me to see things through Willamina's eyes. And what I saw shocked me. It didn't take much imagination on my part to think about what a girl in her position might do if she took it into her heart and mind to set things in a way that she thought was right.

And what about Carmella? Mavis had said she might be connected to gangsters. What part, if any, did Carmella play in all of this? I thought again about the press conference she had held at the house the day before. Could it be that she just wanted to help her stepdaughter find her beloved horse, no matter the means? Or had there been something unseen—something more sinister—underlying her actions?

Of all the things I pondered, only one presented me with a course of action. Mavis had told me that Willamina played tennis twice a week at the Los Angeles Tennis Club on Clinton Street at Rossmore. Unlike horseback riding, tennis was definitely one of the skills that had been taught to me as necessary when I was in school. The last few years I'd often thought that had been a waste of time. Considering the way my life had turned out, there just hadn't been time or money or *anything* for games like tennis since the crash. But now I realized, nothing is ever wasted. Sometimes, you just have to bide your time in order to make use of all that you have and know. And the time for tennis, I gathered, was finally here.

CHAPTER TWENTY-SIX

"You're looking for your *tennis* togs?" Marjorie sounded as though she couldn't believe her ears.

"I know it's been a few years, Marjorie. And I imagine they'll be a bit out of style now. But still, it will be better than nothing."

"I suppose so," Marjorie sniffed, elbowing me aside and immersing herself deeply into my closet.

She surfaced a few minutes later looking pleased with herself, a tennis costume more dated than I'd remembered in her hands.

"Oh dear," I said. "Do you think I can wear that?"

"I do think so," Marjorie said. "You can. You *will.*"

"Glad you're so sure," I said doubtfully.

"I *am* sure, Miss Katherine, and here's why. *You* will know that your ensemble is out of date. But do you know what everyone else will think?"

"I guess I don't or you wouldn't be asking in that way, so do tell."

"They will merely think you are uninformed and have no fashion sense. They won't *begrudge* you that. The worst they'll do is snicker behind your back."

I just looked at her for a moment. "Are we getting to the part that's supposed to make me feel better about this?"

Marjorie just smiled at me and turned and left the room. I knew she was right, but I didn't have to like the idea of having my cover be that of a frumpy spinster. I donned the now unfashionable drop-waisted tennis dress that had been the very height of *haute* when I last wore it to play in 1929 and tried to tell myself that looking like someone's spinster aunt might actually be a good cover.

If anyone at the club noticed my outmoded ensemble, they had the good grace not to say anything. Nor did I, despite my self-conscious fears, see anyone averting their eyes or snickering behind their hands. Like most of the times in life when we are very conscious of our appearance, no one noticed. They had their own concerns.

The Los Angeles Tennis Club is and has always been a private club, one that my family was a member of when the dress I wore was still new and fresh. I had no business there now, though. And I knew that neither Dex nor myself would even be considered for membership, no matter how much money we had. It was just that sort of club. Mavis would have understood and likely approved, and never mind the fact that they wouldn't have approved *her* for membership, either.

On my way there in the Red Car, I'd considered various approaches and had more or less come up with what I thought was an acceptable one by the time I got there. Or rather, by the time I had *almost* gotten there; part of my plan was to *not* be seen arriving on the streetcar, something I was sure Los Angeles Tennis Club members were not inclined to do. I got off a stop early and walked the final block, swinging my racket, grateful that, as far as I knew, tennis rackets had not changed as much as women's tennis togs over the past few years.

Behind the club's broad oak doors, a nattily dressed man sat with a large book. *His* ensemble looked quite appropriate for a game of afternoon tennis, though I had to acknowledge that it was not much different from what he would have worn had the two of us played in 1929. Like most items of fashion, men's tennis costumes had not changed as much as women's.

"Good afternoon," I addressed him, with a smile intended to be haughty, confident, and approachable. It was not as much of a reach as that sounds. I just tried to channel my younger self: the one who really hadn't a care in the world and who understood with a clear confidence that all she surveyed had been put in place to ease her progress. Although, in fairness, *that* Katherine Pangborn had always been properly attired. For everything. "I'm meeting my friend, Willamina Huffle, here for tennis this afternoon. Has she arrived?"

I was relieved to see my words confuse him, but not greatly. Miss Huffle was a club regular. More, she was a young woman of privilege. It was likely she often made plans and then expected the club to fall in line. At least, that was what I hoped.

"She *is* here, but she's not made provision for a guest."

"Fine, then," I said, taking up the pen, then sliding his book around so that it was facing me. I fixed him with my most dazzling smile. "I'll just sign in, all right? Then Wills can sign *me* in on her way out."

As I spun the book around to face him again, he looked doubtful, but only just.

"You know where to go, then?"

"Of course," I said, though I really had no clue. Father had been a member, but he'd been the only real player in our household. I knew how to play. Of course I did; tennis combines healthful exercise with social interaction and thus was taught as a matter of course. But no one had ever taught me to like it or seek it out.

Still, it was not difficult to find my way around, and the fact that I *had* been at the club on previous occasions helped. The clubhouse itself formed the club's central core. Change rooms were attached to that and the courts ran out behind and at either side in a sensible pattern.

I made my way to the clubhouse lounge, picked a table with

a good view of possible comings and goings to the courts, ordered myself a lemonade, and settled in to wait. It didn't take long. About halfway through my refreshingly icy beverage, I saw a familiar head of short golden hair heading in my direction.

"Miss Huffle," I called when she was close enough to hear. "Willamina? Is that you? What a coincidence!"

I don't think she placed me right away—I was out of context, after all—but I saw her face clear after a moment when she'd figured it out.

"Miss Pangborn, isn't it? From the Academy?"

"Quite right," I said. "It's very funny running into you like this, two days in a row. Imagine! As though our paths were meant to cross."

"It's likely our paths have been crossing our entire lives, but we've not paid attention before. May I join you? I was meant to meet Mary-Ann Patterson here—do you know her? Of the Alhambra Pattersons?—but it seems she's stood me up."

"I'm sure she has a stellar excuse," I said. "Please join me. The lemonade is perfect. Let me recommend it."

"Who are you playing today?"

"Well," I said, "you, perhaps? It looks as though I've been stood up as well."

The implication, of course, was that I'd been stood up by someone of the opposite sex. Someone who I would rather not name for fear of bringing further embarrassment upon myself. And, at that moment, I thanked both our ridiculous social conventions and the fact that I knew what they were because Willamina didn't probe further, just as I'd known she would not.

"All right. I've got court nine booked in half an hour. Would that suit?"

"Perfectly," I said, "but I should warn you, I'm not terribly good." Which, considering the fact that I'd not been terribly good the last time I'd played more than two years before so I feared I'd actually be terrible, but I couldn't see how to get out of playing tennis since I was properly—if unfashionably—attired at a tennis club. With a racket.

A white-jacketed waiter came by to take Willamina's order.

"Hello, Jock," she said. He returned her smile. "My friend, Miss Pangborn, says the lemonade here is very good. Imagine! I've never tried it before."

"She's right, though, Miss Willamina. We press it ourselves on the premises. And the lemons come down from Oxnard."

"The things you learn. I'll have one of those please, Jock," she dropped her voice a bit and slid a dollar bill across the table. "But spice it up for me a bit, all right?"

Jock didn't respond, but I noticed the bill was gone when he left.

"I wouldn't have thought to do that," I said, not adding that the thought of her drinking did not alarm me at all. It was possible it would make her more talkative than usual. The fact that it might not do much for her tennis game would be an unexpected bonus.

"You?" she said. "Would you like a spot?"

"I'm fine, thanks. I'm not a good enough player to drink beforehand," I said honestly. "You know, when I ran into you at the barn yesterday I was looking for Flora. And that got me thinking. You and Flora. You told me yesterday that you're not really friends. Yet I can't imagine it: you have so much in common. The horses and everything, mutual friends and so on."

Willamina made a disparaging sound. Something between a fairly unladylike snort and a derisive chuckle. "Hardly," she said. "We're not even in the same social circle."

Her drink came and she accepted it without a glance at her old friend Jock. It looked like lemonade all right, but the sharp, lost scent of whiskey colored the air between us.

"You're not? I didn't know that."

"Well, think about it; where did her people *come from*?"

"I didn't . . . I didn't ask." Here's the thing: you could spend a lifetime knowing things were a certain way but, once it had all unraveled, you could just move on. That's what I'd found, anyway. And, as earlier in the day when I'd spoken with Mavis, I found myself a little shocked and a little rocked backwards to what seemed now an outmoded time.

"Ha! That's it, isn't it? They came from nowhere, that's where."

"Nowhere," I repeated without inflection. "But everyone comes from *somewhere.*"

"Right!" She lowered her voice again, though this time it was for a different reason. "I heard her father started out in a developer's office. He was a clerk of some sort. The lowest of the low."

I wondered what she'd think if she knew I was a shamus's secretary. If a developer's clerk was low, where would that fit me? Or would the facts surrounding my own birth and background save me? It astonished me that there were still people out there who clung so tenaciously to these old beliefs. What I saw: the world was upside-down now. What had made a weird kind of sense before made absolutely none now. I said none of this, however. I just pressed on.

"Lowest of the low," I echoed, watching one of my melting ice cubes chase another down the inside of my glass.

"And that *step*mother of hers. *Carmella.*" Willamina practically spat the word. I was reminded of Mavis's feral hissing. "No, no, but I beg your pardon. Something is not right there."

"What do you mean?" I could have told her what Mavis had said to me, but that only would have added fuel to this fire.

"She's a lot younger than Cedric, for one thing." The way she pronounced his name, it sounded like a diminutive. Cedric.

Like something that was not whole.

"Sure, that's true. But that's not that unusual, is it? It seems to me that it is not."

"You're right. Of course. And the fact that she is a scant dozen years older than her stepdaughter, I suppose that's nothing as well?"

"I didn't say it was nothing," I pointed out. "Just that I don't think it's entirely without precedent. Men do that all the time. But what about Matthew?"

"Excuse me?"

The way she said the two words surprised me. Like I'd hit on something I didn't know was there.

"Matthew Sweet. Flora's fiancé. I thought, all things considered, you two might be friends."

"What do you mean?" Willamina pressed.

"Well, considering his background and everything, I thought you two might . . . have connections."

"Socially, you mean? Or more than that?" There was innuendo in her voice, but I didn't know what it implied.

"Well . . . either way. Or something else. I don't know. I'm only saying. Since you're both friends with James . . ."

"James?"

"Stroud. Since you're both friends with James Stroud, I thought it might be that you shared other things. As well."

She sipped thoughtfully, while watching me over the edge of her glass. I got the idea she was aware that she could go in one of two directions and that she was contemplating which one to take.

"Well, James," she said finally. "He's a sweet boy." Her voice was quiet. Watchful, I would have said. Waiting.

"Seems to be," I agreed.

"He's been friends with the both of us—me and Flora—for a while now."

"I got that idea."

"Well, I told him—James—I told him that I figured that might not be the best idea."

"What?"

"That he should be such good friends with the two of us. There's not room for it, either. That's what I told him; he's got to make a choice."

"He's sweet on Flora." There. I'd said it. And, as soon as I did, I knew I had her attention. I was on to something, though I was willing to allow it was not necessarily what I was after.

"What do you mean?" she said, sitting up a little straighter and putting her drink down perhaps a little harder than she'd meant to. "What do you know?"

"Nothing really," I told her truthfully. "Nothing at all. But I've seen them together. You can't help but notice."

"Notice what?"

"Well, I'd say, with absolutely no authority at all, that he's in love with Flora. At least a little bit."

"In love!" The words had a scornful sound.

"Without authority. That's what I said. I don't know anything. Just something I thought I saw. In his eyes."

"What an imagination you have, Miss Pangborn." She said it pleasantly enough but her smile didn't work its way north of her nose.

I shrugged. "Like I said, I don't know anything . . ."

"I'll say," she interrupted as she stood up. "Listen, I have to go."

"What about our game?" I said.

"Some other time," she replied. And I might have said more, but she was already out the door.

CHAPTER TWENTY-SEVEN

Once Willamina was gone, I sat and sipped my lemonade and thought about what, if anything, I'd learned. I'd been surprised to discover just how deep a chasm separated Flora and Willamina, at least from the latter's perspective. And for everything she'd said, it struck me that there was even more beyond that. Things that had only been implied or hinted at. Did any of it mean that Willamina was actually capable of hurting Flora? Or kidnapping her horse? I didn't know and not knowing wasn't sitting well with me. Though, after speaking with her, one thing was certain: Willamina Huffle would definitely warrant watching.

I was so deeply engrossed in my own thoughts that I failed to notice the man approach.

"Miss Pangborn?" he said, breaking into my musing.

"Matthew," I said, when I looked up, trying hard to control the now almost-familiar flutter in my breast. "Mr. Sweet. How nice to see you. Join me?"

He indicated Willamina's glass. "You're here with someone."

I smiled at him. Indicated he should take the chair Willamina had vacated. "I wasn't before. I am now. Please, if you've time, just sit."

He pulled out Willamina's chair and plunked himself down, picking up her abandoned glass and sniffing.

"Hmmm," he said. "I'd not have pegged you for an afternoon drinker."

"You'd have been right," I said. "That's not mine. It was . . . it was my companion's." I found myself oddly reluctant to come out and tell him what I was doing there. Matthew drew his own conclusions.

"Ah," was all he said.

I sighed and didn't say anything. After all, I reasoned, it wasn't going to be possible to have it both ways. Not while on a case. My schoolgirlish feelings for my client's fiancé had no place here at all. There was probably nowhere that they belonged.

"Are you a great tennis player?" he asked, prodding my racquet with one white-shod foot. I thought he was avoiding looking at my outmoded tennis costume, but that might have been my imagination.

"I'm not, really. To be honest, I haven't played for a great while. I'm probably very rusty, and I wasn't very good before my limited skills fell into disuse."

"Well, that's all right," he said. "I'll give you a lesson."

"Oh, no, I couldn't," I said. "What would Flora say?"

"Oh, Flora, she won't mind. She's a sporting sort, you've seen that yourself."

While I knew he was right on the one hand—Flora was certainly of a sporting disposition—I didn't know how she'd take to the idea of me playing tennis with her fiancé.

On the other hand, there we were, he with his tanned and earnest face, me with my out-of-date costume—all dressed up, as it were, with potentially nowhere to go. I honestly couldn't find it in myself to give him a flat-out "no."

"I really am quite dreadful, you know," I said instead.

He smiled then, revealing fine, even teeth, and I knew it when he said it didn't matter. "The play is the thing!"

Once on the court, I realized I'd been too gentle with myself: I wasn't even good enough to be a "dreadful" tennis player.

Whatever small skill I recalled having while in school had abandoned me. Halfway through our second set, it occurred to me that I was actually a more accomplished equestrienne than I was a tennis player. Since I had very little experience or skill with horses, that would seem to draw an accurate picture of my ability. Still, we laughed a lot as we played. We had fun. In the time we played, I felt carefree. I felt young. And it was only then that I realized I hadn't felt either of those things for quite some time.

We played a full game. I don't remember the final score. It was something ridiculous and not worth recalling: a million to one would have about covered it, though. Afterwards we went back to the clubhouse for even more lemonade, and Matty told me that I hadn't exaggerated.

"You really *are* an awful tennis player," he said, laughing.

"See? I did warn you."

"That you did. I figured you needed a break, though."

"Pardon?" I said.

"Well, it struck me that you'd been working rather hard. And I saw you sitting here and you looked very forlorn. I don't know, I just . . ."

"You felt *sorry* for me?" I was oddly nonplussed by this. "That was a *mercy* tennis match?"

"Well, we're not exactly even players."

"Still," I said, rising despite myself. I could feel my face flush with embarrassment, though it seemed even to me that I was reacting beyond circumstance.

"Listen, I didn't mean it badly. It's just . . ."

"You felt sorry for me! Well, fine. Thank you." When I rose to my feet it was as though I was unable to stop. I watched these actions as though from outside myself. "You've done your charity work for the day." And without even a good-bye or a look in his direction, I made my way directly to the exit, wondering even while I did it what I imagined I was doing.

I was halfway home before I even began to understand what I was feeling. There had been a minute, and perhaps ten of them, all in a row—where I had imagined he looked at me with a certain light in his eye. It was a light I felt I could return easily enough. And then his words brought me back. What had I been thinking? He was affianced to a *client*, for heaven's sake. But beyond that—and here my cheeks glowed red once again—I was no longer someone whom even an unengaged man of his station would consider as a social equal. Oh, sure: a tennis match. Or even . . . well . . . even something more. But nothing real. Not ever. I squelched the way that made me feel. Pushed it down. I watched the shapes of people and buildings flowing past me on the streetcar. I made my mind a blank and tried to think of nothing at all.

Chapter Twenty-Eight

Unaccountably, the next morning, I was still in a bad mood.

"What's eating you?" Dex said, not for the first time even though I thought I'd been doing a particularly good job of hiding my grouchiness.

"Nothing," I said.

Dex just raised an eyebrow. He may be a drunk and I don't always think he's a great detective but he's a fairly good judge of mood and of character, I'll grant him that, even if I sometimes do it begrudgingly.

Before we began our day in earnest, Dex wanted us to exchange notes on the Woodruff case. He was in his rights to expect it and it was even a good idea, but I wasn't in the mood.

"All right, young lady," he said after I'd avoided him and his requests for a quarter hour we could ill afford, "bring your notes into my office and close the door behind you. We're going to talk about this case whether you like it or not."

"Honestly, Dex," I said as I complied, settling myself into the green leather chair opposite his desk, "you act as though I've been avoiding talking about it. I haven't. I . . . I've just got a lot on my mind."

"I'm still your boss, kiddo, and don't you forget it. Who signs your paychecks?"

"Your accountant," I pointed out. "Two Thumbs Tommy."

"Yeah, but who tells Tommy to sign those checks?"

162

"Usually his wife, Hannah, 'cause more often than not you forget."

"Okay, okay," I could see that Dex was not going to be put off the course he'd chosen, "but who found you trying to hawk your mother's jewelry when you were just a kid and gave you a job instead?"

"Mustard."

Dex was losing ground and he knew it. "Look, kiddo: who runs this operation?"

That shut me up because I wanted to say, *Me, Dex. I run this place. When you're off spilling booze down your throat I talk to clients. I answer the phones. I run down the deadbeat husbands who are too despondent to pay up when you've found their wives in the arms of another man. I open this place up in the morning. I lock it up at night. I straighten your tie and remind you to put on your gun and then I drive you around when Jack and Jim and José have clobbered you so hard you start seeing two of everything. But I need you, Dex. Even if I wanted to, a girl can't hang out a shingle in this town and be taken seriously. And you saved me and, for that, I keep my trap shut tight and let you have all the glory and let you keep your pride intact and your reputation clean. You need me more though, because without you, it might take a while, but I'd find another job. But without me, Dex, you'd just be another PI spending his days soaked behind a desk, unable to deal with life as it came at him. Too pickled to remember where he left his hat and wondering if the name on the door was really his.*

I didn't say any of this. I couldn't. And as he waited for my answer, I saw a look in his eye. A glimmer of understanding, maybe. I let it be.

"You, Dex," was all I could bring myself to say. "You run this operation."

"Damn straight." He laced his hands behind his head as he's wont to do and tilted his chair back beyond the place where it was safe. It always looks awkward to me; as though he might topple right over, though he never does. "We've got a case to work here and it strikes me that we're not as far ahead as we should be by now. What did you turn up on the Huffle broad?"

"She's a definite possibility," I admitted. "I think she bears watching."

"And at what point were you planning on telling me this?" Dex asked sharply.

"I'm telling you now."

He hesitated. I thought he might give me a little speech or lose his endless cool, but he did neither. "Yesterday would have been better," was all he said. "Anything on the horse?"

I shook my head. "You?"

"Naw. I drove out to the Palisades yesterday, like I said I was going to, but if it *was* Fritzy I saw, he's not there now."

"So another false lead?"

"Looks like. But then I got the idea to talk to your captain out there some more."

"You mean Major Doak?"

"The same," Dex said. "I got to figurin', you'd said he told you they had a hard time getting their hands on horses good enough for international competition . . ."

I felt myself grow excited. How had I missed this? "But that's an incredible idea, Dex! Get anywhere?"

"Not at all. If someone on the team took that horse, he doesn't know about it. Not only that, I'd say he'd be mad as hell if someone under him did it. See, as he pointed out to me, if they took him, they might be able to forge a partnership with the horse in time for the games—they *might*. The thing is, though, you and me could watch the games and just see a horse and rider, but there are plenty of people who would watch and see it was Fritzy right away."

"People would recognize him, is what you're saying?"

"Right. So that's a no-go."

"So we got anything at all?" I asked.

Dex flipped the morning paper across his desk at me.

"We got this."

It was the society section of the *Register* and the headline was just big enough to catch an eye:

SOCIETY COUPLE PLAN WINTER WEDDING

There was a photo of Flora and Matty looking chummy. It wrenched a little bit at my heart. And there was a couple of inches of copy detailing what was anticipated for the wedding, where the happy couple would be honeymooning and where it was thought they might live. All in all, it was straight up society stuff. I said as much to Dex.

"I don't get it," I said. "Why are you showing me this? None of it is a surprise, right? We knew they'd set the date, we knew all this stuff. What gives?"

"Look at this bit, near the end here," he said, using one nicotine-stained index finger to point the way.

"Why, it's just a quote, Dex. It doesn't seem the least bit out of the ordinary to me."

"Read it out loud."

I sighed while I complied.

Meanwhile, Carmella Woodruff, the stepmother of the bride to be, is said to be very pleased with the match. "Our darling Flora has had a difficult fortnight. We are happy that she is going ahead and that these plans will take her mind off other troubles." Woodruff is referring, of course, to the equine kidnapping that took place at the Griffith Park Riding Academy earlier this week. Miss Woodruff's beloved equine companion was stolen from the stable. Police have no leads and the services of a private security firm have been retained.

I stopped reading and looked up. "I still don't get it, Dex. What's the big deal? These are all the facts as we know them to be. I mean, for once, it looks as though the paper got it all right."

"It does, don't it? But see, here's the thing: a week ago, I don't think it would have been reported in this way."

"You don't? What do you mean? What other way would there have been to report it?"

"Well, as you yourself said, the Woodruffs are something of outsiders; they don't quite fit. Their money is too shiny new, the stepmum is too young and gorgeous and flashy and too exotic. So I'm thinking: something big happens, they get in the front section. But to rate the society page . . ."

"They have to be society?"

"Right. Or something like it. So what's different now?"

"Well, she's marrying Sweet, for one thing."

"All right, there's that. Still, though: I'm not sure his money is old enough to counteract Woodruff's new stuff."

"Oh-kay," I said, but I still didn't get it.

"What's different," Dex said, opting to answer his own question, "is the stolen horse. All the attention." He poked the picture again. "And this."

"Fritzy? I don't understand."

"The whole fuss at the Woodruffs' home the other day, for one thing."

"With the reporters?"

"Right." Dex didn't say anything, just looked thoughtful for a bit. "I don't know," he said finally. "There's something there."

"You're just not sure what, right? Well, let me know when you figure it out," I said. "Meanwhile, what do you want me to do about Huffle?"

"Do?"

"Well, you asked me to have a look at her. I did. And I'm not sure I like what I see."

"Okay. What's the trouble?"

"Well, the trouble is, *you're* the big PI around here. Not me."

Dex looked at me without saying anything.

"I don't know what to do," I said.

"About what?"

I looked back at him, waiting for a light to dawn. When it did not, I spelled it out. "Willamina Huffle. I figure she's got the motive—she's jealous of Flora, every which way. She's got the means—they both had their horses stabled down there. I looked, like you asked, and I found. I just don't know what to do now."

"So you think she could have sent the notes?"

"She could've. Yes. From all that's happened, that's actually the easy part."

"And you figure we should take a closer look?"

"Yes, Dex. That's what I'm saying. But not *we*, Dex: *you*. As much as you've got me doing all this stuff, at best, I'm just pretending. And that's all right for some of it—staying with Flora, for instance. That doesn't take any special skill. But this investigating stuff? I can do it, but I'm always afraid I'll miss something."

"Fair enough," Dex said, nodding. "But we're spread thin and I need your help."

"We're always spread thin, Dex. What's different now?"

He smiled at me. "I don't know, kiddo. Maybe you are." Before I could respond, he went on. "Look, I'll do as much as I can with all this. Meanwhile, you need to get back out to West Adams and keep an eye on Flora."

I started to protest. There was no way I wanted to be anywhere near any place that Matthew might be, but Dex wasn't having it. "No, Kitty. I don't care what excuse you've got, I need you to keep her in sight. We've already lost the horse. We just don't want to take a chance and lose the girl, too. Mustard will be here any minute. He's heading out to the Valley today. I asked him to stop by on the way to pick you up and take you out there."

"She's at the stable?"

"She's at the stable," he said, nodding. "And I just don't think she should be out there on her own."

I didn't argue that she was hardly on her own. The equestrian center had a whole platoon of staff and certainly in broad daylight she should be as safe as houses. I didn't argue because I know Dex when he has his mind made up, and this was what it looked like. Later I'd wonder if he'd had some sort of premonition, but it was a kind of absent wonder. Right then I just had so much else on my mind.

CHAPTER TWENTY-NINE

Mustard was looking oddly spry when he came to pick me up. He looked younger in his plus fours and open-necked shirt than he did in his everyday suit and tie, topped off with a fedora.

"Golf," he said when I asked him where he was off to.

"You seem to playing an awful lot of golf these days," I said as I got into the car.

He just chortled a bit, obviously amused.

"I'm in a rough racket," he said, maybe as way of explanation. "Golf is relaxin'."

I nodded. The little I knew about the sport made me think he was probably right: miles and miles of walking on a beautifully kept course, past little lakes, and every so often you stopped and whacked a ball. I could understand the attraction, especially for someone like Mustard whose work was just shady enough that he never talked about it. In fact, though I'd known him for quite a while, I still wasn't sure what he did or if it was legal. He called himself a "fixer," but I'd never actually seen him repair anything. I'd surmised long before that whatever he fixed had something to do with horses or dogs. Boxing matches or baseball. Things like that. Plus he sometimes fixed things for Dex: getting him cars and thugs when required. Bootleg whiskey, of course. And, quite possibly, lots of other things I didn't know about and perhaps could not even imagine. Perhaps did not *want* to imagine.

For all of that, there was a sweet fairness about Mustard that

169

I'd come to rely on. He would look at a thing, and he'd tell you what he saw. Quite often he didn't see what *you* saw, but that was seldom a bad thing.

We were in a big, dark car today. I didn't know what kind. With Mustard, it was always a different car. I never asked him to explain, though it was clear none of them represented an attachment. For a lot of guys, a car is a personal statement. For Mustard, it was just a way to get around. They tended to be on the new side and in perfect repair, but you never would have said Mustard loved a car. He was more about getting someplace. Fast. While looking reasonably good getting there.

I checked him under my lashes now. For some reason, he looked good to me today. With Mustard, that was never a given.

"Thanks for the ride, Mustard. Even *I* complain about taking the Red Car way out there."

Mustard grinned his appreciation at this. In the office, it was always Dex who wanted a car and me who opted for the streetcar in order to save a few cents. "Well, Burbank. That's a long way to sit next to someone sweating in a suit that's too hot."

I laughed, surprised at how well he'd hit the thing on the head.

"A lot of that," I admitted. "And little kids. I don't mind little kids," I said. "But when they sit near me on the streetcar, they all seem to be coughing their heads off."

"Dex oughta have a little car. That way he could drive it every day and you could drive it in a pinch."

I nodded, liking the thought. "Especially with clients like these. Dex is hauling out to the Palisades two days running. And me out to Burbank. Well, yeah: a car would be good. You tell him, Mustard. He doesn't listen to me about things like that."

We drove in companionable silence for a bit. Mustard is a lot of things, but he's not full of a lot of hot air. And we'd known each other long enough that we were something like friends. Mustard was the one who had found me, at the lowest moment after my father died. I'd been pawning my dead mother's jewelry in order to pay for my father's funeral. Truly, moments in life don't get much worse than that. He got the pawnbroker to play straight with me—maybe even a little straighter than straight—and, in the end, he'd talked to Dex and gotten me my job. So, yeah: he fixed things all right. Even so, after driving a few miles in silence, his next words, when they fell into the quiet car, surprised me.

"So I've been thinking . . ." He sounded a bit tentative, which was unusual for Mustard. I gave him the space and room I figured he needed.

"Oh yeah? What about?"

"I figured . . . you and me? We oughta get hitched."

This seemed to me such a preposterous idea—and was so completely out of the blue—that I could only look at him, at first to see if he was pulling my leg and then to see if he'd lost his mind. Neither appeared to be the case. To say I'd never thought of him in that way didn't even scratch the surface.

"Sure," I joked. "Give me a diamond as big as a doorknob and I'll pack my bags and move in as soon as I find out where you live."

He didn't hesitate in his response. "Oh, it's a nice place. You'd like it fine." And then, after he'd thought about this for a second, he added, "and we could always move. To someplace you like, I mean. I'm not fussy that way."

"No, I mean, I have no doubt where you live is . . . nice," the joke fell out of my voice when I realized he was serious. "I meant that, well, I just would have thought that, before you get hitched, it's important to know more about someone. You see what I'm saying?"

"Sure," he said. "Sure I do. But you and me, well, we know each other pretty good, Kitty. And we get along just fine. 'Fact, we get along swell. I think you're about the prettiest girl I've ever seen, too." He blushed a bit at this, but he didn't stammer. And then he moved on. "We've never had cause to raise our voices to each other even though we've worked together some. And we've seen each other pretty low and still, we got on. And I figure, you know, we could get on pretty well. Through life, I mean. Through life."

I thought carefully before I answered. Though I'd never thought of him romantically, Mustard was very dear to me. And now, when he'd forced the issue, I realized his declaration was not as unreasonable as it had at first seemed. There was a decade between us. Maybe a little more. And our backgrounds . . . well, they were very different. But hadn't I been musing on the fact that that sort of thinking was outmoded? No longer relevant in the modern world? I knew he worked very hard. That was a trait I'd been raised to prize in a man. But what he worked at . . . well, I wasn't even sure what it was but I was pretty sure that no one in my background would approve of whatever it was. Then there was the physical. From under my lashes, I made out his profile—so intent, currently, on the road. *Stalwart* was the word that came to mind when I thought about Mustard and his looks. *Dependable*. Were those really such bad things?

"I'd never thought of you," I said honestly. "That way, I mean."

Mustard didn't seem put out by this.

"Well, that's all right, isn't it? We've never played that game, you and me. See, that's good too."

"It is?"

"Sure. Lotsa folks, they have what you call, you know, the freezon. They have this sorta dance back and forth. But not you and me, eh?"

"Frisson?"

"What?"

"You said we have the 'freezon.' I thought maybe you meant *frisson*. It's a French word. It means, I guess, like spark of connection or something very like that."

"Sure. That's just what I said. And that's another thing I like; sometimes you know what I mean better than I do." Though he smiled at me a bit when he said this, I had the feeling it was not a joke.

"Wait; you're saying we *don't* have *frisson*. And that's meant to be a reason to get married?"

"Well, sure. We get along, is what I'm saying. What I *did* say, if you think about it."

"That's true," I agreed. "You did."

"I think we'd make a nice life, you and me. I could get you a little house someplace nice. Wherever you liked, really. I'm set up okay. You know that's true. And I'd get you a little car. No Red Car and barking dogs for you." I blinked and looked straight ahead at the road while the picture Mustard was building started to form. It frightened me a little that he was almost making sense. "Maybe we'd have a squirt after a while, if it was what you wanted. Or a couple—a girl and a boy, one for each of us. And we'd laugh a lot, you and me. And we'd be friends, just like we are. And we could get old together."

We could get old together.

"Oh Mustard," I started to say, but he stopped me.

"Never mind, Kitty. Don't answer right now. I don't even want to hear it, all right? You keep your answer inside for the time. You mull it over—on the inside, mind? After a while, if you're sure it's a bad idea, you tell me so and that'll be that, all right?"

And he said this with such kindness, such true gentleness of spirit, that there wasn't much I could do but shake my head.

How could I do anything other than what he asked? Such a small request. Just think—consider, really—think about it in a serious, meaningful way. Then give him my answer. Before I even got out of the car, I resolved to keep my tongue for a couple of days and then tell him he should go and find a different, perhaps more worthy, girl.

He let me out at the front of the stables and I waved him good-bye. But I didn't go directly to the barns as I thought I might. Instead I found a big sycamore tree that shaded one of the paddocks. And I sat beneath, contemplating the horses; contemplating the sky. I sat and I thought. And some of those thoughts were surprising. Even to me.

CHAPTER THIRTY

The shade of the tree I sat under sent dappled rivulets of sunlight dancing across my limbs. I watched the dust motes chase through the wash of sunshine, heard the warm and comforting sounds—distant laughter, echoes of neighs, the bark of a dog—and felt something like comfort. It was an odd sensation.

Could it be I was actually considering Mustard's proposal? Because what was he offering me, really? In certain lights, he could be seen as a thug. Surely my father would not have approved. Marjorie certainly wouldn't. And I could only imagine what even Dex would say. Still, there was a part of me that *did* consider what Mustard had proposed. I thought about it and recognized the possibility of peace. Would that really be such a bad thing?

"A penny?" The voice—husky and quite male—brought me back. I looked up and saw only a masculine-shaped outline. Whoever it was, he was backlit against the sun.

"Still worth a penny?" I quipped, trying to figure out who it was before I gave away the fact that I didn't know. "Even these days?"

"When they're your thoughts, Miss Pangborn," he swung himself down next to me on the grass and I could see him clearly now: Matthew Sweet. "When they're *your* thoughts, I would think they would be worth something more."

I loathed myself for simpering up at him in the way that I'd been taught at Mrs. Beeson's School for Young Ladies, but old habits die hard. Sometimes, though, instinct is the first place we go when other ways are unclear. And other ways *were* unclear. I had managed to come through all of my years with a minimum of masculine attention. Then, on a single day, to get both a viable proposal of marriage as well as the flirtatious attention of one of the most eligible bachelors in the city was more than I could think about in a single go.

Wait: *viable?*

"They're not thoughts I could share," I said.

"I was glad when I saw you sitting over here by yourself," he said.

"Glad?"

"Sure. I wanted to apologize. For yesterday. At the club. To be very honest, I'm still not quite sure what I said wrong. But, whatever it was, I didn't mean it and I'm sorry." He smiled at me then and I had to stop myself from smiling right back at him, so compelling was the look. "Forgive me?"

"I'm sure there's nothing to forgive," I said rather more stiffly than I intended.

"Still. If you could say the words . . ."

"All right. I forgive you. Happy now?"

"Very." Another smile. It lit his face and I cursed the color I felt rising to my cheeks as I noticed. "Now tell me why you're sitting under a tree?"

"It was just such a beautiful day," the lie coming easily, "I just wanted to relax for a minute before getting to work."

"Flora's been asking after you." I still saw warmth in his eyes, or thought I did. But now I saw something else, as well.

"She has?"

"Yes. She's found another note."

CHAPTER THIRTY-ONE

To my eyes, the note was like the others Flora had received. Crudely lettered, but in an artful way, as though the person sending them meant to disguise their own hand. It seemed to me that the art of the thing was different, but I recognized that could be my imagination.

"It's a ransom note," Flora breathed. She was standing in the aisle outside Fritzy's stall looking exhilarated and frightened all at once. I understood the look. On the one hand, it meant the game was afoot. On the other, it seemed almost a sure sign that the horse was alive. Either way, motion felt good after the hopeless looking and endless waiting.

The note demanded that a satchel with ten thousand dollars be placed in the deepest part of the Bronson Caves. I looked up quizzically at that point, but neither Flora nor Matty had any trouble with the reference.

"It's an old quarry," Matthew explained, "right in the park. They stopped working it a few years ago. All that's left is a small system of tunnels."

"People call them the Bronson Caves," Flora added.

"When they say, 'the deepest part,' does that make sense with what you know of the location?"

"Sure," Flora said. "You couldn't leave a sack of money there for days on end without expecting it to get taken, but for a short time? That would be a good spot."

"That part of the park is very quiet," Matty added.

There were a few other, very typical, requests. Small bills, of course. And the police should not be notified. The drop, the note said, should be made at exactly sundown the following night. Provided all went as expected, there would be a note there telling them where to find the horse. And Flora should come alone.

"Under no circumstances is Miss Woodruff making that drop," Dex said when he joined us less than an hour later. I'd gotten lucky; when I called the office, he'd just put his nose in, having once again come up dry in the Palisades. After I spoke with him, he jumped into his loaner car and roared out to Burbank to "get a gander" at the ransom note with his own eyes and formulate a response.

"Oh, but I am, Mr. Theroux. I'm going to do just what they ask. I'd do anything to get my horse back."

"But they know that, don't you see? That's why they insisted it be you. No, I'm sorry, Miss Woodruff. It's out of the question." Flora started to say something, but Dex steamed right through. "The horse was taken on our watch, you understand? There's no way on God's green earth I will allow anything to happen to you. Kitty will go."

"What?" Flora and I were echoes of each other, scant seconds apart.

"You heard me," Dex said. And then with a smile, "*Both* of you heard me."

"We heard you all right, Dex," I said. "I guess we just couldn't believe our ears."

"That's right," said Flora. "Why, Kitty and I look nothing alike. She's much taller and . . . and more slender and I'm darker and . . ."

"Look, it's going to be late in the day, right? Sundown, as the kidnapper requested. There won't be much light left. They'll just see a youthful feminine form. Kitty will make the drop. If the horse is there, she'll lead him out. If there's a note or something, she'll take that, too. Meanwhile, I'll be standing by with a couple of torpedoes waiting to jump on whoever takes the cash."

Dex looked pleased with himself and this simple-sounding solution. But even I knew that in those few short words a lot could go wrong.

"I don't think they'll make it that easy for you, Dex: just waltz in and let you take them and the money, do you?"

"No, Kitty," Dex looked dimly amused with me, "you're right: I don't figure there'll be a lot of waltzing involved. But, like it or not, that's our plan and we're stickin' to it. Miss Woodruff: the ten thousand dollars. Is that a sum you can get your hands on? In time for this exchange, I mean."

"It's a lot of money, but yes: I'm sure my father would be able to get that amount of cash."

"I understood you hadn't told your parents the whole story." Dex was being as diplomatic as possible, under the circumstances.

"That was before Fritzy was taken," the girl said. "Once he was gone, I told them everything."

"And once she told her father, he insisted on paying your fees, as well," Matty said, sounding a little aggrieved. "Though I was happy to pay."

"Oh, Matty, let that go now," Flora said, clearly vexed. "It doesn't matter who pays."

"If that's the case, why didn't he just let me do it?"

"Never mind that now," Dex said. "Let's deal with what we've got. Can we get the money for the ransom together in time?"

"If Flora's father can't put his hands on the sum, I can get whatever is necessary," Matty said chivalrously. "Or my family can. You can go ahead and do the balance of the planning knowing that, between us, we can take care of that part."

Dex went on to tell them that there would be a few extra expenses on our end: the aforementioned torpedoes, for one. Matty said he understood completely and peeled another few hundred dollars out of his billfold. I wondered at the sensation of that: how it must feel to always carry so much money, you didn't need to think twice about anything you wanted. I surprised myself by thinking that I wasn't sure the feeling would be entirely rewarding.

The day passed slowly, as only a day filled with waiting can. As expected, Flora had no trouble raising the ten grand. While that was going on, Dex organized his backup boys while, under his direction, I followed up on a few leads.

"But the horse is already found," I pointed out when Dex told me to tag along to Flora's house. "Tomorrow night, Flora will have him back."

"If we caught a break and found him today, it would be so much the better, Kitty. It would mean we wouldn't have to go through with all the ransom shenanigans. You go and keep your eyes peeled. Until we figure out who's been doing all of this, we're not out of the woods; it could all happen again."

Back at Flora's, Carmella was waiting for us. She approached us the moment we walked in the door.

"Flora, dear," she said, visibly excited and dripping honey, "there's a reporter coming from *Town and Country.*"

"What?"

Carmella's eyes seemed to gleam in a way. If she was a cat, she would have been purring. "That's right. *And* a photographer."

"Carmella, *please.* What are you talking about?"

"She's coming to talk to you, Flora. About . . . all of this business." She waved a hand airily, vaguely in my direction. I gathered I had become the symbol for "this business."

"Whatever for?"

"Why an *article,* dear. Of course. They're going to write about you. I told you. In *Town and Country.*"

"But I can't imagine," Flora said. "What would they want to talk to me for? Isn't that all cotillions and fashion and who's doing what to whom and where?"

"Honestly, Flora: you make it sound like a *gossip* rag. It's hardly that. They write only about . . . well, about *our* kind of people. And things that would be of interest to *us.*"

"Our kind? Carmella, please just come out and say it; they write about people with money."

"Money's not enough," Carmella said, and there was a bit of a blaze in her eyes when she said it. I tried to remember what it looked like; I figured Dex would want to know. "They write about people with money *and* substance. And now . . . now they're going to write about you: the competition. The German horse . . ."

"The kidnapping," Flora put in quietly.

"Everything. About you. About *us* in a way. And they're going to photograph you. Come to your rooms. I've put out that violet dress. It looks so wonderful on you. So *regal . . .*"

"I'm not doing it," Flora said, her voice a single dark note.

Carmella had started moving more deeply into the house, towards Flora's rooms. She stopped now, like a stock horse at the end of a rope, when the steer is caught but not subdued. She stopped like she'd hit a brick wall.

"Oh, but you are." Carmella's voice was deadly quiet. Even so, I didn't have to strain to hear the steel.

"It's a ridiculous waste of time, Carmella. I have so much to do. Why, I haven't even had the chance to tell you what happened at the stables today and . . ."

"You will do it, Flora. You will do it for your father. And, God help you, you will do it for me."

"For you? Why would I do it for you?"

"Because, in the course of things, I ask you for very little. You go about your headstrong way and do whatever you like. But this time? This time *everything* is at stake . . ."

"Everything?" Even I could hear the jeer in Flora's voice.

"Yes. Yes! *Everything.* Your whole future will be decided with this one interview. Your future and where you fit into it. Where we *all* fit into it. Now Flora," Carmella hastened on. I could see that Flora found the conversation distasteful and was preparing to leave it behind, "I know you don't want to do this thing, but you *shall* do it. I have created this opportunity and I will *not* see you throw it away."

Flora was deadly silent for a second that stretched into five and then twenty. I could hear the ticking of a large clock from somewhere farther down the corridor. Laughter from outside where the gardeners were sharing a joke. A creak from within the house as it settled on its foundation. The sounds—the echoey, resonant sounds—of silence.

"What do you mean 'created'?"

"All the things I said—all the *valuable* things I said—and *that's* the one you hone in on?"

"What. Do. You. Mean?"

"Nothing. It was only an expression. Just . . . just words." The doorbell rang and it seemed to me that Carmella sagged slightly with relief. "There she is. Please, *please* Flora, don't be a headstrong girl. Do it . . . do it for your father if you won't do it for me. Or yourself. This sort of exposure could mean a great deal to his business."

"Oh bloody *hell*, Carmella! Daddy won't give a damn and you know it."

"Please, Flora," Carmella said as she headed towards the front of the house where one of the maids was probably already answering the door. "Don't embarrass me."

"All right. If it means that goddamned much to you, I'll do it."

"Flora! Your language."

"Goddamned much!" she repeated. "But I'm not wearing that damned dress. In fact, I'll wear what I like," Carmella's eyes opened wider at this, but she seemed to think better of arguing. "And I want to be outside. Please have her brought poolside. And we'll have drinks. With ice."

Carmella didn't look quite approving at either of these suggestions, but she acquiesced. Even I could see it: half a victory was certainly better than no victory at all.

When Flora headed to her room, I hesitated in the corridor.

"You," Carmella said, "you go with her. The Pangborn thing, you know. It won't hurt either."

I followed Flora to her room, keeping enough distance between us that the black cloud of the girl's mood couldn't touch me, all the while wondering at just what Carmella had meant.

CHAPTER THIRTY-TWO

Oseana Wickingham-Stout was as thin as a greyhound. She had the same long nose and hungry look. You got the idea that if a rabbit were to cross our path, she would bolt, hunt it down, and kill it without missing a beat.

Oseana was British, though with a name like that, I knew she'd either have to be or would have to pretend it. She had the kind of plummy accent that made her sound like she was trying to talk around a mouthful of marbles. Her voice made me think of Mustard: how amused he'd be to meet this woman. How he'd manage to make fun of her without her even knowing it. And when I realized the way my thoughts had gone, I tried to banish them. Was I really considering what he'd proposed? It seemed as though I was.

Flora hadn't given the violet dress a second glance, wearing instead the same getup with which she'd greeted Dex the other day: the bathing suit so scandalous, I could barely look at her without blushing, covered by the same robe she'd worn on that day.

"What about you?" she'd said, indicating my jodhpurs. "You can't go out like that. Mumsy wouldn't approve." She'd come up with another bathing costume, a similar robe, but in a dark pink shade I would not normally have worn. I just had to convince myself the bathing costume provided the underpinnings for the robe, and then I was fine, too.

"Miss Woodruff," Oseana Wickingham-Stout fairly shouted

184

when she greeted us. I tried not to flinch as she spoke. "How very lovely to meet you! I've heard so much, of course. So sorry that our introduction should happen at such a *trying* time!"

"Pleased to meet you Miss Wickingham-Stout," Flora said, gripping the woman's hand, "may I present my dear friend, Miss Katherine Pangborn."

I saw Oseana's eyes widen at the name but, mercifully, she was not compelled to ask if I was "*that* Pangborn?" I thought maybe she took it as read and that, as Carmella had surmised, my presence—and my name—added heft to Flora's pedigree. I hoped not.

"Charmed!" Oseana said, gripping my hand in one disagreeably moist paw.

Flora indicated we should sit, and the moment we did one of the maids came out of the house with a tray of iced lemonade and some fine little cakes.

"My stepmother said you wished to speak with me?"

"Oh, quite, quite!" Oseana enthused, while sorting out a couple of madeleines and some lemonade. "I read about you in the newspaper, you see. And it seemed to me that *your* story had the makings of a *story,* if you follow."

"I think I do," Flora said. I tried not to be alarmed at the quiet of her tone.

Maybe Oseana heard what I heard, because she backpedaled a bit.

"Now don't get me wrong," she said, "I think it's awful—just awful!—that your horse has vanished. But you *can* see how it would all make such an interesting story?"

"Quite," Flora said, still not very loudly.

"And then there's the matter of possible Olympic competition and your father's *connection* to the Olympics and your pending nuptials . . . well, you see? You're a society writer's *dream* subject."

"Ah," Flora said.

"Well . . . well, then," Oseana began awkwardly. I had a hunch she'd anticipated a warmer response, perhaps usually got one. She'd taken a notebook and pen out of a seemingly bottomless bag and set herself up as though to write. I thought at least part of the posture might be for self-comfort. Flora hadn't said much, but her attitude was close to Siberian. As Oseana herself had pointed out, she was a society columnist. One would think she wouldn't have much opportunity to test her sleuthing skills.

"You were saying," Flora prompted, suddenly seeming as though she were beginning to enjoy herself, just a bit. "A *dream* subject . . ."

"Yes. Well. Perhaps we could begin with the horse? You mother has given me pictures . . ."

"Stepmother."

"Pardon?"

"Carmella. She's not my mother. She's my stepmother."

"Oh, yes. Well, I see. That is, I *did* know that, but just surmised you would prefer . . ."

"Stepmother."

"All right. In any case, Mrs. Woodruff has given me photos and was telling me a bit about the horse. I *do* hope you get him back."

Flora softened visibly at this. It was just a wish, but she seemed to take it to heart.

"I have every hope of that myself, Miss Wickingham-Stout," Flora said with less fever than I'd feared.

And so on. Flora didn't give much that Oseana didn't have to pull from her and, to her credit, the reporter did a good and patient job.

While this was going on I sat quietly at the sidelines sipping my iced lemonade and watching their interaction. To my astonishment, the more distant and haughty Flora allowed herself to become, the more the reporter seemed to respond to and respect her. By the time the interview was complete, Oseana Wickingham-Stout seemed a soft fish in Flora's hands, prepared to do anything the young woman requested.

After Oseana had concluded the interview, the photographer came forward and spent an hour with Flora, photographing her in suitably glamorous poses.

"Well, that went well, don't you think?" Flora said after the *Town and Country* entourage had gone.

"We'll see, I guess, when her article comes out." Me: always the pragmatist.

One of the poses the photographer concocted featured Flora sitting on the diving board, but not on the business end. She's in that turquoise robe. Because the photo is in black and white, you can't tell the color. But it's hinted at just the same. The house is spread behind her sphinx-like: an icon. And at just that moment, a slight wind came up and moved her hair about just so. You've seen the shot, I know. Everyone has. And for all of us it represents a particular time and place, a moment in history, really, that Flora held in her hand.

Chapter Thirty-Three

All the business with first the reporter and then the photographer passed the hours urgently enough so that, by the time we'd done with it all, the bulk of the day had moved on and we were less than twenty-four hours from the time the ransom was to be dropped off.

Flora ignored her stepmother for the balance of the day, but when she heard her father come home, she rushed through the house to meet him, anxious, I supposed, to make sure all the details surrounding the ransom had been taken care of.

While she did this, I stayed poolside with the book I'd been perusing on and off since the reporter and photographer had left. It was called *The Good Earth* and it was by a writer named Pearl S. Buck who I'd heard of but never read. Since a lot of my reading material these days came to me secondhand, it was a rare treat to get my hands on some very current literature; something I'd read about in the newspaper and had been told that I must read. Reading it, I could see why, so it wasn't difficult for me to let Flora flit about her various interests in the house while staying deeply into my book . . . and not disobeying Dex's order.

"That's that, then," Flora said, returning to my side less than an hour after her father came home and flouncing down in the chair opposite me.

I put the book down. Clearly, Flora wanted to talk.

"That's what?"

"The ten grand. Daddy says he'll bring it by the stables himself at the appointed time."

I raised an eyebrow, but didn't say anything. It struck me as an odd plan. Flora must have seen my reaction, because she went on.

"He's worried, don't you see? He's afraid I won't listen to Dex and will take off on my own to make the delivery."

"I do see," I said with a smile, "and I think he's probably right to worry."

"Oh, you!" she scoffed. "You're as bad as . . . well, as bad as everyone. Look, Katherine, I don't know about you, but I can't stay cooped up here all night while I wait and worry."

"Sure you can." I indicated the novel I'd put down on the table in front of me. "Read a book."

Flora rolled her eyes. "You sound like someone's maiden aunt. Reading a book is *not* what I had in mind."

"So I gathered."

"I want to go down to the *Tango* tonight. Dance a little. See and be seen, you know. I figure I can call Matty, or maybe even just go on my own."

Her mood shocked me a little. There was such a frenetic quality to it. The time was at hand, in a way, that's what I thought. The horse no longer needed to be found. We just had to get through one more day. Trust Flora to try and do it up in style.

"Well, I'm not sure what the *Tango* is, but I do know that—whatever it is—you are *not* going alone."

"How can you not know about the *Tango*?" The girl looked genuinely shocked.

"I don't get out much." It sounded flippant, but it wasn't far from the truth.

"It's a boat. It's anchored outside the three-mile limit. Such an adventure! We go down to the Pleasure Pier and take a water taxi."

"From the Santa Monica Pier?" I asked. "At night?"

"And then the water taxi skims you through the waves," she did a fairly expressive rendition of waves with her hands, "and deposits you out at the boat."

"Oh, I get it: it's one of those gambling boats I've read about."

"Well, that's what they say. But there's really so much more. Such fun! Dancing and dinner. Drinks, of course. The very best steaks. And gambling. But I mostly don't bother with that part. There's so much else to do that's fun."

"I don't think it's a good idea."

"You don't think *what's* a good idea? Fun? I can believe that!"

"No; fun's all right. It's just you. Going anyplace like that right now. There have been threats against you. It sounds . . ." I tried to push down the part of me that felt like the maiden aunt she'd accused me of sounding like, "well, it sounds dangerous."

"Oh, phhhh," Flora said dismissively. "I've been a million times before. It's not the least bit dangerous."

"Well, despite you having been a *million times before* . . ."

But whatever it was I started to say was bowled over by the force of her personality.

"Listen, Katherine, I *am* going. You can't stop me," and as she said this, I recognized the truth of her words. "Now you can join me if you like; I've invited you. But I *will* go, whether you come or not."

When she got up, there was no anger in her movements, but I knew she'd meant every word. At the doorway she stopped and addressed me again.

"I'm going to change. If you'll be joining me, you'd best come so we can find you something to wear because—obvi-ously—you can't go in either jodhpurs or a robe."

And then she was gone. I picked up my book and tried to

focus, but the words kept swimming. I found that more irritating than anything else, because I'd been enjoying the story intensely up until that point.

I got up with a sigh and, bringing the book with me, headed into the house. I was apparently going to make my first trip to a gambling boat. Though part of me was irritated at Flora's youthful vigor, another part was excited. I was going on a boat!

CHAPTER THIRTY-FOUR

Before we left the house, I had the foresight try to call Dex at the office, but no one picked up. Next I tried Mustard's office, but he wasn't in either. I figured they must be together. When I called Mustard's office, one of Mustard's young associates answered. I left a message saying where I was going and that Mustard be told either as soon as he came in or if he called into the office, but I knew it was entirely possible he wouldn't get it until the following day.

Since I'd exhausted all my options for contacting Dex, I tried to put it out of my mind. Flora hadn't given me an alternative. I could come with her . . . or not. It didn't seem to make much difference to her one way or the other what I did.

We took a taxi down to Santa Monica because Schuster was busy driving Carmella someplace and Flora said she hadn't been able to get in touch with Matty. There were cars at her disposal, but she said she disliked the long walk down the pier followed by dicey parking.

"This way we get dropped right by where we get the water taxi," Flora said, "like princesses."

I'd wanted to stay at Flora's until she got in touch with Matty, but she had pooh-poohed my objections.

"We're modern girls, Kitty!" she said, "we don't need a man to have a little fun."

That hadn't been my point—needing a man to be able to enjoy ourselves—it was just that, considering all that had happened, a few precautions didn't seem out of place. Flora wouldn't hear it, though.

"We're perfectly safe," she said, stepping onto the water taxi, careful to lift the hem of the beaded evening dress she wore. The dress was of a blue so deep, it perfectly matched the indigo of her eyes. Was there an extra brightness to her that night? A brittleness, maybe? I'd ask myself that later. At the time, though, all I was thinking about was keeping up. "You don't even know *how* safe. Just stop worrying and we'll have us some fun. I left a message for Matty at his house. Who knows, he might even join us when he gets it. Would you feel better then?"

I barely had time to think about answering, as I maneuvered myself onto the boat, careful to avoid crushing the delicate material of the dress I was wearing. It was one of Carmella's— all of Flora's things being exactly the wrong size for me. The dress I wore looked as though it had cost three months of my salary but when I'd protested the loan, Flora's hands had formed dismissive gestures, as though imitating small birds.

"Don't even think of it. That woman spends a fortune of my daddy's money on clothes. It's only right I should get *something* out of it."

Her eyes, when she'd said this, had narrowed evilly and I determined the wrong side was not the part of Flora to get on. The dress *was* pretty, though, and was loose enough on me that a precise fit was not demanded. That was a good thing because Flora's stepmother was a darn sight better endowed than was I.

As the water taxi sped across the inky bay towards the distant lights that I took to be the *Tango,* I felt my excitement rise. The noise from the little skiff's engine was too loud to permit easy conversation and it was just as well; I feared Flora would laugh at me if she saw my rising excitement. I felt like a child.

When we approached the *Tango* I had a sense of a very long, low ship. As the boat's shape formed something solid at our approach, it seemed smaller than I'd imagined. When we boarded, however, I could see that this was an illusion. The *Tango* was large and sturdy and from where we boarded it ambled off in several directions.

We were met by a man in a uniform. He looked military but I realized by the lack of insignia—and his location—that it was probably only dress.

"Evenin', Miss Flora," he said, and he doffed his hat to me, "Ma'am. Welcome aboard again." And though he looked the part of a military man, his voice and inflections betrayed a wisdom of the street. "You two on your own tonight?" he asked.

"For the time, yes."

"What's your pleasure this evening? Can I have someone escort you to the gaming rooms?"

"I believe we'll sup first, thanks. And I know my way."

Flora headed off and I scurried along behind, trying hard not to gawk at the interesting things and people along the way.

"What was that about?"

"I dunno. He's always there. I think they greet everyone as they come on board. Probably have an eye out for dry agents. And I've seen them take guns off men who tried to bring them aboard. They're pretty strict about that here."

I felt my eyes widen and I looked at Flora. "I can see why!"

I knew that the shady types who ran these boats had the police well in hand, but it would make it necessary to do your own policing when it came to keeping your patrons from killing each other. Dry agents were something else again, a law beyond the law. Fuelled by the might of the right, they were relentless in their efforts to stop the flow of illegal booze. But the flow was so dense—a river, a waterfall. This deep into Prohibition, the organization that kept illegal booze flowing into Southern California was much too vast to dam.

I stopped thinking about all of these things when we reached the dining room. It seemed to me a floating miracle and almost as fancy as anything we would have found on land.

We were seated at a large, oak table, easily big enough for a half dozen more, but the few tables for two were already taken. Above us, a chandelier glistened silently while the room's gleaming wood paneling and green leather upholstered chairs gave the feeling of being in a gentlemen's club.

"They make a good steak here," Flora said as she looked over the menu. Considering the clientele, I had no doubt they would. Flora must have seen me hesitate, because she continued. "Go ahead. My treat."

When the waiter came, Flora ordered a broiled steak for each of us. And she ordered a bottle of red wine. She laughed at my lifted eyebrows.

"I don't think it's even against the law out here," she said earnestly. "Remember: the three-mile limit?"

"I keep hearing that term. What does it mean, anyway?"

"Oh, geez, Kitty, I don't know. Something to do with international waters. We're not in America anymore! And if we're not in America, Prohibition doesn't even factor in."

It sounded hinky to me, but I kept my trap shut. After all, from the deck of the boat, I'd still been able to see the lights of Santa Monica; the pier and the city behind it. How far from America could we really be?

"And anyway," she went on, "haven't you been to Europe? Why, they drink wine with all three meals in some places there."

"I'm sure they don't. Not at breakfast, certainly!"

She shrugged as the waiter brought the wine and two glasses and poured a bit into each. While I didn't immediately cotton to the taste—acidic and with an odd dryness that almost left me thirsty—I followed Flora's lead and had a sip after I'd buttered a bit of bread and eaten a small bite. The taste of the wine was suddenly palatable. More: it made me appreciate subtle nuances in the flavor of the bread that I would not have noticed without the wine's enhancement. I felt I had made an amazing discovery and busied myself taking small sips and miniscule bites, and didn't notice Flora wave at someone across the room until he joined us.

"Ladies, what a delight! The brace of you would brighten any room."

The warmth that rose to Flora's face when she greeted James Stroud was quite beyond anything I'd seen whenever her eyes rested on that of her fiancé. I wondered if it meant anything.

"Who are you here with?" Flora asked.

James pointed across the dining room at a young man with smooth pale brown hair and a pleasantly bland face. "That's Allan Hancock."

Hancock smiled and waved distantly when he saw us all look.

"Why don't the two of you join us?" Flora said, completely ignoring the look I gave her when she said it.

"That sounds a smashing idea," James said. "Jolly. Let me just ask Allan, but I'm sure he'll think it's fine."

"What on earth do you think you're doing?" I hissed when James had left to talk to his companion.

"What?"

"All things considered, and under the circumstances, the invitation was not an appropriate one."

She smiled at me in the way I imagined a cat might. "Maybe that's just why I did it."

"Don't you *ever* worry about what people will say?"

"You don't really expect an answer to that, do you?"

"What about Matthew?"

"What about him?"

I looked at her then, completely at a loss. What about him, indeed. It really was getting to be a different era. I understood that but, certainly, there had to be limits. Otherwise, what was the point? A certain amount of independence seemed a good and even desirable thing. Look at me; I had it. But there was a point beyond which it was careless disregard. We were two young women alone, one of us affianced, having dinner on a gambling boat while two eligible young men were about to join us. It was behavior that went against everything I'd been taught since childhood.

"Allan, meet my friends Flora Woodruff and Katherine Pangborn."

Up close there was something seal-like in the length of Hancock's limbs, the smoothness of his hair. Something even blander in his pleasant features. Though he was dressed much as James was—neatly pressed dark suit, shirt with a white collar, tie, dark shoes, hat in hand as he approached us—it seemed to me that the cut of his suit was not as good as James's, the cloth not as smooth. If these things were true, Hancock himself seemed unaware of it. He approached us with the kind of confident arrogance James always exuded in such quantity.

"Charmed," Flora said with a smile that bordered on a simper as the two men took their seats.

Our food arrived at that moment: two large plates covered almost entirely by a steak edged in bacon. A piece of parsley provided a contrasting note of green and a few broiled mushrooms decorated the top of the steak. Other than that, each plate seemed little beyond a huge expanse of meat. Enough of it, I thought mildly, that our two meals represented sufficient meat to keep the boardinghouse going—and Marjorie in raptures—for a week, perhaps two.

"Well, we can't just eat these huge slabs of meat while you men look on with nothing in front of you," Flora said as the men took their seats.

"We've already eaten," James said.

"Of course you have. Still," Flora said, beckoning a waiter

with the motion of a single finger. "Indulge me?" Then to the waiter, "What can you offer us that's both fast and light? For the gentlemen. Just to keep them from being rude." She said it with a smile that stole the sting from her words.

"We have some mushrooms under glass, ma'am. Or perhaps oysters in spinach?"

"Both sound nice. Bring one order of each, please." And then to James and Allan, "That way you can pick and we two—being well brought up young ladies—don't have to feel self-conscious while we devour our half cow apiece."

Flora and I still had delicately stemmed wine glasses in front of us, while both men had brought cut crystal lowball glasses from their table. Each glass contained a generous portion of some amber liquid.

"It's Canadian whiskey," Allan said, following my glance. "You get the good stuff out here."

"That's right. Not the rotgut you mostly get right now at the speaks in the city." James lowered his voice. "Tony the Hat brings this stuff down by the boatload from Canada. He owns this tub. And another one, too. And he controls all of the good liquor that gets into Los Angeles these days."

"Why 'the Hat'?" I'd been wondering since I first heard his name.

The two young men looked from one to the other and shrugged.

"My father owned a haberdashery." The voice, deep and exotically accented, seemed to float out of the darkness at us. A moment later, the voice's owner appeared. I didn't need to be introduced. Had not his dark looks spoken volumes, his air of ownership would have. "In Piedmont, before we came here from Italy when I was a boy."

Face to face, there was something familiar to me about Tony the Hat. I felt almost as though I'd met him before, though I knew for certain that I had not. Something in the cast of his eyes, the jut of his chin. Something pulled at me, though I couldn't think what it was.

"Is that true?" Flora asked. "That your father was a haberdasher?"

He smiled at her deeply and the smile, I could see, went all the way to his eyes. "It is not true," he said with a glint in those dark eyes. "My people were simple farmers. Surely you can see that in my stance?"

Flora shook her head.

"But the haberdashery? That's a good story, no? A better story, I think, than the one that makes the truth." I was relieved when the men's food arrived and whatever Flora might have responded was cut off. Having a gangster so notorious he was identified by a nickname this close to us was making me uncomfortable. I'd feel better, I knew, when we were left alone with our steaks.

"Enjoy your evening," Tony commanded with a smile for each of us before he melted back into the shadows.

"Quite the gall, busting in on our conversation like that," Hancock squeaked once the mobster was out of earshot. The three of us ignored him. It was clear to us that if Tony the Hat wanted to bust in on a conversation, that was just what he'd do, and you'd better like it.

Flora didn't say anything, just started delicately on her giant steak. I followed her lead. My own was buttery soft, practically fork-tender, and cooked and seasoned to perfection.

"Good, isn't it?" Flora said with some satisfaction. "That's why this has gotten to be *the* place in the Southland to have a steak."

"For those who know," Allan said with a smirk. His voice was soft and girlish. Though that combination can be endearing, from him it was like nails on a chalkboard.

I took another bite of my steak. It was just as good as it had been, but I was wishing Flora hadn't invited the men to join us. I didn't like the way James looked at Flora, nor the way she giggled back at him. And I just didn't like Allan Hancock's looks at all.

Somehow, too, I felt like a fourth wheel: which is ridiculous, since there is no such thing. At least, not in a negative context. Still, I felt it. It was as though a conversation needed to take place, one that couldn't happen while I sat there. I had no proof of this. I saw no sign: no glances exchanged, no meaningful looks. But I felt it, just the same.

I began watching Flora very closely, but she seemed completely comfortable and in her element. She coquettishly skewered mushrooms and sipped oysters, managing to make both food thefts look like seduction. Every so often even that activity would seem to bore her and she would peer off into the dark. I had the feeling she was waiting, but I couldn't imagine for what.

I sat quietly and ate my steak, perhaps pulling a little too hard on my wine at times. I was unused to alcohol and, after a while, I could feel the effects. I wasn't drunk—I hadn't drunk *that* much—but I could feel a warmth and movement I was unused to.

Despite my discomfort, I knew that, from a distance, we would have made a tableau of laughter and enjoyment: though none of the laughter was mine. When Matthew appeared—stern-faced—at our table, I started guiltily. Flora, for her part, did not. "Matty, darling!" she said, perhaps a little tipsily. "What a surprise! Join us."

He didn't say anything. Just stood scowling at Flora.

James sat back in his chair and smiled at Matty in a way that struck me as both unaffected and sinister. He sounded friendly, but I thought I could hear reverberations below the surface. Of just what, though? I didn't know.

"Yes, come on old man; take a load off," James reached over and speared a piece of meat that Flora had just cut off her steak. "The food here is good. As always. You'd enjoy it, if you gave yourself a chance."

Though James's comment seemed innocent, Matty's face darkened at the words. I couldn't help but think that, even with anger on his face and in his heart, he was beautiful. Something in the way his features came together lifted them beyond the everyday. I tried not to sigh into my wine.

"You look a thundercloud, darling! Stop it. You're spoiling the party." Flora laughed, though I could hear the edge in her voice. "Sit down."

But Matty didn't sit down.

"She was right about you," he said darkly.

"Who?" Flora demanded, looking at me. "Who was right?"

I shook my head, indicating that it certainly hadn't been me.

"If this is all it's ever meant to you," Matty said, the quiet in his voice betraying only carefully controlled anger, "and if you would have me look the fool—perhaps there are things that should be rethought."

He turned on his heel then, and left the dining salon.

"Aren't you going to go after him?" I asked after a full minute had passed and Flora had done nothing but return her attention to her steak.

"Hardly," Flora said, looking around without embarrassment, "I don't know what's eating him. He'll come 'round later. He always does. Shall we order some coffee or tea? Perhaps a nice dessert?"

I looked down at my half-eaten steak with regret. I was still hungry but, quite suddenly, I couldn't eat another bite.

CHAPTER THIRTY-FIVE

It was easily ten degrees colder on the *Tango*'s open deck than it had been back on shore. We were more than three miles out and, from this distance, the lights of the city were a visible but distant blur. It was a quiet night, but I could feel the deck move under my feet. I'd taken the steamer from Los Angeles to San Francisco a few times, and I'd once spent a few uncomfortable hours aboard a luxury ship moored at San Pedro, but I'd never gotten used to that unnatural movement of a boat on the sea. At best, it made me want to sit down. At worst, it made me want to unload what I'd eaten of my steak.

I held on.

When we'd gotten on board earlier in the evening, we had been part of a bustle; a cheerful melee. An hour or so later and things had quieted down quite a bit. I figured that when we'd arrived it was early enough that people were just settling in. Now, at nearly nine o'clock, a lot of people had gotten down to the serious business of gaming. It was what most of them were here for.

I didn't intend to follow Matty from the dining room. That is, I can recall no clear plan. But Flora had been so odious and Matty looked so stricken and pathetic that I just followed my urge and looked for him outside after he left. I didn't see him at first though, just the quiet misty decks and the rows of deck chairs, empty now, with the sun tucked away.

I saw the cherry-glow of a cigarette end before I saw him

standing in dim light at the port bow, smoking, staring out to sea.

"She doesn't mean it, you know," I said, not entirely certain I was right, but thinking they were the words he needed to hear. "Sometimes when she speaks I don't think she means anything by it at all."

Trying to console him, I felt conflicted. On the one hand, did I *really* think it would be such a bad thing if he and Flora broke things off? Would that leave a wedge for me and was that what I wanted? On the other, he seemed to have so much of his happiness tied to her, I just wanted the pain I saw on his face to go away.

"I know you're right. That's just the sort of girl she is, isn't it?" He took a hard pull on his cigarette and the cherry glowed even more madly in the darkness. "She's a free spirit, in a way. I guess . . . if I'm very honest, that's part of what I've loved about her. She isn't . . . well, I suppose she just isn't like other girls. She's . . . she's different, somehow. More special. I'm sorry. I forget myself. It's not that you are not special, Miss Pangborn, it's just . . ."

"Oh, never mind explaining. I knew what you meant." Even so, I was glad of the dark. I could feel my eyes swimming slightly. Feel an odd heaviness in my heart.

"No, really." He placed one solid hand on my arm where it rested on the railing, while with his other he flicked the cigarette into the sea. I watched as the glowing tip tumbled, end over end, toward the water. It was such a peaceful night, I could even hear the small hiss as the sea snuffed it out. "I sometimes forget myself. When Flora and I are together, sometimes it pushes everything else out of my mind."

It was a moment not like others. There was moonlight, buckets of it. It spread across the water like a fan. The *Tango* wasn't underway, but it was in slight motion. It bobbed gently in the water like a toy.

There was a wind, but it was gentle. Secret. It carried the scent of the sea, of course, but also whispers from places that I had never been.

Matty's eyes had always moved me. His hands, when they touched my face, were not a surprise. And they were warm and strong and, at that touch, they pushed aside other things—duty, friendship, personal ethics—without even a moment's thought. If I'd had the presence of mind for it, I would have been ashamed.

I was not myself.

"Yet you," he said, closer now. His voice husky against my ear, the scent of an aftershave—minty, yet touched by a forest floor—"you also fill my mind, do you know that?"

I felt myself murmur something. Something that was probably quite incoherent. Who was I in that moment? I don't know. I was taller, more beautiful. A girl in a film. I only know that because I did things I would not normally have done, things quite beyond myself. I reached up and gingerly touched his chin, his jaw, the place where his neck came to his collar. Light fingers guided by instinct, fueled at least slightly by wine. But only slightly. It seemed I'd waited a long time for this moment. In some ways, I'd waited my whole life.

And then his mouth was crushing mine. Beyond expectation, this passionate kiss. A raw violence beyond the damp exchanges that film kisses had led me to expect.

This would have gone on, I know it. And it could have gone to other, for me unimaginable, places. But I heard a voice then; an all too familiar voice. I jumped as it found me.

"Kitty, what the hell?" And I knew that though I would spend a hundred—a thousand, a *hundred* thousand—moments in my life unobserved, this one would be interrupted by Dex.

Matty straightened at the sound of my name and Dex's voice. He straightened and he took a step back. A bar of cold crept into the place where he had stood.

I looked up to meet Dex's eyes, to face my music. I looked up and there was Dex, looking back at me in a way that let me know that everything was not good. Worse, though, and the thing I should have anticipated: Mustard stood next to Dex, his soft shadow. The look on his face chilled my soul.

CHAPTER THIRTY-SIX

"I didn't think I was seeing right," Dex said. "I mean, I thought I recognized you—the both of you—but I didn't think it could be right."

Mustard hadn't stuck around. He'd headed to the nearest door and gone inside. The door closed behind him with a gentle puff. I think I would have liked it better had it slammed.

"Well . . . turns out your eyes are better than you thought," I said pertly.

Despite my saucy reply, my heart was heavy with shame. Anything Dex could think to chastise me with didn't have a patch on the beating up I was giving myself. A client's fiancé, for God's sake. What had I been thinking? All of Dex's horrible antics over the years seemed nothing in the shadow of this indiscretion. And Mustard's eyes. In that moment I couldn't imagine a time in my life when the disappointment I'd read on Mustard's face wouldn't tear at my soul.

Dex looked as though he would have responded to my tone, but thought better of it. Instead he asked an entirely sensible question. "What the hell are you doing here?"

"I didn't want to come, Dex. Flora dragged me."

"Flora did, huh? Did she also ask you to feed her boyfriend your lipstick?" He gave Matty a contemptuous look that started up and ended down. "Seems possible to me you oughta find her, boy. If you plan on keeping her, that is."

For a moment, it looked as though Matty were going to say

something back, but Dex shot him a look that said *keep it to yourself.* Matty didn't need a second opportunity. He fled into the night. Part of my heart broke then. I felt it, just a splinter. I knew he was rushing back to Flora and I realized then I'd just wanted him to stay.

"I'm sorry," I said quietly when we were alone.

"Sorry doesn't get us anyplace close, kiddo. He's a client's fiancé. But, more than that, I just wish Mustard hadn't been here to see."

"He told you what he said to me?"

"Yeah. Well, he told me what he hoped. If there was more than that, he didn't say."

"There wasn't more than that."

"All right then," Dex said. "Well, clients first. Let's go find Flora. However this plays out, I've got a hunch she won't be as choked about it as even you are."

There was no sign of Flora in the dining salon where I'd left her. James and Allan were gone, too.

"That's funny," I said. "I wasn't really gone very long. She was just starting to call out for dessert when I left."

"Whattaya got against dessert?" Dex wanted to know.

"It's nothing, only . . ."

"Let's try the tables," he said. I got the idea he'd rather not hear whatever I might say.

But Flora wasn't at the tables, either. Nor in any of the gaming rooms.

"She can't have just up and disappeared," I said when we'd exhausted all our options.

"Well yes, she can, Kitty. Especially when she's been threatened by a kidnapper."

The import of what Dex was telling me sank in quickly.

"Oh, Dex," I said, "you don't really think . . ."

"Right this second, Kitty? That's exactly what I *do* think. I think it could very well be our worst nightmare. And it happened on your watch."

CHAPTER THIRTY-SEVEN

We were frantic. Or at least, *I* was frantic; Dex was livid and Mustard was in some cold and unreachable place that made me sad beyond sad. And Flora? Well, that was the question of the hour, wasn't it? Though we carefully searched the portions of the ship available to us, and though Mustard managed to talk to Tony the Hat himself, not only did no one know where Flora was, they couldn't even imagine where she'd be.

Between the time I left the dining table and the time we found that Flora had disappeared, for me the *Tango* had gone from pleasure palace to haunted house. As we frantically searched the ship, room by room, I no longer saw the imported crystal chandeliers or the expensive felt gaming tables or the exotic inlaid floors. I saw the hidden cracks that had been caulked around the old tub's windows, the collected grime of a hundred thousand cigarettes on the casino ceiling, and the underlying stench of money badly earned and easily spent.

I was aware of doing three hard circuits of the boat in the hour and a half immediately following our realization that Flora was gone. And, of course, no one knew anything. No one had seen anything. No one really even wanted to talk to us. It was as though she had never been there at all.

And then we gave up. At least, we gave up on finding her on the boat. Flora was gone, but neither could we find a trace of James Stroud or Allan Hancock. I thought it all smelled funny, but Dex told me not to jump at shadows that couldn't be seen.

I didn't know *exactly* what that meant, but I figured it had to do with things not always being what they seem.

When we went to take the water taxi back to the mainland, Dex queried the captain, but the man claimed he hadn't seen anyone that fit our missing trio's description. Did his eyes jump around too quickly as he answered Dex's hard questions? Did I see his Adam's apple bump too quickly in his throat? I was tired and frantic enough that I no longer trusted my own instincts. Was it dissembling I saw, or the natural nervousness of a man whose passengers quite often carried guns? I couldn't be sure.

After he'd questioned the man, Dex continued silent as the water taxi bumped across the bay taking us back to shore. Dex was silent and Mustard had stayed behind. When he'd told us he wouldn't be joining us, he hadn't met my eyes. And when I tried to speak to him, he just turned away.

Once on shore, I followed Dex to where he'd left his borrowed car. "What about Mustard?" I asked. "You came together, right? How will he get home?"

Dex looked at me fully for the first time—really looked at me—and said, "He'll manage. He's a big boy. Now get in."

And I did.

I didn't say anything for a while. Neither of us did. I didn't speak until it became apparent we were going to neither the office nor my house.

"Where we going?" is what I finally said.

Dex took his eyes off the road and gave me a long, hard look.

"West Adams," he said finally. And he wouldn't say anything more.

It made sense to go see Flora's parents. It would be a starting point. But, sitting there as I was, in Carmella's own dress, and having been charged with having my eye on Flora—and having made an *astonishingly* bad job of it—well, it didn't mean I had to like the idea of going there. At all.

A uniformed maid ushered us into the same sitting room where Flora and I had met the press just a few days before. It was very late and I found myself wondering if someone was assigned with standing by in uniform twenty-four hours a day to deal with anything that might come up. In this house, it seemed a possibility.

We were left to sit there for a surprisingly long time. I imagined nightcaps and sleeping gowns being put aside and clothing being donned. Finally, Carmella came out to meet us. She was alone and looking smooth and beautiful in a delicately sewn peignoir set that made Dex look twice. The cloth was of a pale lavender, almost white, especially against her nearly black hair and olive skin. Feathers fluttered over her collarbone and plunged to decorate her décolleté. On seeing her, I reflected that she looked like a movie heroine, awakened from sleep. Not a real person. At least, not like me. I didn't own a peignoir set, for one thing. And if I did, I would be unlikely to wear it even to the drawing room if people were there.

There was a practiced smoothness to Carmella Woodruff tonight. She looked, well, perfect. The middle of the night and Carmella had not a hair out of place.

"Forgive me," she said when she joined us, "my husband seems indisposed. I tried and tried to wake him, but he had a very long day. It seems to have told on him. What is it you require?"

"Is Miss Flora here, Mrs. Woodruff?"

She looked from one to the other of us, perhaps searching for something more, but I didn't think we were giving anything away.

"I don't see why she wouldn't be. Let me check."

She left the room, but the maid was on her heel. I figured if there was any running being done, it was the maid who would be doing it.

Carmella came back in a surprisingly short time, looking not at all out of breath. She stood close enough that I could catch the drift of her scent. A bright floral top note, under a base note of Fougère.

"She is not here," Carmella said. "Her bed has not been slept in. What is going on? Is that my dress?" She looked from one to the other of us as though she would demand an answer.

"Might we have a seat, Mrs. Woodruff?" Dex said. He held the brim of his hat in both hands as he stood, working it ever so gently so that it moved in a clockwise motion as though wired from within.

At first Carmella looked like she might deny his request, insist on being told whatever we were holding back. Then she thought better of it and ushered us through to the drawing room, taking Dex's hat and handing it off to a maid as we moved more deeply into the house.

As we settled ourselves on a couple of sofas in front of a fireplace that looked like it was made more for gazing at than for warmth, Dex pulled a pack of cigarettes from his breast pocket, offering one to Carmella before he lit up himself. She took one and lit it solemnly, only taking her eyes off Dex to indicate the maid should bring an ashtray. The one that came was ornate and deep, a fanciful creation of abalone and onyx and with sufficient weight to kill a man. Carmella smoked silently for a moment, just regarding Dex with that unwavering look. It might have come from desire or it might have been distrust. I couldn't be quite sure, not then.

Dex didn't see any of this interplay. He gave no sign of it, anyway, and once we were settled, he took a big, reassuring hit off his smoke before he spoke. "What I'm going to tell you is alarming, Mrs. Woodruff but—understand—we have no reason to think the worst at this point. All right?"

Carmella nodded, but took her own drag, sending the smoke

at the ceiling in an excited elongated cloud. She looked as though she were bracing herself for something. Considering the hour and our line of work, I figured she probably really did have cause for concern. After all, it was a safe bet we weren't there selling cookies.

"Go on," she prompted. She exhaled again as she said it. Lit from behind as she was, the smoke seemed to swirl up and around to form a halo through her dark hair. It was perhaps unkind of me to wonder if this was a practiced effect.

"It's about Miss Woodruff."

Carmella's face told a story. She did not say, "When is it *not* about Flora?" But I heard it just the same.

"Flora and Miss Pangborn here went down to the *Tango* tonight . . ."

"The gambling ship?" she said breathlessly, though there was something in the way she said it that gave me the idea she knew exactly where—and what—it was.

"That's right. They had dinner and, while Miss Pangborn left the table for a short time, Flora disappeared."

"Disappeared?" she repeated. "How do you mean? Like vanished? Without a trace?"

"I'm afraid that's right, Mrs. Woodruff." Dex leaned back in the well upholstered seat and exhaled a column of smoke. To look at him you would have thought he was relaxing. I knew better. I knew he was thinking hard. "We saw nothing to indicate she'd been taken—no disturbances, no one saw Flora being forced away—but it happened in such a way that we felt you should be notified. Under the circumstances."

"The circumstances?"

"The kidnapped horse. The threats. And so on."

"How could you not see anything?" This was directed at me. "Weren't you supposed to be with her night and day?"

I felt the blood swirl around in my head a little at this

because, of course, she was right.

"I wasn't gone long." My voice wasn't very loud. I couldn't seem to turn it up much above a scratchy whisper. Dex saw this and raised his eyebrows. He's a detective. Sometimes he gets what stuff means more than you do. It can be disconcerting.

"What's going on?" Cedric Woodruff joined us in the drawing room, looking much less composed than his wife. You could tell he hadn't been expecting company. The belt of his silk dressing gown dragged on the floor and his sparse salt and pepper hair stood up on his head like two weeks' worth of unmowed grass.

As he entered the room, his wife stood up so quickly, I thought for a moment she would lose her footing.

"Nothing, my dear." Her smile was hard and plastic. "You go back to bed. I'll take care of everything."

Dex ignored her. "It's your daughter, sir. She's missing."

"Missing? What do you mean 'missing'?"

"I'm sure it's nothing, my darling," Carmella insisted. "Please go back to bed. It'll all be sorted by morning."

For just a second, it looked as though he would do just that; the weight of the decision seemed to rest on him more heavily than the weight of the body he was currently having some trouble with. In the end, though, he pushed himself to where we all sat and plunked himself down on the sofa next to me. Close up, I could see that his eyes were bloodshot and his hands shook slightly.

"Now tell me about Flora," he said, his voice slightly stronger but still shaky. "You said she's missing. What does that mean?"

Dex went through it again, from the top, without impatience. I watched Cedric's face carefully as Dex told it, but all I could see there was worry.

"Carmella, did you know she was going down to Santa Monica tonight?"

"No, dear. That is, I knew she was going out, but I didn't know where."

"I wish you could have convinced her to stay home. And with all this danger about, too! Someone needs to keep an eye on her."

"It wasn't my fault, Cedric! Don't sound like that."

"That's not what I meant, my dear. I'm just saying . . ."

"And we *had* someone keeping an eye on her," Carmella said crisply, while dragging her eyes over me with meaning. "We *had* someone, didn't we?"

"Now, now, Carmella. Let's not blame. What matters is finding her." And then to Dex, "Any chance she just slipped away for some fun?"

"I don't think we should rule out the possibility. Has she done things like that before?"

Carmella snorted but Cedric silenced her with a look. "Now, now, Carmella," he said again. And then to Dex, "Should we call the police?"

"I wouldn't want to advise you about that, one way or the other," Dex said. "As your wife indicated, Miss Woodruff is a high-strung young woman. I should think there's a possibility that she went off on her own."

"What about young Sweet?"

"Hmmm?" Dex said.

"Might she have gone off with him?"

"No. It appears they had some kind of fight."

"A fight? But they get on so well." Woodruff looked suddenly older, as though all of this was catching up with him. But he looked more sharp at the same time, the sleep he'd been trying to throw off finally conquered. "Listen, Theroux," he said now, his voice edged in steel. *This* was the Cedric Woodruff who had managed to make a fortune when other men were losing theirs. "You've gotten good money to look after my little girl. Her horse is gone and now she's missing. Everything you've touched has turned to disaster. You've got exactly twenty-four hours to get something done or I'll have you and your lot in the hoose-gow so fast it'll spin your head."

"You'd throw us in jail?" I'd finally found my voice. "For what?"

"Fraud, missy. Some detectives! Why, it seems you've been stringing me along. From what I've seen, you couldn't find a bootleg whiskey bottle even if the bottom of the bag were wet."

I spared a glance, then, for Carmella. She had subsided into silence once her husband had awoken, but I could see it was not from awe or distress. As he worked himself up, she pushed herself more deeply into her seat. I tried to decode the look on her face. Was it concern or smug satisfaction? Was she a frightened kitten, or a cat contemplating a decision: canaries or cream?

Dex had gone deathly quiet through Cedric's little speech. And he'd gone deathly pale. I wasn't sure if it was anger or embarrassment or some of both. I was aware, only, of one thing: whatever had gone wrong with this case—and it was more than a single thing—had pretty much been my fault. There just weren't a lot of ways of looking at that. To his credit, Dex let none of this show in his voice.

"I'm sorry you feel that way, sir," he said tightly. "I'm not inclined to argue with your assessment, though I certainly disagree. However, you've given us twenty-four hours and—by crikey—we'll take it. Good night to you sir," he said, rising, simultaneously doffing and tipping his hat to Carmella once he'd retrieved it from the maid. "Ma'am. Come along, Miss Pangborn. We've work to do."

Chapter Thirty-Eight

Fortunately the ride from West Adams to Bunker Hill was not long. If it had been, the silence would have frozen my heart. As it was, my mind was full of things that perhaps *should* be said or *could* be said, but whenever I came close to spitting something out, one glance at Dex's stoic profile stopped my tongue.

Dex pulled up right in front of my house, but he didn't move and he didn't say a word. I sat there for a couple of minutes in silence, too, not quite sure what was expected of me, not quite sure what to do.

Dex caved first. "It's late, Kitty. Go on, get out. We'll both be more able to cope with all this after a good night's sleep." When I still didn't get out, his voice got sterner. "Look, Kitty: you really don't want to make me talk tonight. This is all a big mess, but I know it can't all be your fault, all right? Maybe I give you too much leeway, sure. And, okay: that's gotta stop. But you're a sweet kid with a good heart, that's what I keep telling myself. That's what I tell you sometimes, too. You didn't mean to mix all of this up like this. Didja?"

"No! But I *did* mix it up, I know I did. And I'm so *dreadfully* sorry, I don't know how it all happened. One thing just seemed to lead to another." I knew I was thinking of Matty specifically now, but it could apply to almost every other part of the mess as well. "And then, well . . . here we are."

"Yeah, that's right; here we are. And, you know, a lot of it really is my fault when you think about it."

"Oh no, Dex."

"Sure. Sometimes you act so grown up, I forget you're just a kid."

"I *ain't* a kid!"

"You know what I mean, Kitty. I gave you a bit too much slack, is all I'm sayin'. I shoulda kept a tighter rein on things."

Somehow his taking his share of blame for everything only made me feel worse, if worse was a thing it was possible to feel. I couldn't think of a response, though, and we continued to sit there in silence. Me, again, running through the things I should/could say.

"You're not gonna get outta the car, are you?" Dex said eventually.

I shrugged. I hadn't really taken the thought all the way through.

"Look, if you ain't gonna get out of the car, maybe I have an idea." His earlier coolness seemed to have been left behind. It was possible he'd thought about it and decided I'd been punished enough. Or that I'd punish myself more than his silent treatment ever would. And he was right about that, too. "There's a speak down in Venice I'm gonna go check out. Might be useful if you tagged along. You game?"

I nodded enthusiastically, knowing Dex was including me so that I could try to redeem myself: to me if to no one else. And I was properly grateful for the chance. Besides, I knew that if I went home now, I'd never be able to sleep anyway. Better to be moving forward and trying to discover what had become of Flora.

"All right then," he said, turning the key in the big car's ignition, "that's settled. And you're already wearing the duds for it, so that's good."

I looked down at the lovely dress and thought I should have offered to give it back to Carmella. Then realized that it probably hadn't been the time.

Then I forgot about the dress. Settled in for the ride. Felt excitement claw at my gut, despite myself. It was nearly midnight in a life that usually saw me in bed before ten o'clock. Nearly midnight and I was on the passenger side of a big, dark car heading off to go to an illegal drinking and gambling club. There didn't seem to be much for me to do right then but sit back and hang on.

CHAPTER THIRTY-NINE

We drove back to Venice, making me feel like it was a night that might not ever end. That it might just move into some odd circlet of time, with ebbs and flows of love and loss and highs and lows. And then it would all begin again.

We were quiet on this trip, as well. But our silence didn't share the sharp quality of that earlier barbed silence. I can't explain it better than that. This silence had a smoothness, and that is all.

Dex slowed the car when we got to Windward Avenue. Despite the late hour, the street was lined with cars, the sidewalks awash with people. I looked at Dex, but he wasn't giving anything away.

I saw a man stumble drunkenly over an uneven sidewalk. His companion steadied his elbow while her laughter echoed shrilly into the night. Three sailors walked arm-in-arm towards Main Street, the streetlights reflecting off the white in their uniforms and the shadows made by their curiously belled pants. An old man walking his old dog was the only odd note. Perhaps the beautiful clear night and the forced continence of the aged driving them out.

Though I didn't know where we were going, I suspected we'd have to walk for a bit when Dex parked the car and grumbled about not being able to find a spot. We traipsed about a block back to the Antler Hotel, a short stout pile of a structure. The hour was late and even from the street I could see the lobby was dim and quiet. It didn't look like much was going on.

"Rest your dogs here," Dex said, leaving me under a lamp-post while he went inside. I took one look around the dark street, shadows at every corner, and scampered in on his heels. I got there just in time to hear him say the most inexplicable thing to the man behind the desk.

"Bob's your uncle," Dex said.

The guy looked up from the newspaper spread out on the desk in front of him. He looked Dex and then me over critically, his mouth the sort of mean straight line that hasn't seen a lot of smiles.

"But he's got a mean left hook," he said when he'd satisfied whatever question he'd asked himself.

"Thanks," Dex said and headed back outside. And then, to me, as we walked, "Couldn't stay put, huh?"

"Umm . . . you left me under a streetlight in front of a hotel in the middle of the night."

"Wanted to see if you really meant what you said about coming along," he said, grinning. "Come on, follow me."

I only hesitated for a moment when Dex looked quickly left, then right, to see who was looking in our direction—no one—then darted into the alley. I followed because, by this point, it was fairly obvious to both of us that my choices were limited.

Dex moved down the alley at a brisk, unhurried pace—me hard on his heels—not stopping until we were directly behind the hotel. Dex indicated I should follow him down a narrow staircase. And there we stood, the two of us, in front of an almost hidden doorway to what looked as though it was a maintenance room.

"What are we . . ." I started to ask, but Dex shushed me with a motion and a look.

He gave the door a gentle but confident rap. Almost immediately, it opened a crack. We couldn't see who was on the other side.

"Look what the cat dragged in," said the gruff, unseen voice. Friendly enough words, but they were uttered absolutely without inflection.

"But he's got a mean left hook," Dex responded, just as though he were making perfect sense.

The door opened wider—just wide enough to let us pass— and I followed Dex into a warren that looked like it had fallen out of some dissipated dilettante's imagination.

From the first, I had a sense of being at the business end of a tunnel. Not far from where we'd entered, the tunnel widened out into a medium-sized room. The customers were like fireflies in a dungeon, their affluence and determined revelry a sharp contrast with the rough walls and bare floor. The crowd was beautifully dressed and perfectly focused on the gaming taking place at various tables around the room and down other corridors.

The most distinctive thing about the place was the smell. Tobacco smoke. Bootleg whiskey. Perfume: cheap and other kinds. Men's cologne. But overriding all of these things was the odor of sea-tinged damp. It wasn't an awful smell, but it was a scent that stuck with you, like a warning. You had the feeling that, when you left, that deep damp smell would cling to your clothes and linger in your hair.

"What is this place?" I said to Dex.

In response, he took my hand, as though we were lovers, and led me to a dark corner where he smiled deeply, seductively. It was enough to make my heart flutter, even though I knew the smile was intended for anyone who might be watching.

"Now listen, kiddo, and listen good," he said around that smile, " 'cause I'm only gonna be able to say this once, okay?"

I nodded.

"We're under the canals. It's a network of tunnels that were built for maintenance. And, in case you're wondering, no: this is not a legal part of the Antler's business."

The thought that this might be a legal operation had never crossed my mind.

"What are we doing here?" I asked.

"Lots. Stick close to me, okay kiddo? And follow my lead. It might feel funny, but I won't steer you wrong, got it?"

Still holding my hand, he led me to the bar and helped me solicitously onto a high stool. A waitress with long legs and a short skirt came by. She had pretty eyes in a sad face. Dex ordered without consulting me: three fingers of bourbon, neat, for himself; a kir royale for me. He already knew that was the one alcoholic beverage I'd encountered that didn't make me wrinkle my nose. In fact, it was pleasant-tasting. Like fizzy juice with an invisible kick. A girl had to be careful around a drink like that.

"Haven't seen you in here for a while, handsome," the girl said to Dex when she dropped off our drinks. She spoke to him, but she was looking at me. And she was looking at me like she didn't much like what she saw. I felt myself bristling. Dex wasn't my boyfriend. Of course he was not. Still, how did she know that? She oughta show a little respect.

"Naw, that's right. My girl here is looking for a friend of hers."

"Anyone I'd know?" the girl asked.

"That's what I'm wondering," Dex replied. "She's a good-looking girl, close to underage. Dark hair, expensive duds."

She looked around the room. "Could be almost anyone here."

Dex just shrugged agreement.

"Alone or with someone?"

"Well, that we're not sure of. Could be either way. And this girl's a swell."

The waitress seemed to consider before she answered. "You know, I don't think we've had anyone in here like that tonight. You wanna ask John?"

"Sure."

"He's in the office. You want I should pull him out?"

"Naw," Dex said, dropping a few coins into the tip jar on her tray, "I'll find him all right," and then to me, "You stay here, sweetness. I'll be right back."

As Dex headed down one of the corridors, the girl stood next to me, watching his back.

"You're a lucky twist, you know that, kid?" she said. "Dex Theroux, now he's a gentleman. All of them ain't, you know. All of them ain't. Not like him."

"Thanks," I said, hoping it would be answer enough. Now that Dex was out of the frame, she seemed a little more willing to be friendly. I felt myself thaw towards her, but just a bit. I knew that girls like her needed watching. She wasn't just here to sell drinks and cigarettes, I could tell that straight off. I had the idea that before she hung up her short skirt and her big tray, someone would be calling her missus, at least that was the plan.

With Dex out of the room and the girl thawed, I was so sure I had her figured that when she changed direction, it took me off guard.

Dex had been gone a while and I'd been alone, sipping my drink for maybe four or five minutes. Returning to the bar with her empty tray, she stopped in front of me and regarded me thoughtfully before speaking.

"She wasn't in here tonight, but I figure maybe I've seen her before."

"Who?" I asked, not immediately following her leap.

"The girl Dex said: young, pretty, dark hair. Rich. We don't really get a lot of dames that are that whole package."

I looked around at the gamblers and realized she was right. It was mostly an affluent crowd, sure. Intent on spending their money. But it wasn't the sort of place young people went to kick up their heels. I'd been to a few of those and could see the difference. This was a place serious gamblers could go to gamble seriously. A young woman would be remembered in this place, that's what the girl was telling me. The presence of a young woman would be noted, filed away. It seemed possible she was telling me more than I could see.

"But this one is?"

"Yeah: if it's the one I'm thinking. She used to come in here with a good-looking young guy sometimes. I heard her call him 'Matty.' "

"That's her," I said breathlessly.

"Then, for a while, she would come in here alone."

"For a while?"

"Yeah. Last couple times I seen her, though, she wasn't alone at all, if you get what I'm saying."

I looked the girl over closely and she looked back at me. She could clearly see that I did not.

"The good-looking guy you mentioned?"

She shook her head and dropped her voice a couple of notches. "Last couple times, she was in here with Tony the Hat."

"What are you telling me?" I said, dropping my voice to match hers. Moving close enough to whisper in her ear. Close enough to smell something like lilies over her own musky scent.

"I'm not telling you anything, sister," she said, just as closely. "I'm not telling you anything more than what you wanna hear."

"Tonight," I pressed on. "Was she in here tonight?"

"Not tonight, no. I ain't seen her. Her *or* the Hat."

I pulled a dollar out of my purse. Looked at it thoughtfully, then brought out a second one and pressed them both on the girl, scratching our office number on a matchbook as I did so.

"She comes in here again, you call me at this number?"

The girl shrugged, but she made the number and the two bucks disappear all right. Then she went on about her business and I sat there and sipped my drink and mulled over what she'd told me. Flora and Tony the Hat. Was it even possible? And, if so, what did it mean?

Not too many minutes later I was anxious for Dex to come back. I had so much to tell him. Plus, with the information I'd gleaned from the girl, I felt as though there was no reason to stay and, after a while, I came to the conclusion that I did not like the place. The air was too thick, we were perhaps down too low, and after a while of just sitting there and sipping, I'd come to understand that the atmosphere was not of glorious revelry, but of sharp desperation. The people at the tables didn't really look as though they were playing. They all seemed to be riding on every toss of the dice, every spin of the wheel. You could feel it in the air.

After a while I was so anxious to get out of there that, when Dex appeared, I almost knocked over my stool.

"Harrah hasn't seen anything," Dex told me. He indicated I should retake my seat, and he sat down himself. "It took me a while to get in to see him and when I *did* see him, he didn't have much to say."

"I had better luck," I said quietly, indicating Dex should come in close. "The girl says she's seen her," I indicated our waitress. "But not tonight. She said she figures Flora has been in here before, though. With Matty . . ."

"Natural enough."

". . . and with Tony the Hat."

He pulled back and looked at me. "What?"

I shrugged. "That's just what the girl said."

"Are you sure she was talking about Flora?"

I shook my head. "No way to be certain. It sounded a lot like her, though. Said she was rich and young and dark-haired. Even said she called the good-looking young guy she came in with a few times 'Matty.' "

Dex whistled and pushed his hat back on his head. Took a pull on his drink and lit a smoke in an efficient and practiced set of movements.

"Well how do you like that?" he said finally.

"Not much," I admitted. "What now, boss?"

Dex laughed out loud. The sound was surprisingly happy. I figured maybe something inside him had finally snapped.

"Hell, Kitty, I'm just thinkin' this up on the fly. If what you say is right? It changes the game some, don't it?"

"I guess. But how do we find out?"

"If we're right? We don't, really. Not with Tony the Hat. At least, not right away. Normally I'd say we ask Mustard to nose around. See what he can see. But under the circumstances . . ."

I felt like cursing the blush that stained my cheek at the reminder and hastened another question by way of a subject change.

"So what now?" I said, hoping Dex didn't notice my discomfort.

"Out to the stables, I guess." He sipped his drink. "They've promised us a tradeoff in less than twenty-four hours."

"They promised *Flora* a trade. They've changed the game up by taking her."

"Would you say you're sure the same people have Flora and the horse?"

"I'm not sure of anything anymore, Dex, but it would follow. What about you? What do you think?"

"I think we have to assume it's the same people. It's too much coincidence for there to be *two* kidnappers out there targeting the Woodruffs."

"But what about if what she said is right?" I said, indicating our waitress on the other side of the room. "If Flora has been coming here sometimes with Tony the Hat, that means it's a whole new game, doesn't it?"

"Does it?" Dex said thoughtfully. "Maybe yes and maybe no. We'll have to think on that some. And ask some questions." His glass was empty. He looked around for the girl with the tray and, when he saw her, he held three fingers into the air. Made a tilting motion. She got it and nodded back at him. Three fingers of bourbon was ordered. Even I got that. Being able to easily decipher Dex's drink sign language made me wonder if maybe it was time for me to start thinking about a different job.

"But wait," I said, "the notes that were left after every incident."

"Right." Dex could sense right away where I was going. "They were all the same, weren't they?"

"Well, they were the same enough. Crudely lettered. Child-like."

"Right." Dex nodded, smiling at the girl while she dropped off his drink. "Especially since it's always seemed like whoever was leaving the notes was targeting the Woodruffs."

"Targeting Flora," I amended.

"Huh?"

"Well, you said targeting the Woodruffs. But unless there's something we don't know about, it's Flora that's been getting targeted."

"True enough. So? I assume this is going somewhere?"

"Well, I've just been trying to think: who of all the people we've talked to has something to gain by either Flora losing her horse or Flora herself being taken out of the equation?"

Dex took a surprisingly short time to respond. "That girl," he said. "From the stable. The big-boned one in love with the

Stroud kid." I was impressed. He had actually been paying attention.

"Willamina Huffle."

"How the hell did I forget that handle? But, yeah: you'd said you figured I ought to dig deeper on her. Then the horse disappeared and, I dunno, seems like we've been running around like chickens with our heads cut off ever since." He paused thoughtfully for a second. And then, "Remind me not to take another job where everything's so far apart, will ya? It seems like I could've gone to San Francisco and back. Twice. For all the driving around I've been doing on this job." Another thoughtful pause, "Oh wait: *I* didn't take this job, did I? *You* did."

"Yeah, yeah," I said with a dismissive wave, "we've been all over that. And I figure we'll probably be all over it again. But, if I hadn't, think of all the grins you would have missed."

Dex smirked. "Well, anyway," he said, "if we have to have a suspect, the Huffle broad would seem to be a likely one all right. Her and Stroud, I guess."

"How you figure Stroud?" I asked.

"Well, he was there when Flora disappeared."

"So were a lot of people. It doesn't necessarily mean anything. And I don't see what he'd have to gain by taking either Flora or the horse. And what about Tony the Hat?"

"What about him?"

"Well, if the gal there is right and Tony and Flora have been keeping company . . ."

"Is that what she said?"

I thought about it. That was definitely not what had been said. It had, I realized, been what I inferred. But was that just my own desire talking? The one that would like to see Matty clear of encumberment?

"Okay, no. Not in so many words," I admitted.

Dex looked at me closely again for a full half minute. I thought maybe he was going to say something, then thought better of it and went a different way.

"Okay, kiddo, look: here's a plan. Tomorrow's a big day. You're beginning to look a little peaked . . ."

"Have you looked in a mirror recently, Mr. Theroux? Looks like your eyes have packed up for a long voyage."

". . . and it would be best if you were fresh and ready to deal with anything that comes up."

"Like I'll be able to sleep a wink."

"So from here, I'm going to drop you off home. I think the best thing you can do is get some shut-eye."

"What are you going to do?" I asked, because it seemed quite obvious to me that shut-eye wasn't in his plan.

"Well, like I said, I'm going to go out and poke around at the stables. I feel like there's something we've been missing."

"Mustard," I said, but Dex understood even that single word.

"I know, kiddo. I know. Maybe I'll stop by his place on the way out, see if he wants to tag along. Don't feel too bad about him, Kitty. He had some ideas, but I never really saw it anyway."

"You didn't?"

"Naw. You and him hitched? That doesn't even sound like it makes sense. What was he thinking?" He reached over, ruffled my hair. I pulled my head away and smoothed things as well as I could. Dex chuckled. "See what I mean? It'd be like marryin' your kid sister. Some things? Just oughta be left alone."

We'd long since finished our drinks by then, and Dex indicated we should leave. I got up happily, anxious to put the place behind me. There was a coldness there, a hollowness. Despite all the people. There was an emptiness even though the place was packed.

And though she was busy carrying a tray full of drinks as we made our way to the door, I felt our waitress's eyes on us. It made me feel bad. Like I had something she didn't. Even though it wasn't true. Like I'd pulled down a jackpot without even half trying. Her eyes told me she knew that part, as well.

When Dex dropped me off at my house, he repeated what he'd said earlier. "So, you go on in and get some shut-eye. In the morning, see if you can get anything on the Huffle broad. Between us, maybe we'll turn something up. The answer is out there, Kitty. There's something we've been missing."

CHAPTER FORTY

I went from thinking I'd never be able to get to sleep to blinking the morning sun out of my eyes. It was streaming through a crack in the curtains and I knew that, though I could put a pillow over my head and try for another half hour of sleep, I was done for the night.

Dex had told me to follow up with Willamina Huffle. At first I didn't even know where to begin. Our last meeting had not gone well, after all. The more I thought about it, though, the more I realized that I knew just what to do.

Taking the Red Car to Windsor Crest was pretty simple from Bunker Hill. A half hour and a couple of changes. Then I hiked a few blocks over from Wilshire until I got to the Huffles' address on Longwood Avenue. The place was breathtaking. It was smaller than the Woodruff mansion, but not by much. What it lacked in square footage it made up in style and a more traditionally prestigious address. Clearly the Huffles' fortune had deeper roots than did the Woodruffs'. That was something I knew I would have cared about a few years before. Now I simply noted it as another fact in a complicated case.

The house was set deeply on a big lot with a long driveway that curved into a big horseshoe at the front of it. A low evergreen hedge separated the house from the street. All I wanted to do was watch the house for a while; just see what I could see. At first I wondered how to do that. It seemed to me that with a house this grand, loitering in front for very long without attracting attention would be impossible. But it was morning and you could feel the affluent neighborhood getting itself ready for another day of excess. Vendors of every sort were delivering their wares up and down the street, providing enough traffic to cover my inactivity, at least for a while. I figured that a short while was really all I needed. From my vantage point, I could get a pretty good look at the place.

The large house dominated the lot, but didn't cover it completely. There were gardens, an open area that I surmised held a swimming pool, and, at a corner of the yard, something incongruous in this day and age but not impossible: a paddock and, at the corner of the paddock, a small shed, suitable in size to house a single large horse. The Dutch doors that led from this structure directly onto the paddock were closed up tight.

While I chided myself about the impossibility of what I was thinking—the unlikelihood, the coincidence, the pure, blind luck on my part were it to be true—I noticed a horse trailer at the far corner of the property, just peeking out from behind the barn. Not only a place to quietly keep a horse, but also the means by which to transport him. I felt my heart lift and race. I had to see what was inside that little barn.

At a different time, I'd have filed away what I had found and come back after dark or—better still—gotten someone to come back and do the snooping for me. Someone Mustard would likely have found. Or maybe Dex himself. But that was a luxury I couldn't afford. By the time evening rolled around and it was dark, the game would be over. I needed to know what was in the little barn right now.

So I set my course, trying to look as much like a piece of outdoor furniture as was humanly possible while maintaining my position and contemplating my options. While I did that— and before my very eyes—life at the big houses on Longwood Avenue began to shift into gear for the day. Little by little, the traffic slowed as the day's deliveries had been made, masters and mistresses seen off to their days of working or social wallowing, and children trucked safely off to posh private schools.

I had only been out there for a half hour when I realized that things had quieted down a lot since I'd arrived. Then I saw Willamina herself driven away in a beautiful dark red car. On her head was a jaunty dove gray hat, something that was clearly too old for her. Too old, as well, was the smug, self-satisfied smile on her face. I turned away quickly, but if she saw me, my identity didn't register. I wasn't in a context she would have expected.

While I stood and further pondered, I saw gardeners tucking tools into a jalopy and driving away in a storm of backfires. Not long after that, two maids left the big house by a side door. By the time they reached the sidewalk, their arms were linked and their heads were wreathed in laughter. I suspected they were heading for a day of fun or maybe shopping for their mistress. Their errands didn't matter to me, though. What did matter: I could tell from their dress and demeanor that they'd be out of the house for a while. I realized that if I was going to get a peek inside the small barn, this was probably it. With the gardeners gone, Willamina herself and her maids off on errands that looked as though they would consume some time, I was unlikely to get a better chance.

What did I risk? I tried not to think about it as I walked as nonchalantly as possible up the curving driveway. I'd taken off my cloth hat and tucked it into my purse, hoping that, if anyone noticed me, they'd see I was hatless and take me for a domestic. It wouldn't be hard to do: bareheaded and in my simple dress and serviceable but inexpensive handbag, I certainly looked the part.

But I realized that though my heart pounded with the expected fear of potential discovery, it was unlikely I'd get into much trouble if I were found out. I was a passing acquaintance of Willamina's. Perhaps slightly more than that. Were I discovered on the property, it would be more embarrassing than felonious, I knew that. Somehow that didn't still my heart.

All the while as I walked down the driveway, crossed the yard, and moved through the garden, I expected a stern voice: *Hey. You. What are you doing there?*

But none ever came. The house seemed every bit as still as I'd imagined—as I'd wished it to be—and, on my way to the little barn I felt sunshine on my head, but no ill wind at my back.

As I crept closer to the barn, I knew that at least one part of all I'd imagined was correct. From the familiar odor in the air, there was no mistaking it. The sweet, ripe summer grass smell. Based only on that, there could be no doubt that a horse was housed here.

With one hand on the stall door, my courage nearly gave out. *What if I was wrong?* Then I heard it: the unmistakable sound of a horse turning around inside. The heavy stamp of feet, an impatient whisking sound, and the crunch of straw under hooves.

I could barely contain my excitement. After what seemed like days and days of nothing going right, finally—*finally*—something was working out as planned. *Beyond* the way I'd planned, really, because I'd set out for the Huffle mansion this morning not daring to anticipate anything like this.

It took me a minute to determine how the door was secured. A couple of latches on a Dutch door. I was about to swing open the top portion when a voice stopped me.

"And just what the hell do you think you're doing?"

And there it was.

It sounded so much like the voice in my imagination, at first I almost didn't credit it as real, though I turned so quickly towards the sound that I nearly lost my footing.

"Willamina," I said in confusion. She was wearing a housecoat over silk pajamas and clearly hadn't been anywhere yet today. "I saw you . . . that is, I thought I saw you drive away."

"My mother," Willamina said coldly. "People say we look just alike. Now, again, tell me what you're doing here."

"I came . . . that is, I came by to say hello," I began weakly. And I could tell it was weak because Willamina raised one carefully shaped brow. The morning sun enhanced the gold in her hair, caught the translucence of her skin. She looked formidable. Like some substantial Norse goddess.

"Really," she said. "That doesn't explain why you were skulking around back here."

"Hardly skulking," I said in protest. "I just saw this cute little barn . . ."

I didn't finish the thought. It sounded preposterous, even to me. Had I not been sure, her stance would have instructed me. She stood in front of me, her silk-clad legs wide apart and firmly planted, arms crossed in front of her, needing only a breastplate and a fur-trimmed helmet with horns.

"Yes . . ." she prompted.

"And I . . . I thought I would come and . . . see it. Up close," I finished lamely.

"Ah," she said. I don't think there was a second where she believed me. "And now that you've seen, what do you think?"

I was saved answering by the loud, clear neigh of a horse, probably responding to the sound of voices and wanting to know what had become of his breakfast.

My eyes met Willamina's triumphantly. I wheeled before she could stop me and finished the movement that had carried me earlier: I wanted to open that door.

So sure that I would find Fritzy, and so much had I expected to see his dark brown coat that it took me a moment to reconcile the deep red bay in front of me. The brand plainly visible when

236

the highly strung animal did a turn around the stall. Not the brand that Fritzy bore. Similar. But not the same.

"It's my Alfie," Willamina clarified when she saw my confusion. "When Fritzy disappeared, I had him brought home."

As I looked at Willamina, I felt the beginning of understanding coloring my cheeks.

"You had him brought here?"

"Right. I kept a pony here when I was a kid. The city changed the bylaws in the last few years. I can't really legally keep a horse here. But I thought, under the circumstances, it would be all right."

"Under the circumstances . . ."

"Right. With horses disappearing. What safer place for Alfie than here at home? Why? What did you think?" Her features drew back in a smile that was not altogether attractive. It allowed me to the see the tips of sharp, white teeth. I almost felt an aria could not be far behind. "What were you expecting to find?"

I didn't answer. The look on her face told me she knew. It also told me that, though I hadn't found what I'd expected, I should not put Willamina Huffle completely out of my mind.

CHAPTER FORTY-ONE

By now it was getting to be mid-morning and the sun was almost directly overhead. It was suddenly unbearably warm. I felt a trickle of sweat between my breasts. My brain felt like it was going to cook. Whatever light breeze we'd felt just a few minutes before had fallen off, so we stood in a cloud of hot stillness, the scents of oil, fresh cut grass, and horse penetrating the air between us.

"I asked you a question," Willamina insisted as I stood there in front of her. "What did you expect to find?"

I studied my feet for a moment, the dark outline of my shoes marred by the paddock dust. When I spoke, my voice had an unused quality, as though I hadn't called upon it for a long time.

"I think you know," I said quietly, still studying my feet. And then, when she didn't answer right away, my courage flooded back. I raised my head and met her clear, blue eyes. "I think we've not got reason to play games."

She fixed me with a look of distant triumph, but she stayed mum.

"And just because I *didn't* find it," I said with confidence, "that doesn't mean it's not somewhere to be found."

The look she gave me had a lingering, withering quality, as though she couldn't imagine a sorrier excuse for a girl than me. In that second I felt it, too. I felt the reflection from her eyes.

"You think you've got it all figured out," she said finally. "You thought I had Flora's horse," her voice was deadly quiet. I had to strain to hear each word. "It's always been that way. Everyone thinks I want what she has. You're just like all the rest of them. You look and you look and then you see what you want. Well, damn you for it, Katherine Pangborn. Damn you straight to hell."

And without another glance at me, she turned and walked calmly back to the house, her slippers silent beneath her. I heard a side door close with a delicate thud.

I stood there in the garden for a good five minutes, the sun beating down on me, the odors of the day more intense, and I felt something very like shame.

Chapter Forty-Two

The encounter with Willamina made me realize several things, though only one of them was immediately relevant.

Because Los Angeles had grown so rapidly and the distances between places can be vast, we had adapted to the age of the automobile quite quickly. While most people no longer kept horses at home, and while I could barely remember a time when draft animals were a regular feature on city streets, in reality, it hadn't been very long. Lots of people still had the capability of keeping a horse in their own backyard: small barns, old coach houses, and paddocks just like Willamina's probably littered the Southland. Some of those had been converted, of course. I'd seen many that had been converted to garages and even cabanas. But many, many others stood empty. Just waiting the opportunity to harbor a stolen Hanoverian. The realization was not a happy one, however. My spirits sank as the fullness of what this meant washed over me.

As I made my way back to the office, I examined and tossed away plan after ill-conceived plan. Clearly, it would not be possible to check every little barn in the Los Angeles area in the attempt to discover where Fritzy was stashed. But there were some useful things I figured I *could* do. I decided to focus on these.

Mustard's office was out of my way, but I figured that, under the circumstances, I should make the effort, even if I wasn't sure he'd be there. The office was over a garage on Alameda.

You reached it by way of a narrow stairway that clung to the outside of the building like an afterthought.

I clambered up the stairway at the side of garage with some effort—it was a lot of stairs and the tread was open, clearly not intended for easy negotiation in heels. After the bother of getting up there, when I tried the door, I was grateful to find it unlocked. Mustard was standing at the window behind his desk, just watching a moving oil derrick in the field next to the garage. At the sound of the door opening, he spun around. When he came out of the spin he was holding a gun in his hand and it was pointed right at my heart.

"Jesus, kiddo," he said, reholstering the gun when he recognized me. There was a look of fright on his face. I could tell it wasn't because I'd scared him, rather because he knew better than I did how close I'd just come to getting dead. "You really oughta knock."

I didn't say anything. Not at first. I just went to him, held him, feeling the vast strength and the essential goodness in him. He held himself stiffly at first. Distant. After a while, though, I felt his hand, tentatively, at the back of my head, touching my hair.

"I'm sorry," I said after a while. "And I was sorry to hurt your feelings. I love you, Mustard. I've always loved you. Like a brother. Like a . . . like a friend. I don't want to lose that. Not ever. But it's not a big love, Mustard. I don't . . . I don't love you the way I'm supposed to love the man I'll marry."

"The Sweet kid." Mustard held me now and the words he said were muffled against the top of my head. "You love him that way? With a big love?"

I pulled back and away from Mustard. I wanted to look into his eyes and see how much what I said cost him. See if it was a price that I could pay.

"I don't love him at all, Mustard. I don't love him *even* as much as I love you. But what I feel for him . . . well, it's different, I guess. Can you understand?"

"Sure, Kitty. Sure I do." He sat down now, his chair creaking heavily under his weight. "I guess I knew it all along. I just thought—you know—lotsa people get married for that—for the big love—and after a while that's just gone and their lives are hell. I tried to tell you all this in the car yesterday. Maybe I didn't say it right."

"Naw, you said it right. It's just . . . well, I don't know, Mustard, maybe it's just my age? But I want that; I want the big love. And maybe it's just from reading books and magazines; they've taught me to expect it. I don't know. But I have to . . . I have to try, at least. I'm sorry. And I'm pretty sure Matty isn't it, but I want . . . I want to be able to find out. Get hurt. Love and lose, you know? You've done all that, but I haven't. I didn't realize that before all of this, but I haven't done that at all."

Strangely enough, as I said this, Mustard looked more hopeful, like what I'd said made sense. I saw it on his face and I pressed my advantage.

"Still friends?" I said.

He stood up and hugged me again, a brotherly hug. It didn't entirely fool me, but the words he said were the right ones.

"Absolutely, kiddo. We'll always be friends. But if you change your mind . . ."

"Ha! By then, you might have changed yours."

He grinned at that, a warm grin. And I knew then that everything between us was still a little shaky, but it was going to be all right.

CHAPTER FORTY-THREE

"Hold on: the girl said Flora had been to the club under the Antler with *Tony the Hat?*" Mustard sounded incredulous.

We were streaming along in the same dark car he'd driven me out to the Valley in the day before. I was pleased that the detour out of my way had come with the best possible outcome: Mustard and I were friends again. Plus I didn't have to take the streetcar back to the office. Sometimes things just work out swell.

"That's what she said all right."

"Did she say they were . . . you know . . . romantic?"

"She didn't go that far. But that was what I took it to mean. Something in the way she said it, I guess. But Dex thought maybe that wasn't it."

"Hmmmm." Whatever thoughts Mustard was having, he was keeping them to himself.

When we got back to the office, I was disappointed to see Dex wasn't there, but I wasn't surprised.

"He said he was going to go back out to the Academy and have a look around. Last chance before the ransom drop-off, I guess."

"What do you want to do?" Mustard asked, plopping himself in the single waiting room chair while I hung up my coat and took my usual seat behind my desk. I saw him hook his index finger under his collar and run it towards his lapel. It was a nervous gesture. I'd seen him do it before, but I wondered why he was doing it now.

"Me?"

"Yeah. I figured, you know, this one has been pretty much your case. I thought maybe there was some grand plan you had in motion."

"Aw, c'mon Mustard. Don't tease. You know I ain't got any grand plan. Tell the truth, at the moment, I don't even have the foggiest."

As I said this, I realized I was distressingly close to tears. It looked to me like Mustard saw this—saw it and took pity on me—because he rushed in with a plan of his own.

"Aw, c'mon, little one: cheer up. We've still got a thing or two up our sleeves."

I looked at my bare arm and smiled despite myself.

"We do?" I said, embarrassed at the shaky hopefulness even I could detect in my voice.

"Sure. Tony the Hat, for one."

I looked at him wide-eyed, remembering. Dex had said Mustard had an in there.

"Yeah? And you stayed on the boat last night after me and Dex left. Did you turn anything up?"

"Naw. I'd have told you already if I had. I just laid low for a while. Played a bit of blackjack, a bit of baccarat. I thought, you know, if I kept my head low and quiet, maybe I'd see something."

"But nothing, huh?"

"I didn't see anything of our girl or any more of Tony. And there was no sign of the young guys you said were there, too, for that matter."

"So what do think we should do now? You mentioned Tony the Hat. Do you think we should try to see him again?"

"Not 'we' Kitty Cat. Me. You sit tight here and I'll take a taxi out to the boat and have a snoop around. If he's there, I'll ask him about your friend."

"Just like that? Ask him?"

"Why not?" Mustard said. As usual, the source of confident calm. "How you going to get an answer if you don't ask?"

"What about me?"

"You?"

"Yeah," I said. "You said I can't come with. What am I supposed to do?"

"Same as always, I guess. Answer the phones. Type. Make coffee when Dex comes back. I'd bring you along, but I think this is one I'd best do on my own."

I had half a mind to stop him and insist I go along—considering the weakened state of his heart, I figured I could have bullied him into it—but, in the end, I supposed he was right. Going out on a water taxi to talk to Tony the Hat in broad daylight was probably something he'd be more successful at without me tagging along, potentially gumming up the works. On the other hand, I figured there were probably more useful things for me to be doing than sitting around the office waiting for someone to come along so I could make them coffee.

I sat at my desk and drew myself a picture because it was starting to feel like the answer was right under my nose amid all the pieces dancing there.

I thought, again, about Willamina. Despite all I'd learned, it was still possible she felt she would have much to gain by Flora's removal. And what about James? Did he, perhaps in some convoluted way, want to discredit his rival, Matty? It was farfetched, but it seemed to me we'd come to a time when every possibility had to be considered.

Of all the players in this thing, the one person who seemed to me to be completely above suspicion was Cedric Woodruff, Flora's father. There was no motive connecting Cedric to any of the odd circumstances that had been flying around Flora. And neither were there any loose threads that had drawn my attention. At the same time, almost from the very beginning, I had been possessed of the idea that I knew more than I thought I did about Cedric and his business dealings. As I thought hard about that now, the outline of an idea crept into my mind. Not even an idea, really. More like the dim shadow of one. Suddenly I knew just where to go. I checked the clock: it was early afternoon. I had plenty of time to get to my appointment with a kidnapper. First, though, I needed to go home, just for a little while.

Then after that, the Baldwin Hills.

CHAPTER FORTY-FOUR

I found Marjorie on the stairs, a tub of beeswax in one hand, a soft cloth in the other. The stairs were ancient redwood. My father had them milled for the house when it was built. The beauty and purity of the wood had been a point of pride for him and I'd heard the story often. The millwright. The giant trees. And, finally, the Swiss craftsman he'd employed to design and then build the monster staircase.

There was a price to pay for such a beautiful staircase. Well, several. But at the most basic level, it was apparent that woodwork like that needs to be respected, even loved; or so Marjorie had instructed me since I was old enough to understand what the words meant. And now, lacking a staff of housemaids to do her bidding and with the beautiful staircase—her pride—in her own possession, the titanic job of maintaining it had fallen to her. And she did it with love, but she did it endlessly. If she wasn't in the kitchen, it was usually a safe bet that she was somewhere with beeswax near at hand, polishing, polishing, polishing.

"Well, hello my dear," she greeted me with affection as I came up the stairs to find her. She straightened up painfully, as though she'd been at her labors for too long. "Isn't this a nice surprise. You're generally buried in that office of yours at this time of the day. Whatever brings you home now?"

"Well, it seemed a good idea to rescue this banister," I said with a smile, running a hand over the gleaming polished wood.

"You polish it so much, I fear you'll rub the finish off!"

"Pishaw!" Marjorie snorted. It always made me smile when I could get her to make that sound.

"Well, you're right: I *am* teasing. Truly? I came home to talk to you. I wanted to ask you some questions. About . . . before. When my father was alive. And I know you might not have the answers, but I thought I'd give it a try, all right?"

"Well certainly, Miss Katherine," she said, going back to her polishing, but making it clear I had her attention. As she'd pointed out to me often enough in the past, this staircase was not about to polish itself, but it didn't require her full concentration. "If I can help any way at all, you know I will."

"I do, Marjorie. I do know that. The thing is, what I'm wondering about might be something you might not know or recall . . . well, I'll just ask. Did you remember Father ever speaking about someone named Cedric Woodruff?"

"The name *is* familiar," Marjorie said thoughtfully and I felt my hopes rise until she said, "Isn't he the one whose daughter's horse was kidnapped recently? I think I read about him in the papers."

"Yes," I said, "that's right. But do you remember Father ever mentioning him?"

"Why, no. But me not remembering doesn't really mean anything at all, Miss Katherine. I'm sure there were a great many people who went through the house who I never met or whose name I didn't know. You understand," she said without embarrassment, "it wasn't as though I'd sit down with him and take a sherry after dinner."

I kind of smiled at that. The very thought!

"No, I suppose not," I said.

"Or even if I did know it at the time, so much time has passed, it's possible I might have known a thing at some point and just forgotten it by now."

"I hadn't thought of it that way. Well, let me ask you something else. Did you ever hear my father mention a project he was either working on or bidding on in the Baldwin Hills?"

Marjorie mulled the question, but I could see from her expression that I'd not hit any marks. "You know, of course, it's possible. He talked of a great many things, over dinners, at small meetings at the house sometimes. But mostly, you yourself know he avoided bringing business home. If he was discussing a project, why, he'd have done most if not all of that sort of thing at the office."

"Of course he would. I'm sorry, Marjorie. I don't know what I was thinking." Though I tried to hide it, I couldn't help my disappointment; it must have been plain on my face. I'd been clutching at straws coming to Marjorie with this, I could see that now. Of course Father had always done business at his office. All of the people who might have helped me from that time were long gone, spread to the four winds by economic and personal disaster, or so I thought. I felt like weeping all over again.

"No, no; there's no need for apologies, dear. In fact, I know someone who might be able to help."

"You do?" I said, trying to quell the hope that bubbled to the surface at her words, though I couldn't think of who I might have overlooked.

"Of course. And you do as well. Something you've forgotten, I think. Marcus was your father's personal driver for a number of years. He sometimes had reason to know even things he wasn't meant to, if you understand."

Marcus. Of course. As his driver, Marcus had been closer to my father in many ways than almost anyone who still breathed. I thanked Marjorie and headed outside. I didn't even have to ask her where I'd find him.

CHAPTER FORTY-FIVE

Marcus had been like an uncle to me for so long, I'd forgotten to think of him in any other way. Even while he was my father's personal driver, he was also Marjorie's husband and thus an integral part of our household staff.

As a young girl raised without a mother as the focus of a large house, I'd always considered Marjorie as part of my family. I was closer to her than I was to my father, after all. And it just seemed as though Marcus was always about: fixing Father's various cars, doing Marjoric's bidding, sometimes picking me up from the train station when I came home from school for vacations. Father seldom had the time for such things and so there would be Marcus, in uniform, waiting for me on the platform, with a smile on his face and his cap in his hand.

"It's very good to see you looking so well, Miss Katherine," he'd say in his formal yet friendly way. "I can see school has agreed with you once more. You've become quite the young lady. Marjorie will be very glad to have you home over Christmas." And so on. Reconnecting me to my old world in a way that probably nothing else could have done.

It was small wonder, then, that I hadn't thought of Marcus in relation to the business he had done with my father. In my own childish memories and in the self-involved recollections of youth, Marcus's duties had seldom extended beyond me.

I found him in the garage, where there were no longer cars to tinker with. Father's creditors had come and collected them before we'd even managed to plant him in the ground.

The loss of the Packard had been especially painful for Marcus. A black Brougham roof and a body the color of a robin's breast, Marcus had polished the car so well and so often, he'd said the paint was wearing thin in spots. When the men from the creditors' offices had driven the car away, Marcus's face had looked as close to sorrow as I'd ever seen it. I thought his heart would break.

Even though the garage didn't presently house a car, it was still the place Marcus felt most comfortable in the world, among the tools of his trade and all his most precious possessions. He'd gone from chauffeur to owner of a grand, if decaying, home, and, truly, nothing else about him had changed.

"Oh, hullo, Miss Katherine," he said when I put my head in. "I don't see you much out here these days."

Nor had he for a long while. But when I was a child, any time Marjorie wanted to find me, she'd need look no further than Marcus's realm, for the infinite number of fascinating things to be found there and for the calm comfort of being directly in Marcus's sphere. And now, so many years later, those memories came back to me instantly. The smell of metal and axle grease and cars long ago gone off to mechanical nirvana.

"Well, you know, Marcus. My life is different now. But I always think of you out here—pottering—and it makes me remember the pleasanter part of my childhood."

"Ah, well. You mean the schools he was always sending you to. We thought it wasn't a good idea, Marjorie and me."

"You didn't?"

"No, miss. We'da liked you closer, truth to tell. Thought it would be better for you, too." His face darkened a bit. "It wasn't something we could talk about, he and I."

He meant my father, of course. He didn't need to tell me. Father would no more have had that conversation with a servant than he would have with a sparrow. The thought would not have crossed his mind.

"You spent . . . you spent a lot of time with him, driving him about," I began tentatively.

"I suppose I did, it's true. Though I never thought of it that way."

"A name has come up, in a case I'm working on," I began. "Well, actually, a name and a place. I know both will be familiar to you, but I wonder if you'll also know of any way my father might have been connected with them."

Marcus smiled at me then. A good, full smile. "Well, we won't know if you don't ask, will we?"

"Fair enough," I said. "All right. First, the place. It was suggested to me recently that my father had dealings on a development in the Baldwin Hills."

I had hoped that Marcus would have an answer. Had I expected a positive one? In a way, I really had not. So his words when they came—without hesitation—surprised me.

"Why yes, Miss Katherine," he said. "In the months before his death it seemed to me that I was driving him out there more than necessary."

At first I just looked at Marcus. And I blinked. I blinked quite a lot. It took me a moment to gather my thoughts and decide what to do with an answer in the positive. It was what I'd wanted, but not what I'd expected.

"Was he meeting with anyone in particular?"

"Oh yes, there was always a group of them out there. They'd be walking about, making their plans, you understand? Or so I imagined. I'd mostly sit in the Packard, read the paper. Sometimes sit under a tree for a bit, have a smoke."

"So you didn't hear . . ."

"What they were talking about? No. Not ever. Not when they were outside. But the Packard, well, you know yourself. It was a big car. Sometimes he'd offer us up to give a ride there. Or back. And then I'd hear things." He hesitated before adding, "Sometimes I'd hear a lot."

"What . . ." I prompted, not daring to raise my voice above a loud whisper, "what would you hear? A lot?"

"Well, it was all planning then, wasn't it? Nothing much was actually going on."

"For the Olympic Village?" I breathed, remembering what Dex had told me: Cedric Woodruff's company was working on building housing for the athletes in the Baldwin Hills. The comment was, in fact, part of what had brought me to Marcus in the first place.

"That's right. And other things besides. Or perhaps *beyond* is a better way of putting it. Some of it was quite idealistic, you understand: a brotherhood of man. All nations forging bonds of peace together through sport."

"This would have been, what? The summer of 1929?"

"That's right," he said, nodding. "And into the fall." He stopped, his face clouding. "The beginning of the fall. Of course."

My father had died on October 29th, 1929. The day of the Crash. It was on both our minds. I could see it. Marcus didn't mention it. Nor did I. I thought, instead, of my father, cheerful and optimistic. Idealistic, even. Months and even days before he took his own life. I forced my mind back to Marcus's words.

"You seem to remember it all quite clearly," I commented. "The conversations, I mean."

"It was the kind of thing what stays in your mind, Miss. The kind of thing what made you feel good, you know? While it seemed as though the world was getting worse, they were dreaming bigger dreams." He paused a moment, then amended, "Better dreams."

I took this in. Reconciled what I knew about my father and

what little I knew about Woodruff with what Marcus was saying. My father as idealistic, dreaming. His death by his own hand not yet even a shadow on his horizon, yet so very close. It made me want to cry.

"So the talk was of the Olympic Village. Was it a real estate deal?"

"Of a sort, though not exactly. You know, Lucky Baldwin owned the land."

"But he was dead. Long dead."

"Well, his estate then. Yes. I seem to remember something about that. And the estate was donating the land for Olympic use."

"If not real estate, what then?"

"Well, the building, Miss."

"The building?"

"Yes. What would the theatre look like? And the track? And the houses. There was a lot of talk about the cottages where the athletes would stay."

"What sort of talk?" I felt as though I had a glimmer of something: some tickle of understanding, but I couldn't yet quite see it.

"Well the idealistic ones—and I will say, your father was among those—wanted the athletes' housing to reflect the countries from which they hailed. You understand?"

"Tell me."

"Well, Alpen cottages for the Swiss and the Germans and Austrians. Maori bungalows for the Australians. Log cabins for the Canadians. Little villas for the Italians. Tudor cottages for the English . . ."

"Right," I said. "I get the idea."

"But the others didn't want that. They thought it would all be dreadfully expensive."

"And what did they want?"

"They wanted it cheap."

"Who won?"

"Why, I don't know, Miss. At the time, they were years away even from having to build. And I . . . well, I've not had cause to know, really. Since . . ."

"Yes," I said, realizing. "I guess you haven't. Marcus, did my father ever leave these meetings upset?"

"Your father, Miss? Think about it. You know the answer to that."

And he was right. I did. My father had been many things, but he'd always been even. In all the time I'd known him—in the not enough time I'd known him—I'd never seen him upset. His suicide had proven even that a lie. Dispassionate men don't care enough to take their own lives. But on the surface, those he loathed and those he loved: neither ever saw more than a ripple.

Now Marcus, he had never played at being dispassionate. Even now I could see what this conversation was costing him. There was a quaver in his voice and his eyes seemed to shimmer with a grief I knew was deep and more raw than I would have thought, given the time that had passed and his relationship to the dead man under discussion. He looked old to me, I decided. For the first time ever, I noticed the gray that had crept to his temples and the wince he gave when he stood and tried to straighten his back.

"I'm sorry, dear Marcus. Sorry to dredge this all up," I said, giving him a daughterly hug. The move surprised him; I could see that in his eyes. But it did not cause him pain.

CHAPTER FORTY-SIX

"So what does any of this have to do with the price of tea in China?" Dex wanted to know.

"Well," I pondered the question honestly, the Bakelite phone warming in my hand. I was at my desk and Dex was who-knows-where, calling in to see what was going on in the office and what kind of progress was being made. "I'm not sure, really. But it means something, don't you think? It might mean something to the big picture."

"Kitty, we don't have time for the big picture. Big pictures are for the movies. We're down to the wire, anyway, and this ain't no picture show. In a few hours you're going to need to start heading out here."

"Or maybe Mustard will pick me up if he finishes what he set out to do in time," I said hopefully.

"Maybe so."

"But don't you see, Dex? My father and Woodruff had some kind of dealings with each other. And Woodruff is living high on the hog. And my father . . . my father."

I couldn't finish the sentence, but I knew I didn't have to. Dex knew the score and his voice was gentle when he replied.

"Life ain't always fair, Kitty. I know you know that. Better than most. Just because things didn't turn out even doesn't mean Woodruff offed your pop."

"That's not what I'm saying," I insisted.

"Isn't it?" Dex said.

I considered before I spoke. Then, "Maybe a bit. But it's more than that, too. Or other stuff as well. See, why didn't I know any of this stuff before, Dex? This Baldwin Hills stuff?"

"Beats me," Dex replied to the rhetorical question.

"And what's it all mean?"

"That beats me, too."

"I want to go out there, Dex."

"Out where? For what?"

"The Baldwin Hills. I think the answer is there, Dex. My gut tells me so."

"Your gut's wrong, Kitty. You ain't even been at it long enough to have developed a gut for this racket. Anyway, we ain't got time for this, not today. Remember? How the hell you gonna get out there and then out here in time for the business we got tonight?"

I was trying to think fast and think on my feet when the answer walked right in the door.

Chapter Forty-Seven

Mustard was looking a little green around the gills.

"Dex, I gotta go," I said when I saw him. "Mustard is here. He don't look so good."

"Is he shot?"

"No. He ain't shot. He just looks a little sick," I said.

"Well give him a seltzer and get him to drive you around," Dex said, not one to miss a trick. "This way you can have your Baldwin Hills and eat them, too."

"That's what I was figuring," I said as I hung up. Then to Mustard, "What's with you?"

"That's a bad business, Kitty Cat," he said, his voice weaker than normal and for once I didn't correct the name.

"How's that?" I asked, pushing him into one of the office chairs, then hastening to get him a coffee.

"Tony and his boys. Out on the *Tango*. If he's got Miss Woodruff, he ain't sayin'. And he's one cool customer."

"What aren't you saying?" I asked. I'd added cream and sugar to his coffee and was stirring. I looked him over thoughtfully, then added another sugar and gave it a few more stirs before carrying it over to him.

"You know, Kitty, I'm into some stuff you just can't imagine," he said, ignoring my question while he took the coffee.

"That's kinda what I always thought," I said. He rewarded me with a faint smile.

"But these guys? They're in a place beyond."

"How so?"

"Just this 'n' that, Kitty. Like, they've got a place in the desert. In Nevada? They've got plans, Kitty. They're gonna make a Gomorrah out there. That's what they plan."

"Or a Sodom?" I quipped.

"Something like that. But, Tony? He's so young and he's already done so much and the guys that work for him look at him like he's a god. But you know, when you look at him, at the roots of the things he's running? They go deep."

"I don't understand," I said, sipping at my coffee and enjoying the sweet, burnt flavor.

Mustard sighed deeply, took a sip of his own coffee, then rubbed absently at the reddish stubble on his chin. I got the idea he was considering his words.

"You get the feeling, when you spend any time at all with Tony Cornero, that he's part of something old and strong." I must have looked puzzled, because Mustard continued as though I'd queried him. "Well, most of the time out here in Los Angeles, it's a bit of a Wild West show. The crooks and the cops make a lot of noise about each other, but the sides they're on aren't so very far apart." I nodded understanding. I knew what Mustard was getting at.

"Now Cornero," Mustard went on, "what he's part of is something else—and I don't know that the cops know what to do with him, either."

"I still don't understand."

"Well, I guess you won't, Kitty. All that Cosa Nostra stuff. It can seem a bit spooky, even to me."

"Cosa Nostra?"

"It's an old organization. Family-based, near as I can tell. I have heard stories that, to play in their sandbox, you gotta turn someone into Swiss."

"Huh?" I said.

Mustard mimed shooting a gun with his fingers.

"Oh, I don't know, Mustard. That sounds far-fetched to me."

Mustard shrugged. "I'm just telling you what I've heard. And it's unnerving, being around guys like that, I kid you not. We here, in L.A., we have our own ways. But they're something else again."

"They're new then, this Cosa Nostra?"

"Naw," Mustard said, "they've had their hooks in things in L.A. as long as the city has been here. But you keep clear of 'em when you can. You don't get in their way."

"Is that what you did today, Mustard? You got in their way?"

"Naw," he said. "I wouldn't be walkin' if that were the case. Naw. I asked about Flora and, the way they all answered, they don't have Flora, but they know more than what they're sayin'."

"How you figure?"

"Well, it's pretty clear they knew who I was talkin' about. But the fact that she was missing? That they didn't know. And unless I miss my guess, they didn't much like not knowing, either."

I thought about that. I thought about it because something was bothering me, even then. I was just having a hard time figuring out what it was.

Chapter Forty-Eight

It wasn't difficult to talk Mustard into driving me out to the Baldwin Hills. It sounded like Dex was doing everything that could be done out at Griffith Park and both Mustard and I were anxious and antsy. If nothing else, the drive would do something to lure our minds away from everything we couldn't be doing right now.

We followed La Cienega south. For a while we followed a very good road. Once we left the city it was little more than a dirt track that got steadily worse. As we headed into the Hills proper, we passed a road crew. The fact that the eyes of the world would be trained on the Olympic Village not too many months in the future had something to do with all of the roadwork we saw in progress.

I'd never been in the Baldwin Hills before. I'd never had reason to go. Who would? It was Lucky Baldwin's back forty, in a way. Just a small part of the huge spread that had once been the Rancho La Cienega, the Spanish land grant that Baldwin had acquired at the early part of the century. The part that was being used for the Olympic Village was nowhere near that big. Maybe only 300 acres, though when I remarked on this to Mustard he pointed out that a piece of land that big was "still a fair chunk."

It *was* a fair chunk. A beautiful one, at that. The Hills commanded an amazing view. I looked back over my shoulder as Mustard drove and was astonished to see the entire Los Angeles basin, from far beyond the downtown core to the sea.

We knew we'd reached our destination when we came upon a well-marked gateway in an imposing-looking fence.

"Are they serious?" Mustard said, pulling up the car. "I thought it was meant to be a village, not a jail."

"Maybe the fence will only be here during construction?" I said doubtfully, noting the crews of workers beyond the open gate laboring at every aspect of building. It didn't seem likely, but we couldn't imagine what other explanation there might be.

The entire village stood within the confines of the fence, ringed by an immense athletic track. From outside the fence, you seemed to see a town within a racetrack within a fort. The Games themselves were still months away—midway into the following year—and if you didn't know that, you'd have been able to tell from how much work there still was to do. Mustard and I saw that nothing had been completed yet. One large and low-slung building at the core of all that activity looked near enough to completion to already be in use. From the way it was positioned and apparently laid out, I was guessing the pink adobe structure was some sort of administration office. Aside from that one building, though, everything was in varying degrees of chaos. Except that fence. That looked pretty much ready to go. It was open, though, so Mustard pointed the car at the gate and we drove on through, parking it a little ways from the hustle and mess of construction. Like Dex, Mustard didn't like to have to walk too far. The way they both carried on about walking, it made me wonder if men's shoes were much more uncomfortable than women's.

Closest to us, a small crew was busy putting a low fence around the track we stood within. The guy nearest us looked like he was either the boss of this crew or employed by the government; he was actually leaning on a shovel and dragging hard on a smoke while the other men toiled, sinking fence posts and applying rails. Mustard addressed this man.

"Looks like you got work enough to keep you busy for a while," Mustard said with a smile. "That's good stuff in these times."

The man dropped his smoke in the dirt and looked first Mustard and then me over appraisingly. I guessed he didn't see anything to alarm him because after a while he answered.

"Yup. It's true," he said, grinding the butt under one uneven heel. "Not bad work, either, as far as work goes. They pay's up regular enough and gives us a half hour for our dinner. It's all fair enough."

"You almost through?"

"Hell, no. We figures we're gonna be workin' here right until the opening of the Games, between this and that. Takes a lot of man-hours to build a whole town, you know."

"And that's what it's gonna be?" Mustard asked.

"Pretty much, yup," the man replied. He stopped to correct the way one guy was handling the fence post hole digger, then pulled out another smoke while he repositioned himself near us. He took his time lighting his smoke and managed a big pull on this new butt. When he started talking again he didn't miss a beat; there might have been no pause at all. "By the time we're finished there'll be lawns 'n' flowers 'n' such. It'll be real pretty," he said with the air of someone who didn't give too many hoots about pretty when it wasn't wearing a skirt. What he cared about: steady work doing all that prettying for a long time to come.

"Who's the boss here?"

I couldn't be sure, but I thought the man looked crafty when he answered. "Depends on what you're lookin' for, I reckon. Some days, there's more chiefs 'round here than there is injuns."

I thought about the man leaning on his shovel, smoking his

smoke, and figured I could see what he meant.

" 'Zat a fact?" Mustard said, seemingly unconcerned. "Too many cooks, huh?"

The man snickered and blew out another mouthful of smoke. "You got *that* right."

"Is there one who's the boss of *everyone?*" Mustard pressed.

"Well, there's a group of 'em, really. But, on site here, from day to day, that would be Mr. Davis."

"Yeah?" Mustard prompted.

"Mr. H.O. Davis, that's right. Most of the time you can find him in the administration building over yonder," he said, pointing. He saw Mustard look over and said, "But he ain't there now."

"No?" said Mustard.

"No. When he's here, there's a big blue Ford sittin' out front. 'Bout a mile long."

"Well, thanks for your time," Mustard said. "It's much appreciated."

The man looked us over carefully before he spoke again. It wasn't a complicated look. I got the feeling he liked talking to us better than he liked working, even if that work sometimes consisted of nothing more onerous than leaning on a shovel.

"Like I said, Mr. Davis ain't here now," he said as though Mustard hadn't spoken. "An' he's the boss of the site here. But *his* boss? Now that's Mr. Woodruff. And *he's* got a little place down there," he pointed towards the southwest. I followed the motion. "We built him a cabin and a barn and a paddock earlier this year."

In the direction he had pointed, a parched trail headed up and off and then down. Wide enough for a car, but not two passing each other. "He keeps a hoss up there sometimes, Mr. Woodruff does. He likes to ride round the site sometimes. See the work up close more or less."

"To ride," I repeated breathlessly.

"That's right, ma'am. Not lately, though. Ain't seen Mr. Woodruff on a horse for a few months and he hasn't been coming 'round to see the construction so much, neither. Not since we started gettin' real close. Not so much reason for him to come, I guess."

"But the place is still there?" Mustard asked.

"Oh, yeah: I'd imagine," the man said, "lest it got removed by the han-da-god, 'cause I ain't had nuthin' to do with it."

CHAPTER FORTY-NINE

In the end, it was just as simple as that.

When the man finished speaking, Mustard and I just looked at each other. Mustard thanked him. And then, without another word, we turned around and headed back to the car.

"So what do we do?" Mustard said when he was behind the wheel. I perched next to him on the bench seat, nervously nibbling at my cuticle.

"I don't . . . I don't really know," I admitted. "I wish Dex was here."

"Can you call him?" Mustard asked.

"I guess I can try."

We went over to the administration building to see if they had a phone we could use. Inside, it was spartan made to look sumptuous. It was not built to be a permanent building. You could tell that by looking closely at the edges of things.

A clerk sat a desk in the foyer. Terracotta tiles on the floor. A palm fan overhead.

"May I use your telephone?" I asked him shyly.

"Excuse me?" he said with an arch of his eyebrow, as though he'd never heard anything so preposterous in his life. Or, at least, not since lunch.

"The telephone," I indicated the black-dialed creature of which I spoke. "Might I use it? Just for a moment. It's not a toll call."

The second eyebrow seemed to arch up to meet its mate.

"I hardly think so," the man said. The word "hardly" came out sounding like a purr.

"We're here at the invitation of Mr. Woodruff," Mustard said suddenly, taking me by surprise. "Miss Pangborn here is a great friend of Miss Woodruff's."

The receptionist's expression shifted so rapidly, what had come before might have been imagination, a dream.

"You're a friend of Miss Flora's?" the man said. "Why didn't you say so?"

"I thought I just did," Mustard said under his breath. I elbowed him in the side.

The clerk pulled the phone over on its long cord and plunked it down it front of us. Mustard and I exchanged a look—*so now what?* we seemed to say to each other.

"Where did you say he was?"

"At the stables," I said, picking up the phone and dialing the number I had in my purse for the office at the Academy. And hoping. Though I knew in my heart that it was not a hope worth having.

"I'm wondering if you've seen Mr. Dexter Theroux around there today?" I asked the bright-voiced young woman who answered the phone.

"Who?" she said.

"Dexter Theroux." I looked around for the clerk. He was at the other side of the office, apparently filing papers. Whatever he was doing, I figured he was far enough away, he might hear the sound of my voice, but he wouldn't catch the words. I pitched my voice lower and continued. "He's the PI working with the Woodruffs."

"I haven't seen the Woodruffs today. Not any of them," she said helpfully.

"Yes, I know . . ." I began. Then caught myself. "Thank you. But I'm looking for the man I was mentioning . . ."

"Mr. Macwith Zero you said, right?"

"No. *Dexter.* Dexter Theroux."

"Ohhhh," she trilled, understanding filling her voice.

"Then you've seen him?"

"No," she replied. "But I know who you mean."

I gave up then, though not before I left a message for Dex that I doubted would have meaning even in the unlikely event that it got to him. I hung up the phone dispiritedly.

"No luck, huh," Mustard said.

"Not at all. I don't know what to try next."

"You try the office?"

"My office?" I asked. "Why would I call there?"

"I take it that's a no?" Mustard said. "Go ahead and try. What do you got to lose? Not even a nickel."

Mustard was right, so I tried the number. Dex answered on the first ring, like he'd been waiting for my call.

"What are you doing there?" I said, so surprised the sense was momentarily knocked out of my head.

"It's my office, Kitty. Where the hell else should I be?"

"Burbank," I said, astonished at the question. "At the riding academy. That's where you said you'd be. That's the only place it makes sense for you to be."

"If that's so, why did you call here?"

The absolute sense of his question shut me right up.

"Cat got your tongue, huh?" he said sounding smug. "I'm glad you called, though. I was just writing you a note."

"Why?"

"I found some things out today, Kitty. And it changes things considerably."

"I think . . . I think maybe I did, too."

"Well, that's just swell, Kitty. But, look: I don't have time to tell you details right now. I've got to get out to West Adams as quickly as possible. I just wanted to get the information to you—that's why I was leaving the note. I wanted to catch you before you headed out to the stables."

"West Adams? What for? What's in West Adams?"

"Flora's house."

"I know that, Dex. I mean, what are you doing there?"

"I think I found the horse."

CHAPTER FIFTY

"But Dex, *I* think I found the horse. Me and Mustard," I added. I checked on the clerk again. He still looked involved in whatever he was doing at the other end of the room.

"Where?"

"Baldwin Hills. Near the Olympic Village."

"You seen him?"

"The horse? No," I admitted. "I was just going to head down there with Mustard. Wanted to see if I could get you first, let you know what I was up to. You seen yours?"

"No," he paused for a second. A big, heavy pause. "We got a bit to catch up on," he said finally. I could hear the grin in his voice.

"I guess we do. But what do we do now?"

"Well, how's this: I'm heading to the Woodruffs' place. If my lead doesn't pan out, I'll head back here. And if yours doesn't . . ."

"We'll head to the office, too. Good idea, because the office will be pretty central and then, if one of us needs a hand, we know how to reach each other. Good luck, Dex," I said, not really feeling as though luck was going to figure in this late in the game.

Mustard pointed the car down the track toward the head fence post that the pounder had indicated. The car bounced through the hills with enthusiasm if not much skill. It was a roadster and the track we were following wasn't much to the big car's taste. We would have been better in a truck or even riding shank's mare, but I knew Mustard wouldn't have even talked about walking so I kept it buttoned and concentrated on holding onto my lunch.

After a while, we crested a small hill and the buildings came into sight in a little valley below us, just as the man had described. A rough little cottage—one really couldn't call it much more than a hut—a lean-to and a hastily constructed paddock. And oddly juxtaposed against this backdrop of near squalor, a magnificent, dark chestnut horse. A million-dollar horse, perhaps, hidden in a place no one would ever find him, but for a couple of spare comments and a bit of dumb luck.

Mustard stopped the car, right there in the middle of the track. There was no traffic and there appeared to be no one around, but we needed to gather our thoughts.

"It *is* him?" Mustard asked, not really needing me to answer. It was pretty plain that this was no common Cayuse.

I nodded. "I think so. I mean . . . look at him."

And we both did just that, watching with pleasure as Fritzy moved around the enclosure, the muscles rippling under the surface of his summer-slick coat as he turned first this way, then that, enjoying the sun, it appeared, and the relative freedom of the paddock.

"So what do we do?" I asked finally, because it was clear we couldn't just go on sitting there.

"Let's get a closer look." Mustard started the car again and we bounced the rest of the way down towards the shack.

"What if someone's there?" I asked as the house got closer.

"I guess we'll go on and say hello," and without taking his eyes off the track he was following, he pulled back his jacket and showed me the butt of the gun he wore holstered over his shoulder. I wasn't sure if the presence of the gun made me feel better. Or worse.

Mustard parked the car right out front of the hut, nice as you please. If I hadn't been sure about Fritzy's identity, I was then because, when he saw us he gave a clear, loud neigh, a greeting I figured I recognized from back at the barn.

I wanted to run to him for a closer look and a hello, but Mustard held me back.

"Let me just have a poke around first," he said. "You stay here."

I didn't argue, but as soon as he disappeared inside, I followed behind him, quiet as you please.

I had to blink a couple of times in the too-dim light before my eyes adjusted. Inside, the hut looked much as one would have expected when you saw the outside. A hot plate and an icebox made up the kitchen, a battered table and chairs stood nearby. A bed—unmade—sat in one corner. The hut was one big open space, with a bathroom in one corner; you could take in the whole place in a single glance.

"I thought I told you to stay put," Mustard said.

"Ask Dex how well I listen," I said pertly.

"Looks like I don't have to."

Though there was a whole lot of nothing going on here now, we could see signs of recent habitation. A bottle of champagne and a couple of glasses stood on the table. The bottle was half empty or half full, depending on what you wanted to see. A chair stood next to the bed and, over its back, a dark blue dress. Beaded.

"She was here," I breathed.

"Looks like."

"And she wasn't alone."

"She stole her own hoss?"

I looked at Mustard and shook my head helplessly. "I just . . . I have no idea."

We went back outside and poked around. Behind the house

there was a pickup truck and a horse trailer. Mustard looked at it thoughtfully.

"Do you figure we could load him up?"

"Load who up *where*?" I asked, even though I pretty much knew the answer.

"The hoss. You think we could talk him into going up there?" he said, pointing to the business end of the trailer.

"I don't think there'd be much talking involved," I said truthfully.

"Fair enough. But you get what I'm saying?"

"I do. I don't want to, but I do. The thing is, though: if she *was* here . . ."

"And it looks like she was," Mustard pointed out.

". . . then who are we to take her horse? Does it . . . does it make us horse thieves?"

"I don't think so, Kitty. Your job was to find the hoss, right?"

"Ri-ight."

"Well, you found him. Now let's load him up."

Part of me wanted to argue with Mustard, but we both knew enough not to need to discuss the alternative; every minute we sat there with the horse might be bringing whoever had brought him here closer. But if we could get him out of here and get him safely out of the way, we'd have the chance to untangle this thing in peace.

"I'll see if I can get the horse trailer attached to the truck and I'll bring it 'round. You go over and make nice with our buddy over there."

"Me?" I said.

"Yeah, you. I figure if you can convince an animal as stubborn as Dex to stop drinking for a day, long enough to take on a case he didn't want in the first place, you can convince a horse to hop into a trailer. Maybe even drive himself home. Anyway, it sure as hell ain't gonna be me, Kitty. Now hop to it, all right? An' let's get out of here."

The trouble was, I'd seen this horse under Flora's control. He seemed a gentle enough animal, but he was spirited and he was a lot of horse. There was no mistake to be made; this wasn't Blinky, after all. But it wasn't as though I had a choice.

As Mustard went around back to see to the horse trailer, I moved towards the paddock. At my approach, Fritzy tossed his head and pranced around a bit, giving another ringing neigh. I could see it wasn't an aggressive move on his part, but rather one of welcome. He was a *friendly* horse, I reminded myself. A social animal, used to companionship and activity. Still, all that neighing and prancing frightened me still more. I wasn't proficient at horse handling at the best of times and this wasn't one of those. And, even if I was, this was arguably one of the top competition horses in the world and he possessed all the brilliance and fire that you'd expect in an animal who could wear that mantle.

"Hi, Fritzy," I said, extending my hand as I'd seen Flora do as I approached.

The horse whickered deeply and tossed his head. I tried not to flinch as a small amount of horse spittle danced across my cheek. How could one ever become used to such a thing?

"Hi, Fritzy," I said again, rubbing the flat of my hand against his forehead the way I knew he liked while trying desperately to remember at least a tiny bit of the small amount of German I'd learned in high school.

"Du bist ser schoene im fraglichziet," I said, knowing that the best German I could reach for was nonsensical, but hoping that Fritzy would find the vaguely Germanic sounds soothing. He might be smart for a horse, but I was confident he was no language professor.

I rubbed the horse's neck and he whickered again, a deep, rumbling sound. It took everything I had not to pull my hand away: not to think of how huge his teeth were and how much damage they could do. I comforted myself with the reminder that horses are strict vegetarians; if he was interested in my presence, it had nothing to do with hunger. It was small consolation.

I was relieved to hear the truck start up—it meant Mustard had either found the keys or had figured out how to get the truck going without them. We'd be making tracks soon, so I knew I had to get a move on and do my part to get Fritzy ready.

A leather halter and a lead rope were hung on a hook just outside the paddock. I had to steel myself to figure out how to get the halter onto the horse's head. When I held the halter aloft, I could see it was vaguely horse-shaped; I could understand the mechanics of it. What I didn't know was how to get Fritzy to cooperate while I convinced him to wear the damn thing.

In the end, Fritzy took care of the matter pretty much on his own. With halter in hand, I approached the paddock cautiously. The seasoned competition horse surprised me by lowering his head in expectation of the halter. I stilled the pounding of my heart and slid the halter over his head with only a couple of wrong moves. They were easily corrected, and soon I was doing up the buckles and standing back to admire my handiwork. Fritzy whickered again. It was getting easier for me to see why Flora was so crazy about this horse.

"Good boy," I said, offering up another awkward pat of his neck.

Mustard had by now gotten the trailer hooked up and the little rig moving. It was time for me to do my part by getting Fritzy on board and ready to travel.

"What do you think, old son?" I said, just making conversation while I slipped into the paddock with the lead shank, a wish, and a prayer. "How do you feel about a ride, hmmm?"

As I clipped the lead to the ring on his halter, Mustard got the trailer set up, lowering the door at the back of the trailer until it formed a ramp into the conveyance. I tried to think of how it had felt leading Blinky on the trail. That had been easy, barely scary at all. As long as Fritzy continued to cooperate, I figured we might just do all right.

"You're looking good there, Kitty Cat," Mustard said leaning against the fence and watching me getting ready to try to talk Fritzy into getting into the trailer. "You're looking like an old hand."

"Shows what you know," I said without changing the cadence of my voice. I'd never seen Fritzy spooked, but I knew it was a possibility: a very horse-like state of being. They were, after all, creatures of flight. "Get the gate for me, will ya? And don't make any fast moves."

Mustard did as I asked and I led the horse through, moving him toward the trailer without breaking stride, then leading him up the ramp. He didn't hesitate. It almost seemed as though he was happy to get up there. And maybe he was, too: ready to leave this dump in the middle of nowhere and get back to his everyday life amid the hustle and bustle of a busy stable.

Inside the trailer, everything I needed to do was self-evident. Another clip-on lead—a shorter one—was affixed to the trailer near the manger. I clipped this onto Fritzy's halter and removed the one I'd used to get him there, taking it with me. There was already some hay in the manger, and Fritzy tore off a snack as soon as he got there, whickering not unpleasantly as I moved carefully under his neck and out the other side.

"Well done," Mustard said quietly and with admiration as I walked back off the ramp.

"Thanks," I said, still keeping my voice even. "Now let's get the ramp up without a lot of fuss and get out of here. This has all gone so well, I'm afraid something will jinx it."

But nothing did.

There were a few bales of hay stacked next to the lean-to and covered with a burlap sack. Mustard hoisted one of these into the back of the truck. "He might need a snack later," he said, showing a purely practical side I'd not often seen.

Mustard tossed me the keys to his car while he slid back behind the wheel of the truck.

"Where are we taking him?" I asked.

"Not sure yet," he said with a grin. "I'll figure it out while we go, though, okay? Follow me. And if *you* get a bright idea of where to take him, you pass me and I'll follow you. Make sense?"

"Sure," I said, and we were underway.

CHAPTER FIFTY-ONE

As our little caravan moved up the hill towards the growing Olympic Village and then back towards the city, I kept my eyes peeled for cars or anyone who might stop us. But nothing did.

My heart didn't stop pounding until we were well into the city and back in traffic. Even then, I didn't entirely relax. I was driving a big black car. I could blend in almost anywhere. But a truck pulling a loaded horse trailer? Especially *that* horse: I feared getting spotted and followed any minute, but it didn't happen.

As occupied as I was with avoiding being seen, I didn't pay much attention to where Mustard was leading us. Once we were downtown, though, my ears perked up. When we got to the office, Mustard motioned for me to park his car while he waited for me at the mouth of the alley. I was out of breath when I jumped into the truck.

"What are you up to?" I asked.

"You'll see," he replied.

And I did, too. Even so, it took a while to figure out.

He parked our little rig directly behind our building.

"Wait here," he said, and when I would have questioned him further, he hopped out. He wasn't gone long, though.

"We unload him here; you figure you can control him as good as you did up in Baldwin Hills?"

"Honestly, Mustard, I just don't know. I wasn't really aware of controlling him, you know? It just seemed like he was doing the whole thing."

"Well, we're gonna take him off the trailer, so hang on to him real good. I guess all we can do is hope for the best."

And that was just what we did.

Fortunately, Fritzy was a pro traveler. I had to remind myself that not only had he been to countless horse shows and competitions, he'd come from across the world. Travel was nothing new to him and he could certainly manage an alley in downtown Los Angeles without panic. He'd been in far scarier places, like boats and shipyards. In that light, all of this was really nothing new.

And that was a good thing, because not only did I have no idea of what I was doing, Mustard now indicated I was to take the horse into the building and load him onto a freight elevator.

"Just what the hell are you up to?"

"Trust me?" he pleaded. I didn't really have much choice, so I followed his advice.

Once Fritzy and I were inside, Mustard followed us in, then pulled the heavy elevator door closed. The horse was fine until the thing started to move. Even then he seemed more curious than frightened. He kept his ears sharply forward as he felt the ground below us move, and I could feel his muscles tense beneath his silken coat. When the elevator sank slowly into the basement, he seemed to relax enough that I was able to, as well.

We went down two levels, one more than I'd ever known there was. Since I'd never ridden in the freight elevator before, that was no real surprise. What *was* a surprise was at the very end of the corridor, in a part of the sub-basement that was clearly never used.

"Why," I said as I led the horse in, "it's a stable. What on earth . . ."

And it was. There were four roomy box stalls and enough standup stalls for another eight horses. There were what I guessed had once been tack and feed rooms.

"I figure the other side of the building was where they kept the carriages and stuff," Mustard said. "Some of that is mechanical areas now. The modern elevators, for instance, would have been added years after the building was built. But they probably just never had a use for this part of this level. Maybe everyone has forgotten it's here."

"Of course," I said, a light dawning, "when this building was new, there weren't any cars, were there?" Our building had been erected in 1904; there was a brass plaque at the entranceway that I'd passed so often, I never even saw it anymore. The age of the automobile had still been impossible to imagine.

"Not at all. These guys would have been the only way to get around. That and the streetcar."

"But how did they get them down here? Surely not the elevator?"

And Mustard pointed to an archway I hadn't noticed before, one that had been bricked over sometime in the not-very-recent past.

"Probably was some kind of driveway down to this level. And the street's been widened since then, too. So you can't see any sign of it from either side."

"It's a mess, though," I said, looking over Fritzy's proposed temporary digs. It seemed likely to me that this area hadn't been used for more than twenty years. Some of the boards had collapsed under their own weight, and all of the stalls had been given over to storage, but two of the box stalls looked sturdy enough to hold Fritzy, and we only needed one.

"We should be able to get one of them shipshape enough to hold our boy here," Mustard said, echoing my thoughts. "And with any luck, it won't be for too long."

At that, Fritzy let out a loud, ringing neigh that I nonetheless had little fear of echoing up into the building. Mustard set to work clearing out the stall nearest the doorway while I held the big horse, patting his neck occasionally and trying not to jump when he shifted his weight. I didn't feel confident enough to tie him, though, and Mustard seemed to manage his part of the operation just fine without any pitching in from me.

When the stall was cleared of debris, I tucked Fritzy into it, happy to see that the sliding lock, though slightly rusty, still looked strong and in good repair. I waited there with the horse while he settled in, and Mustard set off to fill a bucket we'd found with clean water and to fetch the hay from the trailer.

"It's not perfect—and not as fancy as he's used to," Mustard said when we had the horse all tucked in, "but it'll have to do."

"Are you kidding? It's perfect, Mustard. No one will *ever* find him here."

I patted Fritzy's strong neck, feeling more confident with him now than I had before. He circled the stall a couple of times, snuffling here and there, then—world traveler that he was—he seemed to decide there was nothing there that would hurt him, and he settled in comfortably and began to munch on his hay.

"Sure, that's right," Mustard said, "he'll be snug as a bug in a rug."

CHAPTER FIFTY-TWO

"He said he was going to West Adams?" Mustard said. "What's there?"

We were sitting at my desk—me on the business side, Mustard opposite, and each of us with a cup of coffee in front of us. I'd rustled it up when we got back. Sometimes, if an afternoon has been especially tense, a big cup of coffee is just what the doctor ordered, and this had definitely been one of those days. I could see Mustard looking around for something stronger, and though there might have been something in Dex's desk, I'd overstepped the boundaries enough for one week without me going in and rooting around in there for my boss's stash of bootleg whiskey.

"Well, Flora's house, for one. I'd guess that's where he's gone."

"Why don't we just pop over there, see if he needs a hand."

Part of me agreed with Mustard from the first moment, and sitting there sipping coffee wasn't doing anything to make me feel less anxious. One thing held me back.

"This was our plan though, Mustard. When I talked to Dex earlier, we agreed to meet back here and then see where we were from there."

"I don't like it, though, Kitty. What if he's in some kind of trouble?"

"Okay, fair enough. But what if he's *not* in trouble? What if he's on his way back here right now: gets here, doesn't find us, then heads up to Baldwin Hills 'cause it's the last place he knew we were? You see what kind of mad circles we could start making?"

"Sure I do, but I don't much like the idea of sitting here on my hands while Dex might need our help."

That shut me up because I felt just the same way. We sat there in silence for a while, each lost to our own thoughts, which, for me, mostly consisted of wishing Dex would saunter through the door as he had at critical moments so many times in the past. And though I jumped every time the building gave a creak or I heard the elevator go past our floor, there was no sign of Dex. After about five minutes that felt like *fifteen*, Mustard broke the silence again.

"I got an idea, Kitty: you stay here, wait for Dex. I'll go to West Adams and see what I can see." Mustard liked his idea well enough that he was already in motion, putting his hat back on his head, drawing on his coat.

"It's a good idea, Mustard," I said rising and picking up my coat, plopping on my hat, grabbing my handbag. "It's much better than my idea."

"Which is what?"

"I'm coming with you."

CHAPTER FIFTY-THREE

By the time Mustard and I got to the Woodruffs' mausoleum of a house, it was almost full dark. The mansion looked fortress-like silhouetted against the sky. That didn't entirely explain why I felt so uneasy as soon as Mustard turned the car into the driveway. It took another full minute for me to figure out what was wrong.

Not only had darkness fallen in West Adams, the house itself was in complete darkness. For a lot of people's homes, this wouldn't be worthy of comment. With the Woodruffs, though, and their house full of servants, this was odd enough to be worth remarking upon.

While a part of me honestly felt like just staying in the car, or better yet, getting Mustard to fire up the engine to drive us both away, there was never a moment where that was really an option. And if we *had* considered such a thing, there was a clincher; though the Woodruffs' garage was closed, so we couldn't see who among the family members were home by which cars were in the driveway, there was a bright orange Hispano-Suiza parked in the porte-cochere. And tucked around the side of the house, but still plainly visible, was a less distinct car. Mustard recognized it right away.

"That's the banger I had brought to the office for Dex a few days ago," he said.

"Are you sure?" I'd ridden in that car but the one I was look-ing at didn't appear to be any different than the hundred thousand or so other black sedans in the city. A different story from Matty's bright orange chariot. It would have been impossible not to spot that one anywhere.

"Sure I'm sure."

"So Dex is in there . . ."

"Presumably," Mustard put in. Then, after a pause, "hopefully."

". . . so we should go investigate, right? Not just sit here on our keesters."

Mustard didn't answer, just opened the car door and headed for the house with me on his heels so tight, he would have had trouble making a full stride.

We didn't knock. We might've, but the hallway was dark and the door was open. Mustard didn't hesitate, so I didn't either; his heel still seemed the safest place to be.

Inside the spacious foyer, we stopped and listened, but once the echoes of our footsteps had died off the marble, there was nothing much to hear: just the invisible noise every house makes. The quiet inside the quiet, which is like the noise inside your head; it almost isn't noise at all.

"This isn't good." I'd whispered the words, but they sounded loud to me.

Mustard met my eyes and shook his head. No, they said. This wasn't good at all.

"What do you figure?" he whispered back, indicating hallways to the left and right and the curving staircase directly in front of us. That staircase had looked so elegant on my previous visits. Tonight, in the half-light that was almost dark, it looked sinister. Like it was waiting.

I'd been in the house often enough that I knew the lay of the land. I whispered what I knew to Mustard. "That hallway goes to the dining room, then the kitchen, then the servants' quarters. This one goes to the main lounge and the pool."

"And the staircase?"

"Up to the bedrooms."

"I've got a hunch," Mustard whispered, heading towards the staircase. I didn't have any ideas of my own, so I followed, as I had before, right on his heel.

About halfway up, we began to hear the voices: low and muffled, as though avoiding being overheard, yet confident they were alone. A man's voice, pitched too low to identify from where we were. And then a woman's, the higher notes fluting through the quiet air.

I looked at Mustard. "Carmella?" I asked. I couldn't think who else it might be.

"Dunno," he whispered back.

We continued our stealthy climb, then moved along the hallway, with only the distant streetlights to guide our way. And the voices, growing louder and more distinct with every step we took.

They were in the gallery, the two of them. The gallery overlooked the main, large lounge. So certain were they of being alone, their own stealth was simply form. They knew who was in the house, or thought they did. They knew who was not. I thought it likely the servants had been given the night off. That would explain the darkness throughout the house. And that deathly calm.

We crept to where the hallway narrowed to an entrance and we hovered right outside. It was as near as we dared go. For me it was *too* near. I feared that they would feel our eyes on them and turn around. My heart spoke to that; it beat so rapidly and so loudly in my chest, I was afraid they'd hear it. That was one fear I might have quelled. They were confident they were alone. Too confident. It frightened me because, certainly, it must mean something. The first words I was able to hear clearly confirmed my fears and chilled my heart.

"We've got to get rid of him," Carmella was saying. I don't think I would have been able to hear her so clearly but for the marble floor. Her voice carried across the smooth surface like a hand over silk.

"You don't mean kill him?" I recognized the masculine voice, and my heart fell. Matty.

"Don't be stupid." She spat the words out as though she couldn't unload them fast enough. "Of course I don't mean to *kill* him. But he's a PI, a mercenary. I think it will be enough to offer him money."

I didn't say anything, but my eyes moved to Mustard's and his to mine. They were talking about Dex, of course. We realized it in the same moment.

"You mean to buy him off?"

"Yes," Carmella said. "If we offer him enough money, he'll go away."

"Forget what he knows, you mean? It's possible. One thing, Carmella: you can't leave him locked in the cabana all night."

"Don't tell me what I can and cannot do, Mr. Sweet," she said, and if her words sounded mild, her tone belied it. "You're the one who brought him into this. If you don't like my idea, *you* figure a way to get him out. I still don't understand why you hired him."

"It was tit for tat, Carmella. Surely you understand that." There was something in his voice. Something new to me. Unrecognizable. My heart fell further still. I didn't know how I'd been so wrong, but I now knew for sure that I had been. "You wanted Flora to see more than she had on her own. I couldn't allow that."

"So you hired the private investigator so they would discover who was sending the notes. How did you know it was me?"

"It wasn't difficult. Not once I'd figured out your connection to Cornero. Then all I had to do was watch and follow. Mostly watch. Cornero's men did the dirty work, but I always knew whose orders they were. After all, you had the most to lose."

"I had *nothing* to lose, Matthew. I only ever wanted what was best for Flora. And you? You were not that."

Their voices, as we listened, seemed to be joining in a quiet heat. We were moving towards something. Mustard felt it as acutely as me; I could see it in his eyes.

"You—*you*—would judge *me*? Look at me. Look at who I am. And who you are and where you came from. What would your husband say if he knew?"

"But I think you know that, don't you, Matthew? I think you knew that all along, that's why you were so afraid. Cedric loves me and I know you don't believe it, but I love him as well. He would not have believed you, no matter what you said or did. He would not have wanted to."

"But Flora . . ."

"Yes. Flora was a different matter. And once I knew how you intended to use her . . . well, yes, you're right: I would have done anything to stop you. I *have* done everything. Perhaps even more than you know."

Mustard pulled back his jacket and eased a gun out of his holster. I don't know what kind: something big. It gleamed blue-gray and evil in the dim light. Then he surprised me by reaching behind him and pulling a second gun out of his waistband. This gun was tiny, though also blue-gray and to my eyes just as evil-looking, especially when he pressed the gun on me. It was clear from his movements that he wanted me to take it. I moved my hands rapidly across each other in front of me while shaking my head. It was a silent "no, no!" and Mustard understood, he just wasn't buying it. He pushed the gun towards me again, insistent.

"That's why I needed Cedric to discover exactly who was sending those notes."

"You could have just told my husband. You didn't need to go to all this trouble."

"Didn't I? But I think I did. Had I just gone to Cedric, he would have wondered how I knew. It would have implicated me, I think. And I wanted it clear who was doing it, Carmella. I wanted him to know just what sort of ginzo snake he'd wed."

Mustard made a motion as though to move forward, but I stopped him. It was apparent to me that we were about to hear something of import. Something that would change our entire understanding of the case. Had I listened to Mustard—had I followed his lead—things would have had a better outcome. Another regret for a day filled with them.

"It was never I who was the snake, Matty. That should be clear by now, even to you. I only ever wanted what was best for Flora . . ."

"You had no *idea* of what was best for Flora," Matty's voice rose on these last words, and there was anger in it. Mustard shot me a questioning glance. I could tell he was asking if I was ready to move forward now. I shook my head and shrugged. I didn't know what to do.

I didn't know.

"*You* wanted what was best for Flora." Even from the place where we hid, I could hear the venom in her voice. The disdain. "Don't pretend with me, Matthew. We're more alike than I'd really care to admit. You wanted what was best for *you*. You thought no one knew, but I could see how diminished you'd become. And I did my homework; I knew your father had said you'd not have full access to any *real* money until you were thirty-two."

"None of that will matter now, Carmella. It will be a trade between us, Flora and me. Her money, my position."

"You think she cares about position? You have her confused with me. If Flora cared about you at all, it's for who she thought you were. I've done what I could to show her who you are."

It was clear that Mustard wasn't going to take no for an answer and I understood. Even if I didn't use the gun, having a gun-toting accomplice would help us control this situation. I just wished it was Dex here, not me. But what had they said? Dex was locked in the cabana. The thought of that clinched it. I took the gun with a resigned sigh. Mustard grinned, proud as a father might be, and patted my arm. I shook him off. And then things happened quickly. So quickly that the need to decide was taken away.

"You tried, Carmella, but you've been far from successful. And so what has she discovered? What *will* she discover? I'll find her—you know I will. And when I do, I'll lay it all in her arms: how you were jealous of her . . ."

"I *never* was . . ."

"How you hated her and wanted her out of the way. How you would have killed her . . . had I not gotten there first."

The import of his words took longer, in the end, to penetrate our overburdened minds than it did for the bullet to do its lethal work. When the gun bellowed in the confined space, it was loud and unexpected. I looked at Mustard and he looked at me. It could only have taken five seconds, perhaps not even that, but we both saw what we needed to see; we were both standing without pain or smoking holes in our sides. The gunplay had come from that other pair. When we started moving it was as though we were two different parts of a creature with a single heart; we moved forward as one, mindless of our own safety. Neither of us forgetting that where one bullet had come, others could follow.

We emerged into a long gallery, windowless and with a marble floor. Carmella lay at Matty's feet. I could see she was dying. Matty had shot her neatly in the throat. She lay in an expanding pool of her own blood, one hand moving slightly, slowing even as we watched. Matty stood over her, the gun smoking in his hand, a bemused expression on his beautiful mug. He looked as though he wasn't fully certain about what was going on. I wondered what he could be thinking.

His confusion was to our advantage. Mustard disarmed him easily, and I went to Carmella's side to see what could be done. Nothing could. I watched in horror, for only a moment, while the light died in her eyes.

"She all right?" Mustard's voice from behind me.

"She's dead." I heard my voice but could hardly credit that it came from me. It sounded distant, otherworldly. Especially with the bile that rose in my throat.

"Oh Jesus, Kitty. What the hell we gonna do now?"

I thought fast, but it was hard. I couldn't seem to pull my eyes from Carmella's staring ones. There was a wrap over the back of the chair. Possibly something Carmella had been wearing earlier. I dropped it gently over her. Somehow not seeing the eyes didn't help. It was as though I could still feel them. Staring.

"Well, let's think. Let's think. We gonna call the cops?"

"No, I don't think so," Mustard said thoughtfully.

"I don't know where the horse is," Matty said, something new and vulnerable in his voice.

"Oh, we ain't lookin' for the hoss," Mustard said with a smile. "We've already got him. All nice and comfy."

"You do? Well, that's good then. You can just let me go. I'm sure my dad will give you a big reward, and . . ."

"We ain't letting you go. I ain't sure what we *are* doin' with you yet, but you can just lay money on it: letting you go ain't even on the table. Unless you know where the girl is. Play ball and we'll get along all right. C'mon; you know where Flora is, don'tcha?"

"But I don't. Honestly. I haven't seen her since last night."

He met my eyes. I blushed and looked away. "On the boat."

Since I wasn't looking, I heard rather than saw Matty go down. Though I'd heard no gunshot, at first I thought Mustard had shot him, but that wasn't the case at all. Matty lay collapsed in a heap at Mustard's feet, a trickle of blood spilling from under the hand he held over his temple. Mustard stood over him, his gun in his hand and a look of satisfaction in his eye.

"Oh, Mustard." I said. And then again, "Oh, Mustard. *Please.*"

"What? I didn't hurt him. Well, nothing serious anyway. A little pistol whipping will do this boy some good." He nudged Matty with the pointy toe of his wingtip shoe. "Won't it, Sweet? A little discipline. It'll make all the difference. A brat like you." The words—their tone—seemed benign enough. But I know Mustard and I knew what I was hearing and if I was any judge at all, none of what was happening now boded well for the future of the heir of Sweet Oil.

"Mustard," I said again. "Please." I couldn't think how else to articulate this thing. Mustard, who I'd always witnessed to be the most gentle of men—despite his questionable profession— was goading Matty on. And why? That seemed clear. It was for me, for damage endured—no matter how imaginary—and for what had been taken from him, Mustard, despite the fact that this was not true either. From what I could see in Mustard's eyes, though, it was what raged in his heart.

Mustard didn't move back at my words, but I knew he wouldn't hurt Matty anymore. I could just feel the change. When Mustard stood down, he moved back almost imperceptibly and I started breathing again.

Matty was on the floor, a handkerchief pressed to the gash on his forehead. It was bleeding liberally and I was a little alarmed with myself for not feeling badly about that.

Mustard put his arm on mine, ever so gently. I almost didn't feel it. He pointed at the gun in my hand: reminding me that I still held it.

"You stay here with him, okay? Keep an eye on him, but I don't think he'll try anything."

I nodded.

"I'll just be a couple of minutes."

Mustard disappeared into the master bedroom and came out with a handful of Cedric's silk ties. He used them to bind Matty's hands securely at his back, then both hands behind him tied to the banister. I got the idea he'd bound people in this way before, but I didn't ask. When he was done, Matty looked as secure as a two-year-old buck elk on the roof of a big car. He wasn't going anywhere and once we'd made sure of that, we went in search of Dex.

We went out a back door that opened onto the pool area. Outside, the evening air was crisp and fragrant. I didn't realize I'd been holding my breath until we got outside. The freshness of that outside air made me want to gulp great mouthfuls of it. I breathed deeply as we worked our way towards the cabana. I breathed deeply and tried not to pass out.

The pool was dark and silent. The cabana perched next to the pool on the far side of the garden. The cabana door was locked. We peered through the window. Dex lay prone on a chaise across from the door. I hoped he was sleeping or perhaps drugged. I didn't like to think of other possibilities.

It's possible we could have searched around for the key, but it seemed imperative to both of us that we get to Dex quickly. Mustard took out his .38 and I covered my ears, preparing for him to shoot out the lock, but in the last moment he reholstered his gun and elbowed a pane of glass out of the French door. "No sense wasting perfectly good bullets," he said as he reached through the new hole and unlocked the door from the inside. I was alarmed to see that, with all this talk and racket, Dex hadn't even flinched.

I followed Mustard into the cabana, then crossed to Dex's side to see if he was okay. Dex was conscious, but he didn't look all the way there. He looked as though he'd been drugged or given a good bang on the noggin. Either way, I didn't think any of it was good.

"Mustard, he don't look okay," I said.

Together we shoved Dex into a sitting position. Mustard checked Dex's pulse and the color of his tongue. After a while he said, "He'll do, Kitty. Nothing to worry about; he ain't gonna keel over. But let's get him movin'. The sooner we get out of here, the better."

Between us we managed to bundle Dex out to Mustard's car. We tucked him into the middle of the front seat and I sat next to him, nearest the passenger door.

"What about Matty?" I asked, once he'd slid behind the wheel and gotten the car moving.

"He'll keep," he said.

"You figure?"

"Sure. I tied him pretty good. I'll come back later, once we figure everything out. Once we get Dex all filled in, he'll probably have some idea of what he wants done with him."

I looked at Dex, awake between us on the seat, but only barely, and I tried not to register my concern. Dex didn't look so good to me. In fact, it looked like it might be a long time before he was solid enough to have a good idea. I sat quietly in my corner of the car for a while and just swallowed the notion. I figured Mustard had the same idea. But we both kept it zipped, at least for the time being. There were other things to think about just then.

CHAPTER FIFTY-FOUR

Mustard stopped the car at a coffee joint and I went in and got us three big cups of java in paper cups along with a bagful of sour milk biscuits. I was hungry by then—and I figured Mustard was too—but we didn't have time to stop for a proper bite and the biscuits were so much better than nothing—and I was so hungry—that I couldn't recall much ever tasting so good.

Dex didn't eat at first. It seemed all he could do to sit upright and sip at his coffee now and again. I knew he was feeling a little better when he finally piped up.

"Why the hell am I sittin' in the middle here? Like a girl."

"I figured Kitty could help keep you propped up," Mustard said. "When we set out, there seemed a fairly good chance you'd roll right out the door if we didn't take measures to keep you in place."

"That bad, huh?" Dex asked.

Mustard didn't answer for a while. He just piloted the car silently, considering. I knew what was going on inside his head. Probably the same as was going on in mine. We hadn't been entirely sure about how Dex was going to be. Half an hour before, we'd both felt close to losing him. And now, well, we both still thought it was a possibility, but a Dex that could poke fun was probably in good enough shape to pull through.

When Mustard finally spoke, I'd forgotten that Dex was waiting for an answer. "Even worse," was all he said.

By now we'd left the city lights behind and were speeding

down dark country roads towards Burbank. For a while we drove through the dark in silence. Dex sipped at his coffee and even took a couple of nibbles off a biscuit. I knew it couldn't be right, but I would almost have sworn I saw the color beginning to come back into his face as he did.

"You two gonna bring me up to speed? Or am I gonna need to guess?" he said before much more time had passed.

"Go ahead and guess," Mustard said without taking his eyes off the road. "Might be good for a laugh. Let's see if that pound cake you call a brain still knows how to put two and two together and not come up with the capitol of Iowa."

"Des Moines," Dex said. A half-jovial sound that warmed my heart. I figured, sounding like that, he was going to be all right. His next words confirmed it. "A bite of bourbon would cure me better 'n' anything right now."

I arched an eyebrow, but Mustard reached into an inside pocket, pulled out a flask, and handed it across to Dex, who unscrewed the top, took a big hit, and sighed. The smell filled the car—rich and warm—and I found myself shaking my head.

"He might have a *head injury*, Mustard."

"He ain't a baby, Kitty."

"That's right. I'm a big boy and I can look after myself."

He was joking, but I snorted anyway. "Didn't look like you were doing a very good job of it tonight."

"Never mind, you two," Mustard said, "just never mind. It don't half matter anyway. We've only got a few miles to go and we need to bring Dex up to speed." He passed the flask across again and Dex tipped it to me before he took another big drink. Meanwhile Mustard began to tell the story and I chimed in here and there and we filled Dex in as well as we could and as we recalled it. We gave him the short version because, after all, a lot had happened since we'd decided to drive out to Baldwin Hills and then found and stolen Fritzy.

"Where is he now?" Dex demanded.

"In the basement," Mustard explained. "There were stables down there, from the old days. We fixed him up a nice bed and he's in there, cozy as can be."

"No kiddin'? Well, that's something. Maybe I'll stay there on my next vacation."

Carmella's death was more difficult to cover, at least for me. I still could see her staring eyes. See the life drift out of them. I kept my face strong and stoic but a part of me just wanted to curl up and cry.

"So were they in cahoots?" Dex wanted to know.

"That wasn't the idea I got. You, Kitty?"

"Mustard's right. It felt like Matty had something on her. Or maybe they had something on each other."

"How so?"

I thought hard before I answered, trying to recall everything we'd overheard. Lucky for me Mustard had been there and heard everything I had. Together we had a hope of piecing together at least a working transcript of what had passed between Matty and Carmella. Dex listened hard while we told him what we knew. He only interrupted once, and that was just a signal to Mustard to hand over the flask. Mustard did. After we were done, he let out a long whistle, then sat in silence for a moment.

"So let's see if I got this straight," he said after a while. "Based on what you heard, plus what we've been able to piece together, Carmella sent the notes, right?"

"Right. But Tony Cornero—or probably his guys—actually did the deeds."

"And Matty figured it out and hired us to do the finger-pointing. And you figure he did that because he wanted Car-mella out of the way."

"Well, it's the only thing that makes sense, I think. From

what the two of them were saying before he took Carmella out, Matty doesn't have access to his family's money until he's in his thirties."

"That can seem like a long time at his age," Mustard offered. "And he does like to spend money."

"He does," I agreed, thinking about his orange car: just like D.W. Griffith's, he'd said. And there were probably other expenses we'd never seen. "And you know, Dex, I've been thinking about what that girl at the Antler said. She said she'd seen Flora and a good-looking guy that she called Matty. And she saw her with Tony the Hat. Now I'm thinking, she never actually *said* it was Flora. Remember what she said: good looking, dark hair, money. She could have talking about Carmella, Dex."

"By crikey, Kitty. She could have been, at that." He paused. "But all of this, and we've still got one big question, don't we?"

"What's that, Dex?"

"Flora. All this and we still don't know where the hell she is."

I sighed. "I guess I was hoping that's what got you locked in a cabana, Dex. I guess I was hoping you'd give us some good news when it got to be your turn."

"Not that, Kitty, but I do got some things to tell." Dex nibbled at his biscuit, had a few more sips of joe, then plunged into what was a more complicated story than the one I'd been anticipating.

He told us that, earlier in the day, when he'd been out at the Academy looking seemingly in vain for some lead—*any* lead— that would bring him to Fritzy or Flora, the old groom had come to him.

"Doc?" I said. "But I talked to him. He told me he hadn't seen anything."

"That's what he told me, too. And it wasn't a lie. *He* hadn't. But another one of the grooms told Doc what *he* had seen. He was someone you'd talked to, as well. But he was afraid to come forward because of what might happen to him if he said anything against a white man. And he was afraid to talk at all because he wasn't supposed to be there at night."

"Oh!" I recalled what Doc had said, that there were men who slept at the barn because they had nowhere else to go. "What did he see?"

"He said he woke up when he heard a noise—something out of the ordinary. He came out just in time to see a man leading a horse out of Barn Twelve. The guy told Doc he didn't like the looks of things, so he followed. They had a horse trailer pulled up on the far side the arena."

"That means they would have had to case things out in advance," I said.

"That's what I figured, too," he said. "You don't just pull a trailer around for the hell of it."

"But it's not a lot to go on: a white man leading a horse to a trailer."

"That's what you'd think, right?" Dex asked. "But, like I said, the groom followed this guy leading a horse and he knew it wasn't right. When he gets to the rig, there's a couple of other guys there, waiting. The groom says the three guys were pretty het up about something and they kept shouting at each other in a foreign language."

"What?"

"That's what I thought at first," Dex said. "And then, after last night on the boat, I got to thinking: don't we know a bunch of guys what speak a different language?"

"No," I said. "I don't think we do. Wait: German?"

"Not German, Kitty. You really did take a bump on the noggin, didn't you?"

"That was you, Dex."

"Oh, right. But no, Kitty; *Italian* is the language we've been hearing a lot of. So when I came back here, I ran that past our guy . . ."

"The groom."

". . . And he said he figured that could be it. So then, I put four and four together, came up with Des Moines, and that was the end of that."

"Wait." I looked at Dex in the passenger seat while Mustard drove and wondered what I'd missed. "When I talked to you on the phone, you sounded like you'd uncovered something big. You said you were heading out to West Adams and you sounded like you knew something."

"I guess I did, didn't I? Well, see, after I made the Italian connection, I got to thinking: what the hell would Tony the Hat want with kidnapping Flora's horse?"

"And the whole winter fair thing, right?" Mustard put in. "Why would Cornero give a crap about Flora and Fritzy competing in a horse show?"

"Exactly," Dex said. "That's what I wondered, too. More than wondered, really. And I remembered what you said, Kitty, after you talked to Mavis . . ."

"From the paper?"

"Right. She said she figured Carmella was Italian."

I'd forgotten that. "Still," I said, "it's a bit of a reach, isn't it? Connecting Carmella with Tony the Hat just for being *Italian*?"

"Well, it would be, except Tony the Hat kept crossing our path for no good reason that I could see. I mean, it was pretty obvious this wasn't a mob operation."

"True enough," Mustard said. "You don't generally see the Family messing around with horse shows and notes."

"Right," Dex said. "Kidnapping horses. Throwing rocks. If there's something going down with them, there's generally more blood involved."

""The winter horse show," I said, "and the kidnapped horse.

But what's Carmella's connection with the Hat?"

"And what about Flora?" Mustard said. "What did they want with her?"

"All right, all right," Dex said, "I didn't say I'd figured everything out yet. So now you know, Kitty; that's what it had to do with the price of tea in China."

I looked at him consideringly when he said it, knowing there was something veiled in what he said, but it took me a minute, and when I did get it, I figured it hadn't been worth the effort it took to remember.

"What I don't get," I said, "is what we're doing now. We've got the horse. We know who had him and probably who took him. What do we hope to accomplish out at the barn at this point?"

"We know where the horse is at, Kitty," Dex explained, "but they don't. And we've got a hand-off 'sposed to be happening right about now."

"Or maybe it's already happened," I pointed out.

"I had planned on being out there earlier, but something tied me up."

"Fair enough," I said.

"In any case, that's where Cedric was heading with the money. If nothing else, we need to tell him that his wife is dead."

"Oh my gosh," I said. "You mean before he goes home and finds out on his own."

"That's what I was thinkin'," Dex said. "But there are still things we don't know. And something . . . well, something's not right here."

"You *think?*" I said, not bothering to keep the irony from my voice.

Dex ignored my tone. "None of this is adding up. There's still some things we don't really know."

"Like Flora," I said quietly.

"What about Flora," Dex wanted to know. "Where is she?"

CHAPTER FIFTY-FIVE

Cedric was at the clubhouse, waiting for us nervously, a smooth leather valise in his hand. He looked ten years older than he had even the day before. There was about him an aspect of waiting, of anxiety. And the smell of disaster, I caught that as well. Disaster or disaster waiting to happen. Sometimes those are the same thing. I thought about his wife—the beautiful wife he had adored—and I couldn't bring myself to meet his eyes.

"Theroux, thank God. I thought you said you'd be here earlier."

"I got sort of tied up, Woodruff," Dex said, not explaining further. I was glad to see that Dex's movements were stronger, more in control, though I thought he still looked a little shaky on his feet.

"You better bring us up to speed," Dex said, making no effort to bring Woodruff in that direction. After all, the man's wife was dead and his daughter was still missing, though the horse had been recovered.

"Bring you up to speed?" said Cedric. "Why, I don't have anything to tell. I've just been waiting here. For you."

"Good," said Dex. And then again, "Good. Listen Woodruff, at this point, this thing is all balled up and we don't know nearly as much about anything as maybe we should, but I'm glad you didn't go out to Bronson Canyon on your own to drop off the cash."

Woodruff looked at Dex with what would have been amusement on a different day.

"I wasn't even tempted, Theroux," was all he said.

"Well, good," Dex said, offering Woodruff a sniff from Mustard's flask. Woodruff just shook his head. "That would have just gummed up the works. Listen, Woodruff, there are some things we need to talk about. Some things I need to tell you."

"Do we have time?" the man said worriedly.

"Oh, we have time all right," and then a very un-Dex-like sigh. The day was starting to tell on him. It was starting to tell on all of us. "Is the clubhouse open?"

It was not, but we searched down Biedermeier and had him open it up for us. I wished for tea, but another sniff of brandy was what we got. That seemed to suit Dex fine.

I knew Dex was tired and perhaps not entirely well, but I found myself unable to go through the whole story again and I excused myself before they got started. "I'm just . . . I just need some air, Dex. Sir. I'll be out at the barn when it's time to go."

I hadn't gotten very far when Mustard fell into step beside me.

"Long day," I said when he caught up with me.

"Well, there's that," he replied. "But also I thought . . . well, I thought maybe it was news best heard without a crowd there, y'know? Especially considering our part in the whole thing."

I nodded. "I guess that's what I was thinking too. And I just . . . I just couldn't hear about it again, Mustard. Not right now. I keep seeing her eyes . . ."

We got to the barn. Barn Twelve. There were other places I could have gone at the Academy, but my feet knew the way to this spot, it seemed. Aside from the clubhouse, it was the place I'd been most often. The light was on in the tack room and for just a second, I let a ridiculous surge of hope soar. What if Flora were there, just cleaning her tack? What if she'd come back on her own? When I peeked in, though, it was Willamina Huffle's sleekly bobbed head that greeted me. She didn't look too pleased to see me, either.

"What? You thought you'd sneak up on me and see if I had Fritzy in here with me?" she said without much kindness in her voice.

"No, I . . . well, I told you I was sorry about that."

"Anyway," Mustard said without introducing himself. "We found Fritzy."

"You did?" There was genuine interest in Willamina's eyes. And maybe a bit of relief. It surprised me. "Well, that's wonderful. Where?"

"It's a long story," I said. "Willamina Huffle, this is my associate, Mustard."

"Mustard?" Willamina said. "Is that your first or your last name?"

Mustard smiled at her, showing surprisingly white and even teeth. "Which would you like it to be?"

To my surprise, Willamina didn't turn her back on us, nor did she snort contemptuously in Mustard's face. Instead she laughed as though at some wonderful joke. The laugh had a musical quality. I tried not to let the dismay I felt show on my face.

"So, we found the horse . . ." I said, reminding her.

"Oh. Yes. Right. Of course. And Flora?"

"Well, we've not found her yet, though the way things are turning out, we suspect at this point she might not have been kidnapped after all."

"But the horse was?"

"Yes, that's right, the horse was. But as I said, we've recovered him."

"And you're certain she's not been kidnapped."

"Well, not fully certain. Not yet. But it's beginning to look more and more that way."

"And Matty . . ." she prompted.

"What about him."

"Well, is she with him?"

"No. That's something else we're positive of: she's not with him and he doesn't know where she is."

"Well, I'm pretty sure I know where she is, then."

"What?"

"Well, it's where I'd be under the circumstances. That is, if I was wanting to hide, which seems to be the case. If I just wanted to lie low, without discomfort, mind you, without anyone knowing where I was."

"Where," I said, trying not to sound impatient. "Where would you be?"

"Why, San Pedro, of course."

"San Pedro? What's in San Pedro?"

"The *Flora-Mae*."

"Excuse me?"

"Her dad's boat."

CHAPTER FIFTY-SIX

Cedric Woodruff kept his small motor yacht moored at the California Yacht Club at Wilmington Harbor. The boat wasn't much bigger than the skiff that had taken me and Flora out to the *Tango*, but you could see it was a different breed of fish. Teak and brass gleamed everywhere, and the boat looked as though it could win a race all on its own. As Willamina had said, the boat was called *Flora-Mae*. I knew this because the name was lettered neatly over the stern.

"Named for Flora and my grandmother," Cedric said when he saw me notice. I didn't say anything but, considering the boat's wild, racy lines and the way this day had gone, I figured *Carmella* might have been a more fitting name.

Once the four of us were on the boat, Cedric Woodruff surprised me. What on land was a penguin-ish awkwardness proved to be an aquatic elegance when his feet touched the boards of his own good ship. Something in his own construction—low to the ground, not particularly slender—lent him a stability on the water. It was a transformation and it looked good on him. Though Dex hadn't wanted to bring him along, I was glad Cedric had insisted and I'd prodded. After all, what was the man to do? We couldn't very well drop him off at his house on the way there to deal with his wife's corpse and the young man that had very nearly been his son-in-law neatly bound beside her.

"But shouldn't we ought to stop and do something for

Matty?" I'd said to Mustard as we drove. Cedric had gone with Dex in his car, while Dex had instructed me to ride with Mustard. "I mean, he'll have to go to the bathroom by now."

Mustard shrugged and I had no doubt he was as unconcerned as he looked. "That's all right, Kitty. All things considered, that'll be the least of his worries right now."

We'd gotten to the California Yacht Club's marina just slightly ahead of Dex and Cedric and had waited in the car, as per Dex's instructions. It was a beautiful night. Velvety. And the marina lights danced on water that was unusually still. I had a hard time believing that, just about twenty-four hours earlier, Flora and I had been on the *Tango* and this latest nightmare had begun. I tried not to think fruitless thoughts about turning back time, but sometimes it's difficult not to make wishes.

"And if wishes were horses," Dex said quietly, so near my ear, I jumped. I knew he couldn't have guessed what I was thinking. But still.

The boat was empty. The windows were dark as we approached, but still I'd hoped. I'd done nothing but hope. After this, we were out of ideas.

A heel of a bottle of wine was on the table, but that was all. It looked so similar to what had been left behind at the cabin that I asked Cedric if he figured anyone other than Flora could have been here and left it. He couldn't say for sure. A bottle of wine, he said, wouldn't be that remarkable. Not on a day when he'd not been expected. "I have a man come by, to look after the boat. I've always sort of figured he used it when my back was turned." Nor did Cedric look terribly put out by the thought.

"So that's it, then," I said, sliding behind the table in the boat's small lounge area. "We have no idea where she is. We have no clues."

"Now hold on, Kitty," Dex said, a mild reprimand in his voice. "And come on now. It's not like you to just give up like that."

"Give up? Why, Dex? I've been scraping my brain about this since Flora disappeared. I've checked every option. Turned every stone."

"Not every one, Kitty," Dex said with unusual optimism. "If we had , Flora would be here now."

I didn't reply. What could I say? I just looked at Dex, my arms crossed in front of me. Too tired to even think up a response.

"Let's go over everything we've got," Dex said. He indicated the other chairs around the table I'd plunked myself at; then he sent a questioning look at Woodruff.

"Oh sure," he said. "By all means."

Dex took a seat, as did Mustard, while I lay my head in my arms. Woodruff, meanwhile, went to the nearby galley and came back with four lowball glasses and a dark brown bottle.

"I trust you'll have a drink with me?" Woodruff said. There was something tightly controlled about him. I could only imagine. His wife dead. His daughter missing. "Seagram's rye," Dex said, nodding at the bottle of Canadian whiskey approvingly. "Good man."

"To my Carmella," he said when we raised our glasses. The men drank. I raised the glass to my lips, sipped. Tasted the smoky liquid. The warmth. Thought of the woman who had been lost. I thought Woodruff must be doing the same because I saw his eyes shine a little too brightly. He closed them, set his glass down, and rubbed at his temples as though he might push some demon away.

I knew none of this would escape Dex, but he seemed determined to give Woodruff a moment to collect himself by diverting attention back to the matters at hand. In any case, it felt as though time was pressing. If nothing else, how many more hours could we possibly continue before our bodies demanded some rest?

"We've had a lot on our minds," Dex began, "and I keep going over everything. Like Kitty, I guess I feel as though there's something we must have missed. One thing has been bothering me: one thing I guess I should have checked on by now."

"We haven't had much time," Mustard pointed out.

"That's true. Still," Dex went on. "Kitty, you told me that last night on the boat, before we got there, you and Flora were in the dining room with James Stroud and another man. Tell me his name again, please."

"That's right," I said. I barely lifted my head from my arms at Dex's words. The boat was pulling gently on her moorings. It felt like a cradle. And I was so tired. It wouldn't have taken much for me to fall asleep. "Allan Hancock."

"That's what I thought you'd said, Kitty. Mustard, ain't there a Hancock what's a PI in Westwood?"

"Well, I think there is, Dex. But that's a long shot. I mean, Hancock, right? Los Angeles is lousy with guys got that handle."

"Still, maybe it's worth checking out."

I lifted my head towards the end of this exchange. "What are you saying, Dex? You figure the guy with James—the guy I met—might have been a PI?"

"Well, it fits, don't it Kitty?"

I looked at Dex. Thought about what he'd said. "Does it?" I said finally. "I don't see how."

"Well, from what you said, Flora dragged you down to the *Tango* . . ."

"More or less dragged." I considered. "Well, drag might be an overstatement, really."

". . . and you're not there long before Stroud and company show up . . ."

"Long enough to order a steak. And wine. Not much more."

"Then you step outside for a minute . . ."

I avoided looking at Mustard when Dex said this.

". . . then when you come back, Flora is gone."

"Okay, I already understood how it all happened, Dex. But what out of all that makes you think Hancock might have been a PI?"

"Show her, Mustard."

Mustard reached into his inside jacket pocket and pulled out a business card, which he passed to me. There was raised black script on a creamy background.

"Read it out loud," Dex said.

" 'Allan A. Hancock,' " I read. " 'Private investigator.' Where'd you get this?"

"On the *Tango*," Mustard said. "When I went back there. This afternoon."

"And you didn't tell me, because . . ."

"Didn't seem important," Mustard said. "And, anyway, we had other fish to fry."

He was right about that, anyway. But it seemed like they were all fried now.

"What are we waiting for?" I said. And then after a moment, we weren't waiting at all.

CHAPTER FIFTY-SEVEN

It would have been most expeditious to leave Woodruff behind and for the three of us—Dex, Mustard, and me—to pile into one car, but that's not how we did it. I had a hunch Dex didn't want to leave the heartbroken man alone on a boat. And, under the circumstances, there was no question that he not go to his own home. Not until we'd gotten Matty dealt with and everything else cleaned up. So, once again, Dex instructed Woodruff to go with him. When he told me to go with Mustard, I thought I saw a glint in Dex's eye, but I could have been wrong about that; it might just have been my imagination.

The address was on Westwood Boulevard. I figured it was near the Janss Dome. "Pretty posh digs for a PI," I said to Mustard as we drove.

"That's what I thought," Mustard said. "But with that address and based on the company he was keeping last night, I'd figure he does more insurance scams than anything."

"You figure he works for the Janss brothers?"

"Probably more like he *does* work for the Janss family. And they're real estate guys. That seems to keep coming up in this."

"It does, doesn't it?"

Hancock's office was on the second level of a three-story building just down the street from the Janss Building. Westwood was a storybook place. A newly built Mediterranean village within smelling distance of the sea. The Janss brothers' old man had married into the huge acreage even now being cut up into what was being hyped as some of the best real estate in the Southland. It went without saying that the Janss's were making a fortune at this, at a time when some folks were still losing theirs. It probably meant that having a tame PI in the vicinity could come in handy now and again. And I figured Mustard was right; Hancock probably fit that bill just fine.

I thought it was surprisingly easy to find a parking space, until I realized it was late enough that the late picture had probably already let out. We parked, then sat in the car until Dex and Woodruff showed up. Mustard got out to join them, and I started to as well, but Dex stopped me. "Hold your horses, Kitty."

"What?"

"We don't need a whole big crew going in there," Dex said.

"But *he* gets to go in?" I said, pointing at Woodruff.

"*He* is the client," Dex pointed out. "And I already had this talk with him in the car on the way over here, and he wasn't taking no for an answer. But I work for him. And you? Well, you work for me. So you stay put, young lady," he said, probably in response to the mutiny he saw growing on my face. "Please, Kitty. It's been a long day," and I could hear just how long by the sound of his voice. "I'll bet we won't be long. And we'll come right back here and tell you everything we find out."

I stayed put while I watched them leave, though I had every intention of letting them get safely inside and then following, right on their heels. In fact, just a couple minutes after they'd gone inside, my hand was on the door handle. I was ready to jump into action. And then I saw the couple. I'd been wrong, it seemed. Though the other theaters might already have let out, the late showing at the Village Theatre on Broxton hadn't been over. But it was now and people streamed from the building, heading back to their cars. From the looks of them all, it must have been a romantic movie. Something with Fredric March or

Claudette Colbert, because all of the couples lining the sidewalks looked deeply in love.

That was what caught my attention about this one couple. She looked worried, he looked protective. Though I hadn't seen them before the movie let out, I figured it was just because I hadn't noticed them. I didn't think they'd been to see the film; they looked as though they had other things on their minds. And when they stood, for just a moment, directly under a streetlight, and her profile was illuminated just so, I knew without doubt that, no matter what the boys discovered in Allan Hancock's office, Flora had been found.

CHAPTER FIFTY-EIGHT

My only thought was to not lose sight of her. I wasn't sure Dex would believe that, given his instructions, but, in some ways, that didn't matter. Flora had been lost and now she was found. The coincidence seemed extreme, but there you had it: there she was. And I had no intention of letting her out of my sight again.

I followed the couple down Broxton; then they made a left and walked another block or so. I flitted along behind them, keeping to the shadows. I knew that was a dangerous game—a woman alone in the night with a picture show just out—but I held my quarry in sight and, anyway, it was one of the safest spots in town. Those Janss brothers had seen to that. Still, I tried not to let visions of disaster enter my head.

They reached a long, black car in a row of them and he tucked her neatly into the passenger side before crossing the street and hurrying back in the direction from which he'd come. Alone now. I prayed that he didn't recognize me as he passed, but he didn't even glance my way. I recognized him, though: James Stroud, though I wasn't anything like surprised when I caught his long, dangerous stride.

I watched him for a minute, trying to figure out where he was going and how long he might be gone. Considering the proximity of Hancock's office and the fact that we were in Westwood with many restaurants and cafés and bars close at hand, it seemed possible to me that the couple had been discussing their

315

concerns, perhaps over a drink, and that Stroud was now off to Hancock's office to talk to the PI he'd hired who, if my eyes hadn't been lying the night before, also happened to be Stroud's friend. If that *were* the case and Stroud was heading off to talk to Hancock, I knew I'd have a few minutes with Flora. After all, Stroud might have to wait; Dex and Mustard would already have Hancock talking.

I approached the car. The engine was off and it sat there silent and dark. Had I not seen James let Flora in, I would have thought it was unoccupied. I crept closer and, as I did, was startled by the cherry glow of a cigarette: almost neon in the black night. In that glow, a familiar profile: Flora Woodruff, alone in the car, as I'd known she would be.

I made sure of this last—first watching the car, then peeking in the window—before I pulled open the driver's door and plunked myself behind the wheel. A brave thing, when I think on it now. She might have shot me. I didn't know if she'd have a gun. I guessed, though. And I guessed right. She sat in the dim car, smoking her smoke, alone and unarmed.

When I opened the door, she looked startled at first—frightened—but then she recognized me and smiled. "Well, it's the girl detective," she said. "How do you like that?"

"I like it just fine," I said, not knowing what else to say.

"What brings you out here?" Flora said, just as though this was Sunday afternoon and we were meeting in the park.

"Oh, nothin' much," I said. "I figured I'd take in a picture show, but I don't know if there's anything worth seeing. You?"

"I love the pictures. You have a favorite?"

"Well, sure I do. But that's maybe not what I want to talk about right now."

"No?" There was nothing but bland innocence on her face. It wasn't the first time I figured maybe she should forget about the Olympics and try her hand at pictures, instead. She was an actor born, for sure.

"No. I was more thinkin' about the fact that you didn't bother to say good-bye last time I saw you."

"I didn't think you really noticed." Her face seemed to bubble with silent laughter as she said this. I felt my cheeks heat up.

"Still," I said sternly, "you've led us a merry chase! You couldn't imagine the sort of day I've had."

"Oh I couldn't, could I?"

"That's right. And here you sit, taking in the view, like nobody's business."

She smiled at that.

"I do like you Kitty," she said. "I'm glad we've gotten to be friends."

"Is that what we are? Because you sure have a funny way of showing it."

"Okay, I'm sorry I went off. Left you in the lurch. But I had to do it. Is that what you want me to say?"

"It's a start. There's a lot else I want to know, too. But, right now the most important one, I guess, is the answer to why you're sitting here in the dark. In a car."

"James's car," she said, looking straight ahead through the front windshield. I followed her glance. There wasn't much to see. A couple of sailors, with a redhead between them, her face pointed towards the stars in an attitude of laughter, the men's eyes meeting above her head. Who would be the lucky one? I turned away. None of it had anything to do with us.

"James's car, yes. I know." She looked at me quickly. "I followed you. From the theater."

"You *followed* us? My, my, Kitty: you're a better detective than I gave you credit for. I really didn't think anyone knew we were here."

"Yes," I said, thinking about how much to tell her. And then, "Well."

"Even so. I suppose there's a great deal you don't know."

"Tell me, then."

She looked for a moment as though she might, but then she stopped herself in time. "I can't, Kitty. Much as I'd like to. Sometime, I'll tell you it all. Everything. But not now."

"I can guess, Flora. I can guess at a lot of it. And . . . and there are things you don't know," I said after a brief hesitation. "Things you might need to know."

"Things," she repeated. Her face was still but there was a smile in her voice.

"Fritzy, for one," I said.

She was instantly serious. "What about him," she said.

"He's not . . . he's not where you left him." It was a guess, but I figured it was a fairly well-informed one. In my mind's eye, I could see the two champagne glasses, the beaded dress over the back of the chair. It made more sense now.

It made quite a lot of sense.

"What do you mean?" she said, still playing innocent.

"Baldwin Hills," was all I chose to say and was rewarded when I saw her pale.

"It's not what you think," she said.

"What do I think?"

"That I took him. Fritzy. That me and James took him. You know we didn't, don't you?"

"I don't know anything," I said. "Only that he's not there anymore."

"You know quite a bit. And I think you know what happened on the boat."

I colored at that, but asked anyway, "What do you mean?"

"James and I . . . well, our meeting last night, on the *Tango,* it wasn't accidental."

"How could that be? I had been with you every second of the day."

"Not *every* second, Kitty. I was able to make some phone

calls. Take a couple. James and I arranged to meet and I couldn't shake you, so—forgive me—I brought you along. And James's friend, Allan, was not what he seemed."

"We figured that part out. That's why we're here. I guess that's why *you're* here, too. He's a private investigator."

"James hired him, without telling me. He hired him to look at Matty."

"And found so much more . . ." I said, my voice trailing off in thought. So much was beginning to make sense. I had another thought. "What about you? Were you suspicious of Matty?"

"No. I really wasn't. I thought he was pretty much as advertised. In a way that's right, too, isn't it? He's young, handsome, carefree. From a wealthy family. So there really wasn't very much for a surprise." She said this all matter-of-factly, but I could see what it cost her. No one likes to be duped. Worse. No one likes to discover that everything they thought was true was a lie. And worse.

"Carmella knew."

"What?"

"Carmella knew what Matty was. She was trying to protect you."

"I don't . . . I don't understand. I thought she and Matty were doing all of this together."

"No. Not even close. She knew what he was, though, towards the end, and she wanted to warn you."

" 'The end,' Kitty. What do you mean 'the end' ?" There was a look of fear on her face and I realized she didn't know; there was no way she could have known.

"Carmella's dead, Flora. Matty shot her. She was trying to protect you."

Flora's voice was small in the car. I didn't know quite what to make of it. "And now she's dead. Matty?"

"He's there, at the house. I don't think Dex wanted to do anything with him until we found you."

"Just in case?"

"That's right. Just in case."

"But you said the two of them weren't in cahoots?"

"It doesn't look that way. Flora, you said you didn't take the horse. But I know you had him. What did you mean? If not you, then who?"

"Tony the Hat. That's what I started to tell you. James had hired a private investigator . . ."

"But why did he do that, Flora? On his own like that."

"You were right about that all along, Kitty. James was in love with me. You knew it before I did! And he figured Matty wasn't everything he said he was."

"So he hired Hancock to look at Matty?" I asked. Suddenly everything made sense. Despite what Dex had said to me, we'd never looked very closely in that direction. Well, I'd looked, in a way. But I'd seen what I wanted to see.

What Matty wanted me to see.

"Right. And once he started looking at Matty closely, he saw a connection between him and Carmella. And then a connection between Carmella and Tony the Hat."

All of these connections. And we'd seen almost none of them, me and Dex.

"What connection was that, Flora?"

"Come on, Kitty; I thought you'd know that one by now."

I shook my head. "They're both Italian," I offered up, feeling a little lame even while I said it.

"Well, honestly," Flora said, "in a way it was something I'd suspected for a while. About Tony and Carmella, I mean. Just things I'd overhear sometimes. Or little things Carmella would say that gave her away. But when you see them, well, you just can't miss it, can you? So when I met him the other night, when we were eating our steaks? In that instance, everything I suspected—and everything James and Allan then suggested—I knew then to be true."

I was at sea. Underwater. Flora was telling me things. She was speaking in complete sentences and the words all made sense, yet none of it meant anything to me. I told her as much. "I don't understand. I was with you the whole time. You say you put it all together, but I didn't see anything at all."

"Come on, when Tony came out and talked to us. Didn't you see it then? I did."

"What? What did you see?"

"I don't know how anyone could miss it, Kitty. And Allan has proved it now, too. Tony is Carmella's brother. They look *exactly* alike."

CHAPTER FIFTY-NINE

Flora's revelation shocked me into silence because it seemed as though, in a world gone mad, it was one of the few things that actually did make sense. Even so, right away I figured there were pieces missing.

"They're brother and sister? How did you know?"

"Well, look at them, for one thing," Flora said. "Not just their coloring, but the shape of their features, even the way they use the same words. 'I am a hatmaker's son,' he said. And suddenly . . . I just knew."

"Really?"

"Well, like I said, I'd figured it out before, in a way. And then all this happened," she indicated the world in general, but I knew what she meant, "and then things started to make sense."

"Why didn't you say anything?"

"Like what? What could I have said that you would have believed?" I realized she had a point. "And it didn't all make sense right away," she said, "but certain things started to fall into place. We'd never met any of Carmella's family, Dad and I. And she's my *stepmother*. She said her people came from Barcelona . . ."

"She said she was Spanish?"

"Right. But I don't think even my father ever really believed her about that. But what did it matter, anyway? He loved her. He could afford her. When I pressed him on her origins, he told me that the details didn't make much difference."

"Until the notes started?"

"Even then, I wasn't sure it was her. What did she have to gain, after all?"

"Maybe it wasn't what she had to gain, Flora. Maybe it was never about that at all."

And that's when I could see it. See it plainly: the isolation from friends and family. Sure, she had money and she had a husband who adored her. But she'd wanted more and had never anticipated that a social caste no one talked about would keep her from achieving her goals.

"She doesn't hate me," Flora said thoughtfully. "I don't think she hates me."

"She didn't hate you," I agreed. "I think maybe she even loved you, in her way. Wanted to help you, but didn't quite know how."

Flora might have said more but I told her that, for the time being, I'd heard enough.

"Dex will be wondering what happened to me. I didn't stay where he told me to stay."

"And that will surprise him because . . ." Flora said, a smile in her eyes. The smile of a friend, I realized. Something I'd missed. Something I didn't need to miss anymore. Some things in life you don't have to be told.

"Come with me, please. We'll go find him."

"And James?"

"Of course, yes James. And your dad, Flora; he's with them, too."

"Oh my gosh, you're not serious? You are! Well that's wonderful. Who's missing? No one is missing! Somehow you're making this all come out right, despite everything."

"Despite everything," I repeated with a smile, but that one didn't reach my heart. I hadn't been completely honest, but I hadn't wanted to dash the happiness I'd seen wash over Flora's face. Someone was, of course, missing. Carmella. And I had a feeling that if her plans had all come to fruition untainted by a plotting dilettante, everything would have come out right. More right than any of us would ever know.

"I know who isn't here," Flora said suddenly as she and I walked through the deserted Westwood Village streets back to the place where I was supposed to be: back to where we'd left Mustard's car. "Fritzy. You said you had him? I want to see him."

"Of course you do," I said, thinking of her face when we took her down the freight elevator, under the office building to the place where we'd stashed her horse. "We'll find everyone and we'll all go and see him together."

She would be happy when she saw him. Her face would light up, and he would likely give that loud, ringing neigh when he greeted her. And she would say something to him in German. *"Meine liebchen,"* she would say, while she stroked his silken neck and he pushed his muzzle into the palm of her hand. *"Meine suisse* Fritzl."

And everyone would be happy. Everything would be just as it should be. And we'd barely miss those that didn't join us. We'd stand far enough apart that no one would see or feel the empty space.

CHAPTER SIXTY

And that's just how it went. A joyous reunion. A happy round of back-slapping by the guys followed with an inordinate amount of good quality bootleg whiskey shared. Everyone was jubilant.

There was a shadow on Cedric, of course. More than a shadow. I wondered if the sad look one could surmise in his eyes would last for the rest of his days. But, for a while, all had been lost—wife, daughter, horse—and now, things were as right as they could be. All things considered. Under the circumstances. He did not look quite happy, but I had a hunch he would survive.

On the surface of things, I was jubilant, too. Inside I struggled in ways that surprised me. When I played the whole of the Woodruff case through my head I could see all the places where I had made things worse, not better. From the very first moment: my errors in judgment, my arrogance, even my unwarranted jealousy of Flora and my admiration of her fiancé.

The way I had handled things made me feel diminished. It made me feel small. It wasn't that I'd made errors and couldn't see them, more like all my flaws and mistakes were as neatly laid out for me as if they were lines on a chalkboard or paintings on a wall. I could see every place I'd misstepped. And it galled me.

I suspect Dex saw me struggle with all of these unspoken demons because, not only did he not take me to task, but for the first few days, he pretty much left me alone. And I stuck close to the office, the good little receptionist. Answering phones, making coffee, and keeping my yap shut.

Finally it was as though Dex couldn't take it anymore. He called me into his office one clear, blue afternoon and indicated I should take my customary seat. The window was pulled open and the smell of sunshine, dust, and gas fumes rode in on careful beams. I was glad, though, because waves of cigarette smoke and Dex's customary tavern smell rolled out.

Once I was settled, he opened his left-hand desk drawer and pulled out an almost new bottle of bourbon and a couple of lowball glasses. I watched while he poured two drinks—a shallow one for me, one with some depth and kick for himself— then capped the bottle and stashed it neatly back in his desk. He shoved the less-full glass across the desk at me and indicated I should pick it up. When I did, he picked up his own and tilted it at me.

"To a job well done," Dex said, sipping. "I haven't taken the time to thank you for all your help on the Woodruff case, Kitty. I apologize. You worked hard and you deserve acknowledgment for what you did."

"I can't drink to that, Dex." I put the glass back down on his desk and pushed it in his direction with the tips of my fingers. "I'm sorry—and I thank you—but I can't drink to that at all."

He took a sip anyway and then replaced his glass on the desk with a bounce. "Why the hell not?"

"Well, gosh, Dex: look how I bungled things. I took on a case you didn't even want in the first place. You *knew* better, as it turns out. Then I let the horse get kidnapped, I let the girl get kidnapped . . . and I messed up every single thing you ever asked me to do."

"Aw, c'mon, Kitty: don't be melodramatic."

"Huh?"

"It's just that you take on too much of this. Sure, you took a job I didn't want. But you got us paid, didn't you?"

"I got us paid," I acknowledged quietly.

"Sure you did. And well, too. And yeah, there were a couple of times when you didn't listen so good . . ."

"More than a couple."

". . . but I figure, you probably learned your lesson. You probably won't be in such a hurry not to listen again."

"Well, *that's* true."

"And you didn't bungle everything. Not even close. Who found the horse?"

"Well . . ."

"And, for that matter, who found *me*? Why, if you hadn't been making things happen, I might have died in that cabana, Kitty. And just look at me; I'm right as rain."

I did look at him. And I realized, in many ways, he was right. Oh sure: I did have lessons I needed to learn, but I felt I'd learned a lot of things in the last few days. Things about fools and angels rushing in and being careful where you tread.

It was while I was thinking all of this through that the outer office door opened and Mustard came in, making a beeline for Dex's office when he saw I wasn't at my desk.

"So what the hell have we got going here? A tea party. Why didn't I get an invitation?"

"Hardly tea," Dex said, reaching into his desk for the bottle and another glass. "Just a bit of self-congratulations on the Woodruff case. All in all, in the end it went pretty well."

"That reminds me," I said, "I never did ask you what happened to Matty Sweet. Did you hand him over to the cops?"

Dex and Mustard exchanged a look, but neither of them said anything.

"What?" I demanded of Dex. Then, "What?" directly to Mustard's face. Still nothing.

"Come on, you two. Surely you don't think I'm holding a torch or anything. Whatever you did, it'll be fine by me."

Another look passed between them; then Dex cleared his throat and answered me.

"It ain't that, Kitty. It ain't about you at all."

"Well, what then?"

This time Mustard answered, but he wouldn't meet my eye.

"That night, after we all came back here and gave Miss Flora back her horse, do you remember I slipped away early?"

I shook my head. I hadn't recalled.

"Well, I did. I wanted to get back to the Woodruffs and get things . . . well, get them cleaned up before Flora and her dad went home."

I nodded. I didn't remember, but what he was saying made sense. We'd left a mess behind, after all.

"Well, I thought hard, Kitty. I thought hard about what to do with the Sweet kid. And I thought about calling the cops, but I knew what would happen if I did."

I didn't say anything, but I knew, too. Oil money. A handsome young man with a rich daddy. He probably would have been home and sleeping in his own bed before Carmella Woodruff was in the ground.

"So . . . what are you saying? You *didn't* call the cops? What *did* you do?"

Another look passed between them.

"You better tell her now, Mustard," Dex said. "You've gotten this far through."

"I called Carmella's brother." It wasn't much louder than a whisper.

"You called Tony the Hat?"

"Yeah. They came within a half hour, Tony and a couple of his guys."

"Tony himself came?"

"He cried over her body, Kitty. I never seen a man cry quite that way."

"They took Carmella?"

"No. I think he wanted to, but it wouldn't have been right. He left her for her husband to grieve over. They took the Sweet kid, though."

I felt my eyes go wide as I looked at him.

"What are you saying?"

"Nothin'. Just that."

"They took him where?"

"No, Kitty. It ain't like that. They just took him." Mustard looked deeply into his glass, as though he saw something that interested him there. Then he took a sip. Finally he spoke again. "He ain't comin' back."

I tried not to think too closely on that. I tried not to think about what it meant. What it *all* meant, really. About a woman who had loved too well, and a beautiful young man who never loved enough. About a big-hearted girl with a German horse and a dream it seemed unlikely she'd ever be able to achieve. I thought about a world gone crazy on a wave of great change and I wondered if I'd ever feel at home in it. Ever find a place of comfort and ease.

After a while, I decided to let the two old friends drink together, and I went back to my desk to sit quietly and see if there was any meaning I could pull out of the few days I'd spent in the Woodruffs' company. We'd paid our office rent, Dex had given me my salary, and there was money enough to spare for the time being. But beyond that, there was nothing that really made sense.

And I thought, too, about the offer Mustard had made me. *I think we'd make a nice life, you and me* is what he'd said. *We could grow old. Together.*

Was that what all of this was about, then? Is that what I was meant to pull from this part of my life? A place of comfort. But at what cost? And, truly, in the end, did the cost matter?

Fate pushed Mustard out of Dex's office then. There were words on my lips. Something like *if you'll still have me* or *if you really meant it* or even *if you still feel the same way, then maybe* . . .

Did he see it on my face then? I think he might have. Or else, once more, fate intervened in her own mad way.

"Well, I'm off Kitty," he said before I could speak. "Me and Willamina, you remember her? We're going to the pictures tonight."

"Willamina Huffle?" I said, trying to keep the wonder from my voice.

"The same." He looked a little bashful as he said, "We've been keeping company, you know. Since we met that night. At the riding academy. She's a little off-putting at first. Sweet enough girl, though, once you get to know her."

Once the door had closed behind him, I sat and looked at it for a while, wondering at the things I was feeling. Wondering at what it was that I'd come very close to. I didn't think about Mustard and Willamina and what the future might hold for them. Oddly enough, considering the things I'd been thinking just a quarter hour before, it didn't seem to matter much to me. Except I felt lighter, brighter, more myself than I had since I'd ever heard of Flora Woodruff and her beautiful German horse.

ABOUT THE AUTHOR

Linda L. Richards is the editor and co-founder of *January Magazine* and a regular contributor to *The Rap Sheet.* Linda has lived in Los Angeles and Munich but was born in Vancouver, Canada. She currently lives in the Gulf Islands off Canada's west coast with her partner, the artist David Middleton, and their pets, Jett and Tiger-Lily. A faculty member of the Simon Fraser University Summer Publishing Program, she maintains a busy lecture and festival schedule and enjoys working with new writers. When she isn't writing books, writing about books, teaching, or reading, Richards enjoys hiking the wild beaches near her home, quite often thinking about her current work in progress. On the Web, you can visit Linda at lindalrichards.com.